GRAVEDIGGERS
MOUNTAIN OF BONES

GRAVEDIGGERS
MOUNTAIN OF BONES

CHRISTOPHER KROVATIN

KATHERINE TEGEN BOOKS
An Imprint of HarperCollins Publishers

Katherine Tegen Books is an imprint of HarperCollins Publishers.

Gravediggers: Mountain of Bones
Copyright © 2012 by HarperCollins Publishers

Library of Congress Cataloging-in-Publication Data
Krovatin, Christopher.
Mountain of bones / Christopher Krovatin. — 1st ed.
    p. cm. — (Gravediggers)
Summary: During a class trip to the Montana woods, three sixth graders, athletic
Ian, sensitive PJ, and brainy Kendra, are separated from their group and must rely
on each other to survive as they encounter zombies and more.
ISBN 978-0-06-207740-0 (trade bdg.)
[1. Supernatural—Fiction. 2. Zombies—Fiction. 3. Interpersonal relations—
Fiction. 4. Nature—Fiction. 5. Hiking—Fiction. 6. Montana—Fiction.] I. Title.
PZ7.K936Mou 2012   2011044623
[Fic]—dc23   CIP
                                                                           AC

Typography by Carla Weise
12 13 14 15 16 LP/RRDH 10 9 8 7 6 5 4 3 2 1
❖
First Edition

DEDICATED IN LOVING MEMORY
TO THE PINE CITY DANCERS

ACKNOWLEDGMENTS

Thanks to Claudia Gabel for thinking of me, everyone at HarperCollins for their help, and my friends and family for their love and support. Special thanks to Sam Raimi and George Romero, whose undying menace has always driven me to survive.

GRAVEDIGGERS
MOUNTAIN OF BONES

The Warden's Handbook

by Lucille Fulci

Chapter 6: Gravediggers

6.c—On the Law of Threes

The job of a Warden is solitary in its very nature. Only with great concentration can a Warden manage her time and resources enough to complete the task of containment. More so, the Warden's profession requires her to dwell in contaminated zones, which are rarely hospitable to husbands, families, or friends (this only strengthens the superstition that Wardens are inherently cruel and antisocial). Gravediggers, however, almost never travel alone, and are specifically known to come in threes.

Obviously three is an important number in enchantment. Acts of karmic violence are rewarded threefold to those who commit them, and Hecate, goddess of witches, is said to have three faces. But why the law of three seems to apply to these rarely used tools of destruction is still a mystery.

One explanation is that a team of Gravediggers

must be flexible in behavior and practices to accommodate the danger it's dealing with, and a group of three people creates a full balance. It is not enough to have simply strength on one side and wisdom on the other; the heart, middleman between mind and body, must be represented. Wardens and Gravediggers alike often forget that the true enemy of the world, the one that they've been trained to fight, is karmically repulsive, a creature as repellent spiritually as it is hideous physically. The three-person system of Gravediggers brings a completeness to their role in the obliteration of evil.

Trios aren't necessarily required for Gravediggers. Often greater numbers mean a greater reach. If it hadn't been for all eleven of the Beane Family, the Great Rising of Cairo would have proven a much more horrific event, and there have always been rumors of certain lone Gravediggers roaming the countryside, destroying evil wherever they see fit (see *Annie Oakely*, p. 126). But one only has to look at the great Gravedigger teams of history— Las Matanzas in 1698, the Laumpreck Triplets in 1780, the Fugue in 1861 and again in 1888, and the Richmond Team in 1914—to see that a three-person formation has become something of a tradition amongst the hunters of the cursed.

This, among other things, has put the Grave-digger class at odds with the Wardens. Wardens are solitary and sage, while Gravediggers are social and reactionary. Members of both camps believe that working together is key—Alex Wuttinger of the Fugue famously said, "Three and a Warden is how it's done"—but often, one group rejects the other.

In fact, many Wardens—this author included—believe this warrior to be outdated and brutal, and are currently in talks to have the Gravediggers dis-banded. Too often have Gravediggers, driven by boredom and rage, attacked perfectly contained pop-ulations of the cursed. Given recent technological and magical innovations, having random three-person hit squads seems unnecessary. However, since their presence was vital during the darker days of containment, they will be covered in this volume. . . .

CHAPTER ONE

Ian

Okay, that's it, let me out. I'm dying here, people!

The bus doors open, and I'm the first person down the aisle and on the dirt. A blast of warm country air hits me in the face, and just like that, the past two hours of boring bus ride are gone, and I'm in it, man, out in the wild, part of the scenery. There's the other bus slowly spitting out kids, there are the flaking red buildings of Homeroom Earth, but I'm all about what's past that, the swaying lines of trees, the knobby rock outcroppings, the mountains a faded purple-green against the endless blue sky, far off but *totally* climbable.

Everyone else is getting off the bus, stretching,

starting to look for bags, but all I want to do right now is stand here and take it in. The Montana countryside in the distance is beyond anything I'm used to back in the Wyoming suburbs, where raccoons are the scariest thing a kid can run into on any given day. This place, though, it's built for me, and it's like every second I'm outside is made up of this whole place, like each time I breathe I'm taking the trees, mountains, rocks, sky, into my lungs, and making my body a part of them, so I take it all in, close my eyes and clench my fists and breathe, breathe, *breathe.*

I'm here! I'm ready! *Let's get going!*

"Yo, Ian!" Sean Cunningham and Mitchell West, my basketball buddies, leap out of the bus next to me, Sean broad shouldered and flat faced, Mitchell all rake thin, long limbs, and spiky black hair. They're both grinning, cracking their knuckles and necks, and I can tell they're feeling it, too, the total *hugeness* of being out here, the possibility.

"Dude," says Sean, pointing at the mountains in the distance, "we're gonna climb that!"

"Hold me back!" I yell, rushing forward, and they both crack up as they grab my arms to keep me from launching headfirst into the forest. I'm smiling so hard it hurts. For the past two years, I've been able to chill with the other guys on my team only at practice, mostly because they live all the way across town and Mom wants me hanging with PJ all the time, but now, *finally*, me and my teammates have a chance to do something cool together, to *rage* out here in the wilderness.

"We gotta keep our eyes out, though," says Mitch, pointing a finger at me as we wade through our class and dig our bags out of the bus's cargo hold. "Remember: the Pine City Dancers."

Sean nods hard. "How long have they been out here?" he asks, clueless.

I've had the whole story memorized since Jeremy Morris from the seventh grade gave us the skinny in the cafeteria last week, but I play along, down to hear Mitch tell it again.

"They disappeared last year," says Mitch, getting all intense and low voiced. "Whole dance troupe from Pine City, Montana, on a camping trip, bam, just *gone*."

"What do you think happened to them?" I ask.

"No one knows," says Mitch. "One year later, they still haven't found any of the bodies." Sean and I share a glance: *the bodies*. Insane. "The camp made up some kind of lame cover story about why they had to cancel last year's Homeroom Earth, and why there were cops and health officials crawling all over the place—"

"Food poisoning scare, right?" says Sean.

"I think it was a bug infestation," I tell him.

"All lies," says Mitchell, looking devious. "They're out there somewhere. In a cave, their flesh rotting away, probably getting eaten by wild animals—"

Sean puts his fingers to his mouth and balloons out his cheeks, and all three of us make barfing noises between laughs.

"Let's make a bet," says Sean. "If I find the first corpse, you guys owe me a month's worth of dessert."

"Man, you're such a fatty," says Mitch. "Fine. If I find the first body, you guys have to call me Papa Mitch for two weeks. Failure to do so results in a dead-arm." We nod. Sounds fair. "Ian?"

Oh man, do I dare? Been on the tip of my tongue the whole season. It might be too much, but hey, we're hanging, and my pass game has gotten way better in the past month, so why not give it a try?

"Okay," I say, "if I find the first body, you two have to tell Coach Leider that I should start as point guard instead of Kyle."

Sean and Mitchell look at each other and whistle, but then Sean says, "Deal." We all put our fists in the middle, bump them as a triangle, and let out a solid "BOOM!" Now it's settled: I *have* to find the first body.

"Day one of Homeroom Earth: Ian Buckley, our perpetual protagonist, takes part in a male-bonding ritual."

Oh, great.

I look over my shoulder, and there he is, a sore thumb with a chunky black camcorder attached to his face. Immediately, Sean and Mitch moan.

PJ Wilson stands out *hard* in the wilderness—skinny, short, pale, dark under the eyes. On top of that, there's what he's wearing—a green shirt with a bear on it, a tiny pair of cargo shorts, and some ratty sneakers—and how he smells—sunscreen, bug spray, soap, medicine—that make him a walking target. Oh, and the camera, of course. Can't forget that. Even if I tried.

I've got to keep this situation under control. I can't let PJ take too much guff from my teammates—he's my oldest friend, our parents have known each other forever, and he *is* a good dude at heart—but he's not making it easy on me. Come on, you bring a bunch of guys out into the woods, they're going to get a little crazy, and the first thing they'll do is sniff around for the odd one out of the pack.

"Maybe PJ can come with us," I say to Sean. "How about it, man? Want to get some footage of dead bodies? Remember I mentioned the Pine City Dancers—"

The lens of the camera comes up to my face. "You're kidding me. You actually believe that ghost story Jeremy Morris fed you? Come on, guys, use your brains."

I look at Sean and Mitch, smiling like *Can you believe this guy?* But I'm too late. Sean's crouching down, scooping something up in his hands, and then he steps forward and puts the biggest daddy longlegs I've ever seen directly on top of PJ's camera lens.

Of course PJ goes bananas, spinning around and

slapping at his camera and squealing while Sean and Mitch laugh their faces off and my cheeks burn. When he's finally sure the bug is gone, PJ looks up at us with those big hurt eyes and that huge sad frown that makes his whole head look like an upside-down U.

This is PJ when the camera's off—sad, frightened, *super*sensitive, totally unable to be normal. I'm worried he's going to have one of his trademark panic attacks, but never mind, he's just furious.

"You morons!" he shrieks. "What if that thing had bitten me? And I could've dropped my camcorder! Do you know how much this costs?"

"Really don't care," says Mitch.

"Dude, your friend needs to get his situation under control," says Sean, rolling his eyes.

My teammates stalk off, shrugging and cackling, while I'm left with my lame friend who mutters under his breath and goes over every inch of his camera to make sure it's unharmed. Part of me wants to tell him those guys were jerks, but the other part of me wants to snatch the camera out of his hands and spike it like a football so I can watch its seven million expensive pieces fly all over the forest. PJ pulls a square of paper out of his pocket and scans it. "What are those spiders called again? I want to see if they're on here."

"A daddy longlegs? They're harmless, man. What's with the sheet?"

"My folks made me a list of things to watch out for while I'm here," says PJ. He glances around the woods, looking as small and scared as ever. "You don't think there are any spores in the air, do you? My mom gave me a mask, like one of those face masks for surgery. She read this thing about spores in *Growing Boy Magazine*, and how if you wear a mask . . ."

PJ goes on about spores and Africanized bees and grizzly bears, but now I'm back to looking at our surroundings, jacking myself up for my time in the wild. In the distance Coach beckons for us to gather round the fire pit, and I almost sprint over to him.

It's for the best that PJ and I are in different activity groups. Not that I don't like PJ, but it'll let us hang out at our own pace, you know? And I won't get filmed the whole time.

Coach Leider stands by the bonfire pit, a stone-lined hole full of ashes in front of the mess hall. He's dressed in a camo shirt, camo pants, a camo hat, and wow, he somehow managed to find camo boots. The other teachers standing next to him—Mr. Harder, history; Ms. Brandt, English; Señora Alanzo, Spanish; Ms. Dean, biology—look tiny and seriously ungreen. Coach is all bulging muscles, fists on his hips.

"Quiet down, all of you!" barks Coach. "Welcome to Homeroom Earth. For the next three days, you will get some hands-on education about survival in the wild.

You *will* frolic. You *will* love nature. We clear on that?"

Everyone grumbles approval. Next to me, PJ salutes, then looks to see if I've noticed. I keep quiet. A few more minutes, and Coach will be leading the guys and me on our wild corpse hunt.

"Now, I know you sixth graders were supposed to do this program last year but couldn't because of a bed-bug infestation." I glance at Sean and Mitch, and they both make hands-to-the-throat choking motions. "First off, I want you to know that we've been assured that all of the bunks have been wiped clean of the bedbug scourge. Second, I need you all to pay attention to the Homeroom Earth counselors, got it? They'll need your complete concentration for the next couple of days. You make one mistake out here, disrespect Mother Nature, and *BAM*"—he points a finger and thumb out like a gun— "she puts you in traction. So stay alert, and this should be fun. Us teachers are *stoked*." He looks at Ms. Brandt, who grins and rubs her hands together. "All right. Now, allow me to introduce you to your program head, Professor Randy."

Coach steps aside, and this skinny guy with a scraggly beard and a big brown ranger's cap steps up in front of us. "Hey, guys, welcome to Homeroom Earth! Super-excited to have you aboard! From now on, you're my little deputies!"

I look at PJ and roll my eyes. PJ points a finger at his

head and fake-blows his brains out. See, sometimes he's all right.

"Before we get rompin' and rollin', though," says Professor Randy, "I have to tell you the four main rules of Homeroom Earth, 'kay? Rule one: Don't leave the campgrounds and don't stray from the path. This is a nature conservancy, and there are plenty of animals who won't be all that happy if you stumble onto their den. Got it? Super!"

Yikes, this guy's awful.

"Rule two: No personal electronic devices allowed. That includes cell phones, mp3 players, GPS systems, everything. Cameras are acceptable, but anything more complicated than that needs to stay in your cabin and out of sight." Some of the preppier kids groan. "Sorry, guys. You'll thank us later when a bird isn't building her nest with parts of your iPad. Rule number three: Drink plenty of water at all times. The air is thin and dry out here, and dehydration is a serious problem. And that leads to our fourth and most important rule: If someone's having trouble, even if they ask you not to say anything, please tell one of your teachers or a staff member. Nothing ruins a good time like a burst appendix. Everyone clear on the rules? Fantastic."

Up ahead, I can see Sean and Mitchell laughing as they make their way to the bunks, but PJ's like an anchor at my side, weighing me down. I've gotta be patient—once we split into our activity groups, I won't see him again until dinner. It'll be great—PJ's the kind of friend who's okay to hang out with as long as it's not all the time.

"We're still sharing a bunk, right?" he asks worriedly.

"Of course," I tell him. "I'm not going to flake out on you." Not that the idea hadn't crossed my mind—

"Buckley! Front and center!" Coach Leider appears next to me, all muscles and camo, a huge smile on top of his massive chin. He sniffs the air and waves his hand in front of his face. "Yikes, Wilson, you *sure* you're wearing enough bug spray? No one ever died from an insect bite, son."

"That can't be true," says PJ. "I was just watching *Kingdom of the Spiders* with William Shatner, and they talk about how—"

"You know what I mean," groans Coach. "Go on ahead, will you? I have to talk to your buddy here." PJ gives me a nervous glance but keeps walking. Coach and I slow to a stop. He crouches down, and his voice gets low. "How you doing, Ian?"

Uh-oh. Coach Leider doesn't use first names. I've only ever been "Buckley." Something's up. "Fine, Coach. Excited to get moving. We're going for a hike, right?"

"Here's the thing," says Coach. "Michael McDermott has asthma, and I'm the only teacher here with CPR training. That means that I have to trade one person in my activity group for one person in Ms. Brandt's.

14

You follow?" I nod. He stares at me for a second—he almost looks sad—and says, "I know you were really excited to be part of my group, Ian—"

Oh. Now I get it. "Me?! Why *me*?! Sean and Mitch and I, we have this bet going—I wanted to—we were going to—why *ME*?"

He shrugs. "PJ Wilson is in Ms. Brandt's group, and you two are thick as thieves. Right? I figured I'd be sticking you with one of your friends."

"We're not—" The words can't even come out of my mouth, they feel so lousy. *We're not friends.* It's a lie, but right now, missing out on three days of fun with my basketball teammates, I wish it was true. Ugh. And now I'll have to be filmed through all of this trip. "Fine."

"You cool?" says Coach Leider.

Pfff. Am I cool. "Yeah, whatever," I tell him, hoping he hears how *lame* this is.

"Good." He hisses through his teeth. "There's some-thing else, too. Don't get upset, but . . . I heard that you have a history with someone else in Ms. Brandt's group, so I should probably talk to you about her. Apparently, the two of you had a fight in Ms. Dean's class once—"

Oh no. I feel my stomach sink and my heart melt into goo. Off in the distance, marching toward the girls' cabins, I see her big brown pom-pom of hair, and it's bad, man, it's worse than a million and one PJs.

Anyone, *anyone* but her.

CHAPTER TWO

Kendra

According to my *Field Guide to Montana Animal and Plant Life*, there are fifteen species of owl that are native to the mountain ranges that we are currently camping at the feet of, the Bitterroots. And while they only hunt at night, some owls have been known to come out in the evening and scare up prey that gets confused by the dim light but enjoys the warmth of the evening sun. Therefore, the evenings are when I have to be most alert. That is one of my goals for the trip—to see an owl in flight, specifically the flammulated owl, who looks notably like Yoda from the *Star Wars* movies.

There is something about owls that fascinates me,

perhaps because they are historically symbols for wisdom or because they just appear statelier than most birds, their eyes huge and their chests puffed out. I can only hope that when I see an owl, the owl will see some wisdom in me. We'll recognize each other's brilliance. And it doesn't hurt that they're *extremely* pretty.

But I'm *ideating* (that's three; two more times and I've filled my vocabulary quota for the week).

Once we've dropped all our stuff off at our bunks—it appears I'm the only girl who didn't bring any lip gloss or hair accessories (as though I care)—we have lunch at the mess hall, its wooden walls lined with art projects that consist of twigs and leaves glued to construction paper. I use the time to text Jutta and David from the braintrustfund.org message board about DEET (N, N-Diethyl-meta-toluamide) levels in the insect repellents they've used, and about which berries they've eaten on past camping trips. David tells me he usually uses DEET-free spray—his parents prefer organic alternatives—and that he generally enjoys thimbleberries, but that my trip might be too mountainous to find them. No word from Jutta, but that's understandable. David's from Portland, Oregon, while Jutta's from Hamburg, Germany. She's probably eating dinner.

After lunch, we all return to the campfire pit, where we're split up into our sections and sent to stand next to our assigned teacher. Ms. Brandt checks us off her attendance list, beaming. In the classroom, Ms. Brandt is overly rigid—the sight of her small, spherical form next to your desk is worrisome—but the seventh and eighth graders who I spoke to say that she becomes a kindhearted naturist at Homeroom Earth—*naturist* in this case meaning one who worships nature, not one who walks around without clothes on. Or so I assume.

Either way, her face glows with a wide grin and she rubs her chubby-fingered hands together excitedly. Some of the other kids find this funny and giggle to themselves, but watching her take on such a different persona outside of the classroom gives me a warm feeling in my chest. Today, we can be pioneers!

"Okay," she mumbles. "Wright, Kendra. Jones, Leslie. Todd, Barbara. Dylan, Jenny. Richter, Tom. Wilson, Peter Jacob . . ." She trails down the names of the kids around me, then looks over to Coach Leider, who gives her a thumbs-up. "Splendid. And Buckley, Ian."

Excuse me?

Sadly, this is not a mistake on her part—there's Ian Buckley, all skinny muscles and messy blond hair, crossing his arms and looking completely miserable as Coach Leider leads him over to our group. (Let it be noted that Coach Leider's outfit is astounding. I will never own that much camouflage.) Blood instinctively rushes into my face as I catch sight of him—he's all boy, all stupid, lanky, mean, sexist little *boy*.

"Weren't you supposed to be in Coach Leider's group?" asks Tom Richter.

"Well," says Ian, "I definitely wasn't supposed to be here, with . . ." He trails off.

"Go on, Ian," I ask, "with who?"

He laughs and shakes his head, but refuses to look at me.

Relax, Kendra. So, yes, you're in an Activity Group with a loudmouth jock whose primary goal in life is to jump off a cliff and see how it feels. This may be inauspicious *(that's two for inauspicious, you need three more), but it is by no means the end to your work out here.*

By the looks of things, Ian doesn't seem incredibly pleased to be in Ms. Brandt's group either, since there isn't a single basketball player amongst you, just "pathetic nerds" like yourself, which is what Ian called you in science class before you hit him in the face with your textbook so hard that he had to be sent home and you had to spend your first and only afternoon in detention.

So. Maybe his lack of someone to grunt at will keep him quiet and you can work in peace. Forget him. Take a deep breath of fresh mountain air and let it out. Owls. Keep your eyes out for owls.

Professor Randy sidles over to Ms. Brandt and says, "Everyone here? Wonderful! Guys, I'd like you to meet Maris, your outdoor teacher for the day." A pale, acne-spotted girl with black lipstick appears next to Professor Randy and waves excitedly at us. "She's going to make sure you kids have a rockin' time on your first activity!" When he's looking away, I take a picture of "Professor" Randy with my phone and e-mail it to my message board friends. Subject: *This guy's our professor????* Multiple LOL responses follow.

"All right, guys, our first activity is . . .wildflowers!" announces Maris. Every boy in our group groans as one. "I know what you're thinking, guys, *flowers are for girls*, but actually Montana's wildflowers are as fascinating and diverse as its many animal species."

"But twice as boring," grumbles Ian Buckley.

"Mr. Buckley," snaps Ms. Brandt. A few of my classmates giggle, so I shoot Ian a dirty look to let him know his commentary isn't appreciated. He mouths, *What?* at me. My face burns and my hands ball into fists. If only I had a textbook around . . .

Maris leads us away from the main campsite buildings and up a wide hiking trail with deep woods and colorful fields of flowers lining either side of it. The wind is cool but dry, drawing its lazy fingers through the high grass. It's still early spring, but already the air is dotted with mayflies and gnats, early births from the insect world. The trees around us are impossibly tall, their highest branches straining up at least fifty feet overhead; beneath them, in the shadows of the forest, shafts of light dance, birds chirp, squirrels rustle through fallen leaves, and page after page of fascinating knowledge awaits. For some reason, though the sky is blue and bright, a great misty cloud hangs over the mountain, as though it got caught on a tree and can't drift farther without tearing.

This is a researcher's *heaven*, a safe campsite on a nature preserve that was built to provide young people like us with a chance to study the wilderness in all its beauty. Montana is not somewhere like, say, Iowa, some corn-choked wasteland, but instead is home to purple mountain majesties and green woods teeming with life! According to my field guide, there are over three thousand unmarked mountain trails and peaks in this region. I didn't *quite* believe that, but it was interesting to see it documented. Now that I see the size of the mountains surrounding us, I'm inclined to believe it's the case.

I'm about to snap a photo of the landscape to post on my blog when a message pops up. Sender: Dad. *"My computer shows you as online. I thought we talked about this. Turn your phone off! Have an adventure!"* Something like panic sparks within me, and I stuff my phone in my pocket.

Up ahead, Barbara Todd and Jenny Dylan huddle together, whispering about something near a patch of what I think are toadflaxes (toadflaxi? Toadflaces? I make a mental note to look it up later). This is the adventure my father means: the friend adventure, the Normal Kid routine.

Slowly, I approach them, unsure as to why my palms are beginning to sweat, why my mouth feels so dry.

You're an interesting person, Kendra. You know everything about these woods. Just walk up to them and say something.

"Did you know there are over three thousand uncharted hiking trails in these mountains?" I ask as I reach them.

Barbara and Jenny look up at me like my head is on fire. Barbara is all blond and small nosed in a pink sequined shirt; Jenny wears glittered denim from head to toe and has a wholly unnecessary magenta highlight. "What?" says Barbara.

"On those mountains," I say, pointing to the violet silhouettes in the distance. "I mean, that's a lot of terrain to cover. I feel like . . ." What do girls like this talk about? ". . . like my hair's going to be a total mess after this!"

The silence that follows is *excruciating*. (Has that been a vocab word yet? It should be.)

"You're worried about . . . *your* hair?" asks Jenny, raising an eyebrow and observing the top of my head.

"Of course," I say, laughing a little, trying to stop the buzzing in my head. "It's just . . . what a lot of ground to cover for one day. Totally ruins my staying power."

The girls stare at me, then at each other. Jenny shrugs. "Okay, Kendra," says Barbara, looking away from me. "Thanks for . . . filling us in."

Jenny bites her lip to keep from giggling. Barbara nods farther up the path, and she and Jenny power-walk away from me, laughing to themselves. On the wind, I catch one of them mutter, "That was *weird*."

Then the other replies, "I know. What's her problem?"

My cheeks burn. My heart pounds. The question echoes in my head: What *is* my problem?

It's all Mom and Dad could talk about before this trip. *Make some friends. Real friends, not internet friends. Friends you can do stuff with, who can come over after school. It's not hard—just walk up to them and be yourself. You're so smart and funny!*

It sounds easy enough, but here I am, somehow failing, even though I know what I'm saying is *right*, and *interesting*.

Calm down, Kendra. Don't become discouraged just because two girls in your class didn't want to talk to you. Barbara Todd's a ditz, anyway. Distract yourself. Go over the checklist on your phone again, the one you got from Diane from Montreal. You've got your map, compass, specimen jars, granola bars, your notebook, your field guide—

"Ms. Brandt, look!" The voice is right behind me. I

whirl around to see Ian Buckley jabbing a finger directly at the screen of my smartphone. "I thought the rules were no electronics!"

Ms. Brandt approaches me, her happy-go-lucky naturist smile replaced by the stern expression we know so well from English class. "Ms. Wright," she says, extending a hand. "Rules are rules. Hand it over."

"Careful!" says Ian. "Make sure she doesn't have a textbook on her! She's been known to attack when cornered!"

Before I can say a word, Ms. Brandt snatches my phone from my hands and pockets it. As she walks away, my only successful connection to the outside world in her hand, my heart sinks in my chest. I've been talking up this trip to my whole network, my friends from all over the world, and now I won't be able to post a single tweet of my adventures. No one'll know—not Jutta, not David, not Gerry or Alma or Carter. It'll be like this trip didn't even happen.

When I turn back to Ian, he has a mean little smirk on his face, like he can see the roaring fire that's building in my chest and face. My vision begins blurring red. I don't think I've ever been this angry.

"Uh-oh," says Ian, snickering. "She's gonna blow!"

Behind him, Peter Jacob Wilson grimaces at me. "Sorry, he's not usually this much of a jerk—"

"Oh my God, PJ, gimme the camera!" Ian snatches

24

a camcorder out of his friend's hand and trains it on me, a little red light switching on over the glossy black lens. "Dude, look, she's actually turning purple. YouTube, here I come!"

"Ian, cut it out," says Peter Jacob, laughing nervously at me. "Really, I'm sorry. He's not normally this mean. I think it's the air out here, personally."

Suddenly, my blind rage takes over, and I call out, "Ms. Brandt, he has a video camera!"

Ms. Brandt doubles back over to us, her arms holding a bouquet of wildflowers. Being torn away from her flower picking twice has wiped away all remnants of Excited Outdoors Ms. Brandt. "What is it now?" she asks grumpily.

"Wait a second," says Peter Jacob, holding up his hands to me. "That's—"

"He has a camcorder," I say, pointing to Ian, his eyes bulging with faux innocence. "If I'm not allowed to have my smartphone, he shouldn't be allowed to have a camera."

Ms. Brandt groans and snatches the camcorder out of Ian's hand. "Enough," she says. "We are not here to play with electronics or tattle on each other; we are here to bask in nature's unending beauty." She hands each of us a yellow wildflower. "There. *Get basking.*"

We all watch her stomp back toward the rest of the group. When I look back at Ian, however, in the hopes of savoring *his* reaction to losing his precious gizmo, I find him glowering not at me but at Peter Jacob, who stares after Ms. Brandt with a look of pure horror on his face, his eyes bulging, his mouth hanging open.

"I swear, man," says Ian, "if I'd known she was going to rat us out, I would've—"

"*Unbelievable*," whispers Peter Jacob, and then he looks at Ian. "What am I going to do now?"

"Chill, dude," says Ian, "you'll get it back—"

"And you!" Suddenly, Peter Jacob's eyes settle on me, and his expression goes from aghast to enraged. "You complete *spaz*! Just because you got your phone taken away, you have to ruin *my* trip? What am I supposed to do without my camera?"

His camera? My eyes fly from Ian to Peter, then back again, desperately trying to discern what just happened. "I don't understand—"

"Incredible," snaps Peter Jacob. He clenches his hands into claws in front of his face. "No wonder you don't have any friends." He shakes his head and storms off. After a moment, Ian follows him, throwing his hands in the air.

And now I'm alone again. The woods feel vast around me, as big and empty as the pit in my stomach. All my research on camping supplies and survivalist techniques becomes a flash in my mind, a useless blur of facts that I can't focus on right now.

Make some friends. That's the test my parents keep putting in front of my face, and I'm sure there's a method for acing it, but I'm totally lost. I wish I'd studied what to do when someone makes you feel like this. Instead, I'm earning a solid F.

The group trudges onward, and I follow, the vast expanse of the mountain feeling somewhat like my heart right now—huge, dark, empty.

CHAPTER THREE

PJ

Are you kidding me? First, I get tossed into the sticks like some kind of guinea pig used to study the effects malaria and overexposure have on an everyday kid. And now you tell me that the one thing keeping me sane out here—my camera, my eye to the world—isn't allowed, because . . . why? Because I might actually get a recording of something cool that you've never seen in however many boring years you've picked flowers at Homeroom Earth? These counselors probably got sued once because some jerk had his smartphone eaten by a badger, and now I have to suffer for it.

Really, what are they going to do with my camcorder?

At least with other kids' mp3 players and smartphones, you can watch TV or listen to music or whatever. All you're gonna see on my camcorder is Ian and me, a bunch of wildflowers, the opening shots to my were-wolf movie (it's still in production; rewrites have been extensive), and maybe my sister's sixth birthday (I don't know; I might have deleted that).

If I don't get that thing back the *minute* the bus starts—

I'm not completely lost. I still have that little hand-held camera with the pop-out USB drive, the one I got for Christmas. But I haven't yet learned all of its features. And besides, I know the camcorder so well, its weight, its shot radius. And without it . . .

Without it, it's just me, here. Surrounded.

I almost go to Ms. Brandt to plead my case, but she's so intense in her flower picking that I don't dare bother her. Besides, I've got to talk to her later about calling home tonight. If my choices are camera or phone call, I have to choose the call. Kyra is counting on me.

My portable will have to do. It's better than nothing, I suppose, better than *this*, wandering through a field without a real eye to guide me. It's a water wing when I need a life preserver, but it'll keep me afloat. It's just that the resolution on my handheld is so much worse than my camcorder. There's probably no way to re-layer it on my computer.

Maris hands out laminated sheets with medicines we're supposed to create by collecting certain types of flowers. Mine says I have to put together a bouquet that will create a vitamin supplement. "Don't forget," she says, "first one to collect their entire bouquet gets to have their flowers made into an actual poultice to take back to their parents!"

No one's explained to me what a poultice is yet. There are way too many flowers to tell which ones match my sheet. If I were filming this, I could zoom in, study each plant to see if it matches my sheet, but I don't dare lean in that close right now. Flowers are pretty because they're dangerous. That's how nature works.

I put my hand in my pocket and wrap it around my handheld camera, and all the trees and flowers around me seem just the tiniest bit less terrifying.

Sweat beads on my forehead; it's too hot for all this stooping and picking. Some giant poisonous bug goes flying past my face. Every plant I touch spews a cloud of pollen directly into my nasal passages. One part of the path is lined with this vine that I'm positive is poison *something*. What is it—leaves of three, leave it be, leaves of four, it'll make your throat close up and your heart stop?

Ian's not much company, acting miserable because he's not allowed to go hunting for dead bodies with his teammates. (What kind of idiots *want* to go looking for a bunch of people who *died* in these woods?) There was a time when he would stand up for me, tell me not to listen to the other guys when they made fun of me like Sean and Mitchell did earlier. Lately, though, he's either trying to get me to act more like the other guys on his basketball team or he's pretending like he doesn't notice me.

"It's not *that* big a deal, right?" says Ian. "You probably weren't going to get much good footage out here anyway, right?"

"Whatever" is all I can come up with.

I bet at least ten of the things on my parents' list are in the forest as we speak. Mom and Dad were right—it's ridiculous, the school forcing us to take part in this nature program. I wish I was home, in the living room, watching *Night of the Hunter* and explaining the camera work to Kyra.

The woods look exactly like where *Friday the 13th* was filmed. It wouldn't surprise me if some masked madman was sharpening his machete out there right now. Which is a scary thought but could be cool, if I could get it on film.

"It's not even me you should be ticked at," he whines, "it's Queen Brain."

A few yards away, Kendra Wright picks some skinny yellow flowers. Her coffee-colored skin stands out from all the green grass, and her puffball hair looks huge among the flowers, like a giant brown dandelion (Ian always jokes that that's where the Queen Brain is—most of the hair is just a big pulsating megacortex, like the mutants in *This Island Earth*). When she turns toward us, though, her face breaks my heart, mouth tiny and downturned, eyes soft and watery behind her glasses. And then it hits me that I was a jerk to her, and that unlike everyone else, myself included, she's totally alone. No friends, no partners, just her.

She got my camera taken away, which yes, is killing me. But . . .

"I'll be right back," I say to Ian.

"What's up?" he asks.

"Just give me a second."

When I reach her, Kendra holds a yellow flower that looks like a bird's claw. She twirls it in her hands, not really looking at it.

"Which one's that?" I ask.

"A glacier lily," she says softly. "It's used for skin diseases."

"So you're, what, making Neosporin? Or just hand cream?" She doesn't even hint at smiling. I guess honesty will have to do. "Look, uh . . . sorry about yelling at you like that, earlier." She nods, but stays silent. "It's just that my camera is . . . really important to me. It lets me . . ." How do I explain this? Do anything? Remain in control, rule the world? That sounds crazy, even to me.

"Anyway, it was mean, what I said to you. I'm sorry."

She gulps, blinks, and tries to smile. She looks up at me but stares over my shoulder, never in my eyes. "It's fine. If I'd known it was yours, I wouldn't have told Ms. Brandt about it. I thought it was Ian's."

"I totally get that. He was really obnoxious about your smartphone, so you had every right." She nods. "I'm PJ, by the way. I don't think we've ever really talked. Weird, right?"

Her brow furrows. "Wait, I thought your name was Peter. Peter Jacob."

"Yuck, no one calls me that. It's PJ." I hold up my thumbs and pointer fingers to make an imaginary marquee. "Think of a film poster. 'Directed by PJ Wilson.' Sounds a lot better than 'Peter Jacob,' right?"

"I suppose," she says. "I'm Kendra."

"Sure, yeah. So . . . what are you trying to gather flowers for?"

"Boils," she says.

"Appetizing."

This time, it works—she blinks, then smiles, which is the best I'm going to get, I think. "Yes, it's disgusting. I guess that's why they made poultices for it."

"Okay, what's a poultice?"

Blink, gulp. "Oh, it's like a salve? Sort of a soft . . . clump of plants that people used to put on wounds. Before they knew about antibiotics and disinfectant."

"That's cool. I didn't know that."

Her face glows like the sun. Obviously, I've made her day by allowing her to teach me some pointless trivia. "Yes," she says. "Mostly used during medieval times. I actually just emailed with a boy from England who made one for his father's leg recently. I can forward the email to you when we get back from—"

"Guys!" Suddenly, Ian's next to us. He grabs my arm with one hand and points into the woods with another. "Look! Out there in the woods!"

"Back off, Ian," says Kendra, taking two steps away and glaring at him. "Whatever you're doing, I'm not interested." She scowls at me, like I'm part of some prank setup on Ian's part.

"No, really, look," says Ian.

"Why?" She crosses her arms. "You think that if you distract me, you can put a snake in my hair or something, don't you? Just leave me alone."

"Will you just *look*?" he whispers, and his voice is intense enough that Kendra and I finally follow his finger out into the woods. For a second, I figure he's just being ridiculous, and then the crack of a twig off in the forest tells me he's on to something, and we're not alone.

There's something in the woods, walking around us. Something big.

I'm fine. It's just an animal. I'm not going to throw up. No. Wait. Okay. I definitely might throw up.

The silhouetted shape looks enormous as it moves between the trees, gracefully, calmly. There are four legs, a broad body, some kind of lowered head, and something else, hard to see. Kendra and I crouch down next to Ian, doing our best to barely breathe.

"What is it?" whispers Kendra.

"I can't make it out," whispers Ian.

A bear. A dragon. Death on four legs.

No, says a voice in the back of my head, *it's footage.*

My hand scrambles into my back pocket, and I pull out my handheld video recorder, savoring the simultaneous *"Cool . . ."* that Ian and Kendra whisper upon seeing it. The woods appears on its tiny screen, and the familiar feeling drifts over me, washes away the anxiety buzzing in my head and the nausea gurgling in my stomach, replaces it with a calm sense of control. Now the forest has a border around it, a light, an angle, and I'm the master of it all. I'm the director. None of this can harm me because it's just a movie, my movie. I'm boss here.

I step past Ian and Kendra, then kneel low in the tall grass to try to hide the sun behind the trees, get decent enough light to showcase the silhouette. I hold down the power button for three seconds, and the tiny red Record light flashes on—but not before letting out a shrill electronic beep.

The head whips up, and a deer, a buck with a massive

set of antlers, looks directly at us and snorts. Between the crown of horns hanging over his head and the aisles of regal trees on either side of him, he looks like a king of the forest. Black eyes, wet and wide, stare down the long nose, judging us with a weird sense of nobility, like how dare we try to capture him on camera?

Shots don't get much more perfect than this—it's as if the buck isn't looking at the camera, but at the viewer *through* it. His white chest barrels out in front of him, and the whole forest seems to shake as he tenses his massive body.

"Homeroom Earth, day one, just after lunch," I mumble. "Flower picking has been interrupted by the presence of an animal."

"Check it," whispers Ian. "That's a twelve-point buck."

"That can't be true. . . ." Kendra mumbles out a count, and then whistles. "You're right. Twelve points at least. Gosh, and look at his coloring."

All my fear of this creature is gone—now I want more, reaction shots, slow motion. We need full coverage. "Let's get closer," I whisper, inching forward.

I barely move when the buck turns and bounds off into the woods, flashing us the white flame of his tail.

"Wow, how cool was that?" I narrate. "The glory of nature, right before us! On the first day, no less—" Something blue and worn fills the screen—a pair of jeans. "Ian, you're in my shot."

"Come on!" yells Ian, trotting toward the woods. "Let's go after him!"

"Is that a joke?" asks Kendra. "There are four rules here, Ian. This is the *first one*."

I click off my camera, and reality seeps back in— Ian, Kendra, and me, puny against the endless woods ahead of us. For a second, Ian's idea sounded tempting, but now, in real life . . . "Maybe she's right, man. Let's head back to the group."

Ian stares back at us with this look of frantic dis-appointment. "Footage!" he yells at me. "Research!" he yells at Kendra. When we don't move, he mumbles, "Fine, forget both of you." Then he's off, sprinting after the buck with all his might, crunching through a field of glacier lilies and into the trees.

"Oh, wow," says Kendra.

"I know," I say. "Should we tell Ms. Brandt?"

"Maybe," she says, "maybe you're right." She turns and heads slowly toward the path, but when I stand up to follow her, she's frozen in midstride.

"What's up?" I ask.

She looks at me, then out into the woods at Ian's disappearing back. "Well," she says, "it's just . . . "

"You're not actually thinking about—"

She's gone before I can finish the sentence, bound-ing after Ian as fast as she can go.

"Wait!" I call.

"Bring your camera!" she yells back.

Instinctively, I turn to call out to Ms. Brandt, but I'm greeted with an empty field. The rest of our class is gone, along with our teacher, our counselor, everyone. Suddenly, this field of brightly colored flowers is massive and deathly silent, and the only noise I can hear is the wind in the trees and Kendra's footsteps slowly fading in the distance.

What do I do? My options are slim. I can wait here and hope that someone finds me. I can run after our class and either get lost or rat on Ian, maybe lose my only remaining camera. Or I can—I can—

I can run for it.

And that's what I do. I lock onto Kendra's bobbing hair, and I run like crazy after her, gritting my teeth against the snakes and bugs and spores that I know are whizzing past me.

CHAPTER FOUR

Ian

Up ahead, I can see his tail bouncing between the trees, doing his best to outrun us, but I'm not letting him get off that easy, 'cause his body may be built for rough ground, but so is mine, and for every split-second turn or dodge he makes, my feet follow, pushing off rocks and clearing fallen trees. There are no big woods or mountains in the distance; there's just the ground at my feet, the tree in my way, and that little bit of buck vanishing in the distance. Branches scratch me, stones tumble out from under me, but I adapt and keep going. The buck's the prey. I'm the hunter.

This is more like it!

The woods open up in front of me and I skid to a halt, and for a split second, the buck's there in all his twelve-point glory, white chest shoved out, spade-shaped head held high, two gray antlers jutting out from behind his ears like bony tree branches. He poses on top of a ridge of rocks that rises out of the brush, a symbol for everything cool about the wild. Behind him, the sun just *explodes* out over the forest, with beams of light caught in the tips of his antlers, the blue-gray mountains coming up around his shoulders like he's one of them. It's beautiful, man, *exactly* the kind of thing you expect to see on a trip like this, no, on a postcard from a trip to the mountains. Pure wilderness. My heart skips a beat. My eyes water. Doesn't get much better than this.

The buck lowers his head, stares me down; and he seems like he's looking directly into my eyes, like he knows that we're both cut from the same cloth, but like he doesn't trust me, not yet. For a second, we just stand there, eyeing each other. When I take a step toward him, he takes a few at me, lowering those antlers like he's not afraid to use them. His eyes are like black stones shining at me.

"Easy," I whisper to him, crouching low to the ground. "I'm not going to hurt you."

He lets out a loud snort, turns, and bounds in two great arcs down the ridge. I get that flash of white tail and a couple of crunches in the underbrush, and then nothing, like he never existed.

When I look behind me, Kendra Wright's standing there with her eyes bugging out and a hand clutched to her heart, panting through a smile. Behind her, PJ's taken a knee, staring into the screen of his tiny digital camera, face screwed up in concentration.

"That was *awesome*, right?" I say.

"That was . . ." laughs Kendra. "It certainly was . . . something."

"Tell me you got that," I call out to PJ.

"I think so," he breathes, messing with his tiny camera. "Yeah, definitely. Oh, wow."

Kendra and I huddle around the miniscreen, and yup, there's the buck, staring down at me, and there I am, crouched near the grass with a single hand reaching out toward it, looking *too cool*, like some kind of deer whisperer. On the video, PJ mumbles, "Look, look at that," and then coughs, sending the buck off into the wilderness.

"I could only get about nine seconds," he says. "Sorry."

"That's okay," I say, giving him a pat on the shoulder. "Totally excusable. Those nine seconds are worth the whole run."

I'm not lying, either. For once, PJ's camera addiction has worked out. The look on Coach Leider's face when he sees this video is going to be priceless—at first, he's going to be all shaking his head, folding those big meaty arms, *What'd the counselors say about blahdee blah blah*, and then he'll see the footage of this buck, and he'll to show it to Principal Jones when he asks how the trip went, and the school will use it to get funding for maybe another twenty years of Homeroom Earth, and I'll probably get some kind of Wildlife Tamer award and Coach might even start rethinking this starting point guard situation. And hey, *buck* is even in my name, so maybe the team will call me Ian "Twelve-Point" Buckley, and then we'll see—

"Uh, guys?" says PJ.

"What?" I ask. PJ's staring into the thickness of leaves and branches around us, running his hand through his hair over and over. When he doesn't say anything, I call, "PJ? What's up?"

"I just . . . which way did we come from?" he asks, peering into the woods.

"We came from . . . back there," I say, pointing behind me. Already, though, the grass we trampled is bending back into place. My ears strain to pick up Ms. Brandt's sharp voice or one of the other kids in our group, but there's just the creak of trees, the call of a bird. Guess we ran farther than I thought.

"Are you sure?" he says. "I thought we came from over there, by that huge rock."

"Which huge rock?" asks Kendra. "There are a number of huge rocks in this area."

"That one," says PJ, gesturing with his hand.

"No way," I tell him. "That rock? If we came from that direction, we would have had to jump over it, and I don't remember doing that."

"I sort of do remember that, though. I don't know." Uh-oh. PJ's chest begins rising and falling quicker and quicker. "We're lost, aren't we?" His big sad eyes turn on me, like he's giving a dirty look and begging for help at the same time. "This is how it always starts! You wander off the path and then you get lost, then you find some maniac living in a trailer in the woods, then he pulls out a hatchet—"

This is what too many late-night horror movies do to a kid. "PJ, calm down. You got the footage, didn't you? Admit it, you had a great time running after that deer!"

"Now we're lost!" he whines. "We have *no idea* how to get back!"

Before I can ask PJ who put a gun to his head and told him to run into the woods after me, Kendra Wright hushes us both and dives into her backpack. She unfolds a big colorful map, then scans it with her index finger. Her other hand fishes around among her stuff and comes back out with . . . a compass?

"This is all you've got?" I ask her. "What is this, the Oregon Trail?"

"I had a GPS in my *phone*," she growls, giving me the stink-eye.

Given our current situation, I'll let that one slide. Besides, this is Kendra Wright we're talking about, Queen Brain. Her noggin is a mass of numbers, dates, and stupid school trivia. If anyone can triangulate our location and get us home, it's her.

"We headed northeast," she says. "Those mountains"—she points to the faded peaks way off in the distance—"are part of the Bitterroot Range. There are paths all over them. If we keep walking in . . . *that* direction, we're going to run into Wood Chip Hiking Path, which will lead us back to the parking lot where the buses dropped us off. It shouldn't take more than half an hour."

"See? We're fine," I say to PJ.

"Yeah, right," he says shakily. "I'll believe that when we get back to camp."

Yeesh. That kid's got to grow a backbone. If it were up to PJ, all we'd ever do is film other people having fun while we sit around talking about cinematographers and monster makeup.

"Come on," I say, walking in the direction Kendra pointed.

The woods are awesome. The air is totally pure and smells like a million different things at once—fur, leaves, dirt, rocks, water (who knew water had a smell!). Trees drip with sap and rustle with squirrels and birds living it up from branch to branch. Everything's moving, from bugs zipping through the air to plants twitching in the breeze. Even the sunlight on the forest floor looks alive as it quivers and shakes.

Coach Leider was telling us last week that a trip out into nature is what really separates the wolves from the poodles, because a wolf can thrive alone in nature and still find its way back to the pack, and a poodle can't survive without pampering and hand-feeding. Right now, I know exactly what he means. The woods are a big, beautiful playground, and I get a feeling, a wolfish kind of feeling, that we're headed the right way.

Of course, I haven't forgotten about the Pine City Dancers. If Jeremy Morris was telling the truth, they're somewhere out here, even if all that's left of them is bones. Wherever Sean and Mitch are with Coach's group, it's probably nowhere near as deep into the woods as I am. I need to use this as a head start—with PJ and Kendra along for the ride, I'll have witnesses if I do find them. PJ even has a camera, so we can document it. Forget the bet—if I find these missing hikers, Coach will *have* to be impressed enough to make me starting point-guard, maybe even team captain.

Behind me, Kendra waits for PJ to catch up with us. With her hair, she almost *looks* like a poodle, and anyway, there's no fun in her face, no excitement about being out here. I've got two poodles with me now—a brainiac and a scaredy-cat.

But maybe us wolves need to look after poodles. Coach is never down on us when we screw up during practice, he's always pushing us forward, and that's what gets us through. Why blow off PJ, when I can make a wolf of him? It'd be cool if when we got home, he could finally hang with the guys from the team, or at least not make me look like a loser when they're around.

Wow, Wilson, we always thought you were lame, but you really toughened up out in the woods, and PJ would be all *I had a little help,* and he'd wink at me, and we'd laugh.

A few yards away, I see a chance. There's a big dead cedar tree up ahead, the trunk half cracked and splitting outward like a bunch of sharp snaggleteeth. All the leaves and most of the branches are gone, and the only thing keeping it up is the other tree it's leaning against.

"Let's push it over," I say, pointing to the dried-up husk.

"I don't know," says PJ. "Some idiot is always doing something like this in the movies. They hurt someone's sacred tree, and then it releases an evil demon—"

"Dude, this isn't a horror movie. Look at it—it's deader than dirt. And I bet clearing dead trees is really good for the living ones, right?" I ask Kendra.

She stops, her eyes frozen in that creepy nerd stare,

then blinks and says, "Yes, actually. Knocking this tree over would also provide extra burrowing space for animals."

"See? If Kendra Wright says it, it must be true. We're helping the environment." He still looks worried, so I say, in my most encouraging voice, "It'll be *really cool*."

The other two slowly follow me to the gray tree. I lean into it with my shoulder, kind of hoping it'll go right down and I'll look like the Hulk, but the trunk just creaks and sways, so I motion the other two to get in on the action. Kendra gets next to me and starts pushing, and soon we're shoulder to shoulder, giving the tree all we've got. It's not like we're friends or anything, okay, my face still aches where that textbook hit me, but we're out here together, so I guess I'll deal with letting her in on the fun.

I hear a beep and look up to see PJ holding his camera, narrating, "Ian and Kendra here, trying to knock over a dead tree—"

"PJ, forget the footage!" I call out to him. "Put down the camera and help us!"

"We can't do this with just the two of us," says Kendra.

PJ bites his lip, but his eyes finally leave the screen, and he joins us at the tree.

The cedar resists for a second, and then there's a loud crack that echoes through the whole forest, and we leap back as the trunk slowly snaps outward and the tree drops to the earth with a resounding BOOM. Birds fly, chipmunks scatter, the sound echoes for miles. Next to me, PJ dusts off his hands with a proud smile on his pale little face.

"Awesome, right?"

"Yeah, okay," he admits. "That was really awesome."

The trunk of the tree is now an open pit swarming with white termites that crawl over one another and burrow deeper into the ground to get away from the light. Of course, rather than leave the disgusting vermin alone, Kendra's all over it, actually picking up a handful of creepy crawlers and putting them in a plastic jar—"for later."

"What, just in case you need a snack?"

"Don't be *puerile*," she says. "They're fascinating specimens."

"Whatever you say, Queen Brain."

"What?" she says. "What did you call me?"

"What? Nothing. Get back to your bugs."

The more stuff I do, the more they join in. I jump up and swing from a low-hanging branch and PJ jumps to try and reach it (he doesn't, but at least he tries). We find a couple of downed trees and snap off branches to make ourselves walking sticks. An upturned stone reveals a garter snake, and PJ films it instead of having a heart attack about it—from a safe distance, of course; you can't just make a poodle a wolf in an afternoon.

See? There's no reason we shouldn't be having fun! This is exciting! We're forging a path through the wilderness! We're on our own, living it up in nature!

Except . . .

Except according to my watch, we walk for an hour and twenty minutes and there's no Wood Chip Hiking Path, no walking trails, no hunting blinds, no nothing, just deeper woods, bigger trees. We march past endless rows of tall gray evergreens, miles of fallen red and yellow leaves, the occasional patch of bright green ferns, but nothing else. Even the animal noises fade—soon I only hear birds calling way off in the distance, and the squirrels and chipmunks scurrying around earlier are nowhere to be found. The farther we march, the wider PJ's eyes get, the deeper the corners of Kendra's mouth sink, and the taller our shadows grow against the leaf-covered forest floor.

The sound of rushing water perks up our spirits, and we forge ahead to a small creek running through the woods. We all stop at the bank and take a breather, grateful for something different, some kind of landmark. Kendra fills her canteen and drops a huge pill in it. She tells us it's a water purification tablet, which, of course, she has a bunch of, being a weirdo, but okay, it's been a long thirsty walk, and we all take a much-needed drink. PJ takes off his shoes and dangles his feet in the water. Behind him, I tap Kendra on the shoulder, and the two of us sneak off a few yards into the woods. She looks frustrated and hopeless, and to be honest, I'm feeling less like a wolf every minute.

Kendra's eyes never leave her map and compass. Sweat forms on her upper lip.

"So, look, we may not like each other," I begin in my calmest voice.

"Agreed," she mumbles.

"And that's cool, whatever, we can deal with that at another time," I say, trying not to freak her out, "but we might want to get back to the lodge."

She's silent and then mutters, "Right."

"So . . . which direction do we head to get to the nearest trail back to Homeroom Earth?"

She pauses, blinks hard, and then sort of looks at me, not at my eyes but maybe at, like, my chin. "I . . . don't know."

"Well, what does it say on the map?"

"I don't know."

"Are we traveling toward the campsite or not?"

"I don't *know*," she snaps, and finally her eyes look into mine, and they're all big and wet and scared. "If the map and compass are correct, we should've hit the path forty minutes ago. We've been doing everything right according to my calculations; it's just that something's . . . different." She hands me the map and uses the free hand to pinch the bridge of her nose, and mumbles, "Think, Kendra, think, where are we, where are we?"

Uh-oh. So, the one person in your group who can outthink gravity doesn't know where we are, and now *she's* being a head case, too. This isn't the end of the world, people. Maybe the map is wrong, or her compass is on the fritz, or maybe we're in a part of these mountains that hasn't been charted yet.

"Okay," I say. "Well, maybe . . . one of us should break off, see if we can find some help and alert the authorities. Or at least get to a phone."

"That would be ill-advised," she says. "By the time one of us found a phone, the other two could be a long way away." She pinches her nose so hard, it looks painful. "Do you know any tracking skills or anything like that? Like a hunter?"

"Why would I have tracking skills?"

"Because you're very"—she waves her hands around—*"outdoorsy."*

"You're Queen Brain. Shouldn't you know how to find our way home?"

"Why do you keep calling me that?" she asks, annoyed.

PJ and I have called you that for years, I think but don't say. "Because . . . it doesn't matter. We need to do something," I say, because I can't think of *anything*.

"Let's go talk to PJ," she says. "Maybe the three of

us can come up with a plan."

"Right. Just take it easy with him, okay? I don't want him to have a panic attack."

"Understood," she says, taking the map back from me. "How do I look?"

"Uh, fine? I don't know, smart?"

"Good." She closes her eyes and takes a deep breath. "Let's do this."

Kendra and I turn slowly back to the creek, where PJ sits hunched over with his feet in the water, his hands up in two L shapes to create a frame in front of him, mapping a shot (he does that a lot at home—it's a little embarrassing). Finally, Kendra says, "We need to talk to you about something."

"There's a wall up there," says PJ. "Look. Upper left-hand corner, between those trees." We both crouch down next to PJ so we can see through his frame, and he's right—stretching across a little clearing in the foothills is a gray stone wall.

"Indeed," says Kendra.

Then, it hits me. "But a wall means people, right? We should check it out!"

"Maybe we shouldn't," says PJ, dropping his hand frame and looking down at his feet in the water. "What if we're trespassing on someone's property? This has *chainsaw massacre* written all over it."

"That person might have a phone," says Kendra,

standing up. She carefully hops over the creek and motions for us to follow. "It's our best option right now."

"Best option?" says PJ worriedly. "What about the map? Are we *that* lost?"

Kendra and I share a glance, and I know I've got to take charge. "We're just trying our best to find someone else out here," I tell him, and then hop across the creek to Kendra.

Slowly, PJ tiptoes over the creek and pulls his shoes back on. We hike toward the stone wall, me in the lead, trying to quiet down the weird feeling in my guts. It can't be that I'm scared. Me? No way. I'm a wolf. It's probably just something I ate.

CHAPTER FIVE

Kendra

After a short break, we head for the stone wall. More trudging through the woods. My body aches, but my mind is too caught up in our predicament at the moment.

How did this happen, Kendra? You know everything about these woods; you spent hours sitting at your desk and holed up in the library, perusing survival websites and reference books, mentally tallying anything that sounded slightly important. You worked so hard on this. Home-room Earth. The wilderness. You did all the research, and you were about to get a reward: fieldwork. Adventure. Hands-on experience.

And now, there's a wall. In every direction, all you

can see are trees, mountain peaks, rocks, leaves, but noth-
ing useful, nothing that suggests human life, other than a
stone wall probably built some century or so ago by Crow
Indians worried that the white men wandering through
this forest were becoming too bold for their own good. And
yes, maybe if you had your phone, maybe if your compass
wasn't changing its mind every fifteen minutes, you could
find your way out of here. But all that means is that you
didn't need to do that research in the first place, Kendra,
or that you didn't do enough of it. What does Dad say—
it's a shoddy workman who blames his tools.

This is your fault. So, considering your complete
inability to find your bearings, you have to see if this stone
wall can tell you something.

My face burns hot, but my skin feels cold. Everything irritates me: the trees, the forest floor, the
occasional sound of animals (always far off—we haven't
seen another living creature for a while now). Nothing
is worse than this, than being *unsure*, than *panicking*.
Grasping at straws, hoping a random wall will be the
answer.

Is this how adventure feels, like walking into a risky
situation and suddenly realizing you don't know any-
thing? Is this how Lewis and Clark felt? Magellan? If
so, maybe you weren't cut out for it, Kendra. Maybe you
should've stuck with the books and the internet.

"Do people live up in these mountains?" asks Ian as

we walk. When no one says anything, he looks to me. "Kendra?"

"Not too many lived on the mountains themselves, but a number of Native American tribes settled in Montana. The Crow had a real presence here, but they were mostly just following the buffalo." *Spout those facts, Kendra. They're real. You know them; you're positive of them.* "In these mountains, it was probably the Shoshone, and some Flathead. But again, people don't really live up in these mountains. It's too rugged."

"I guess so," says PJ. His eyes are set on the wall in the distance. There is sweat on his brow, on the collar of his shirt. For all my studiousness, I was at least prepared for this trip. Poor PJ is lost out here, and it's showing.

"Aren't there all those old stories of mountain men, though?" Ian picks up a fallen branch and swings it into a nearby tree. "Like, what's his name . . . Davy Crockett?"

"Sort of. The real mountain men were mostly in the Appalachians out east, and they weren't always those adventurous mountain hero types. Most of them are backwoods rednecks who spent too much time alone and went crazy. They would hunt everything they ate, and raise big families . . ."

Midsentence, it dawns on me that the idea of running into some crazy mountain folk is actually rather unnerving, and the expression on PJ's face is terribly sad. I immediately switch tactics: "Anyway, there probably isn't anyone around here for miles."

"Great," says Ian. "We're all alone. Awesome pep talk there, Kendra."

It's true, Kendra, even if it makes you feel like choking him. You're falling behind on this. There is a right answer here. There always is.

The bigger the wall gets, the stranger it looks, and by the time we reach it, my heart is filled with this irrational sense of, of what, what's the word . . . *dread.* The thing is dreadful. It's about three and a half feet high, made of large gray lumps of age-old stone, and it winds off about a half mile in either direction. But . . .

"Something's wrong with it," says Ian. His face screws up, like he's smelled something bad.

"It looks sick," says PJ.

Yes. PJ is correct. The wall looks infected. Weird bundles of twigs and leaves jut from between its stones, and ivy has bred somewhere inside its crevices and pushed out into the daylight, snaking through the stone pile in thick, hairy vines. Ants and termites move constantly over the rocks, marching in perfect lines. Someone has painted something on the wall, too, in a white chalky paste, a weird twisting shape that's sort of like a cross, haphazardly sketched by lazy hands. There's a smell to it, a sweet but sharp stench that reminds me of the eggnogs Dad makes around Christmas.

"It's rum," I say, my mind grasping the odor. "It stinks like rum."

"*That's* what that is," says PJ. He glances down at the ground, blinks hard, and says, "Are these . . . I think there are coffee beans on the ground." We all kneel down, and sure enough, there are coffee beans and peanuts strewn around the wall.

"Odd," I hear myself say.

"Maybe," says Ian, "but it means we're not alone out here!" He stands back up, presses a hand to the cold stones of the wall, and peels it off with a rough sticky noise. "Yeah, it could be rum," he says. "It's pretty fresh, though. That's what matters."

That should matter, shouldn't it, Kendra? Fresh rum means recent application, means someone's nearby. Then why does the wall send ripples of anxiety down your spine and through your ears? No facts are available as to why staring at this wall shakes you, prickles you down to your bones. So why is your rational mind failing you?

My mother, less of a wordsmith than my father but a brilliant woman nonetheless, has said something to me repeatedly over the years—*Sometimes, you need to get out of your head and go with your gut.* That's what's wrong here, in a nutshell. My gut is incredibly apprehensive about this wall and the symbol drawn on it.

Suddenly, my mind snaps to attention. All this fear and worry has distracted me from my job—record the information, study the facts, analyze. I drop to one knee, dig through my bag, and find my notebook and a pencil. As best I can, I copy down the strange lopsided symbol from the wall and scribble "Rum? Coffee? Peanuts?" next to it.

The beep behind my shoulder startles me, and when I turn to PJ, he's filming me with his tiny flip camera. For once, though, the camera doesn't seem intrusive to me, but rather a tool—something with which to record our journey.

"Could you tape this for me?" I ask him. "With something this odd, it's good to document it."

"Sure thing," says PJ. There's the beep of his camera, and a short bit of narration—"We're lost, and we found this stone wall. There's some kind of shape painted onto it, and it smells like rum. Let's hope that means something." Then: "Ian, careful."

Ian has already scaled the wall and stares petulantly back at us from on top of it, trying to play conquistador, oblivious to the damage he could be doing to a historical landmark. Typical.

"You shouldn't stand up there," I yell at him.

"Why?" he says. "We're going to have to climb over it anyway."

"But still," I snap back at him. "You never think about things, you just go ahead and do them. You ought to have some respect for—"

"For a *wall*?" he moans, throwing up his hands. "What's to respect? We have to climb it! Get over yourself!"

That last crack was uncalled for, and I give him the dirtiest look I can before following him. As PJ and I climb up and leap down on the other side, the sun seems fainter, the air feels colder, and the reassuring scent of the forest is replaced with something sour and spoiled. The wall is made not just of stone, but of air, as though an invisible barrier stretches from the ground up into the sky. It's not me alone—PJ hugs himself tightly, his skinny little body shuddering as we walk onward. Even Ian, with his headstrong bluster, frowns and wipes at the soles of his shoes.

The hillside has gotten steeper since the wall, and we're all struggling to keep pace, except for Ian, whose long, skinny legs yank him easily over any rock or felled tree in our path. Every time we pass a large burrow or a thick patch of bushes, he kneels beside it and peers into it, as though he's lost something. As he crouches near a thick hollowed-out tree trunk, I hear him mumble, "Where are you, where are you . . ."

"What are you looking for?" I ask him.

He glances at me over his shoulder, then mumbles, "Nothing. Just . . . if you see anything that looks like clothing, let me know."

"Is this about the Pine City Dancers?" asks PJ, wiping

sweat from his brow. "You're still hung up on that?"

"Well . . . you have to admit, it would be pretty cool if we found them," says Ian.

When I look at PJ, he shudders and looks around himself. "Jeremy Morris from the seventh grade told Ian that a modern dance troupe disappeared in these woods last year," he groans. "That's why we didn't have a Homeroom Earth trip last year."

Ah. Of course Ian has no intention of helping our situation, only hunting down a campfire story and scaring the wits out of his best friend. What a weasel. "That story's not true," I declare.

"But what if it is?" asks Ian. "We could be heroes for finding these poor lost hikers and bringing back proof of their existence."

"First of all," I say, "do you think our teachers would let us go hiking in woods where there might be dead bodies?" I look at PJ and shake my head in a *What an idiot* kind of way. He smiles back. "And second, what would you tell our teachers if you *did* find them? 'I'm sorry I disobeyed the rules and left the path, but look, here's a dead body.' Good luck, Ian."

"You're thinking about this all wrong," he says.

"You're not thinking about it, period," I tell him. "Same as when you ran off into the woods."

Ian gets a dark, mean look on his face. After a moment's silence, he says, "Well, what *are* we going to tell the teachers about what happened today? We need a story, something they'll believe."

"PJ and I can say you ran off after a deer, and we went after you to keep you from doing something stupid," I say. "They'll believe that."

"Yeah, I bet you'd tell them that," he snaps. "Anything to bring me down, huh, Queen Brain?"

"I wasn't concerned with *you*," I tell him. "I'm thinking about PJ and me."

"Right, but look," says Ian, waving his hands in the air. Finally, it bursts free: "If I get the blame for this, there would be, you know, serious consequences." I'm impressed he knows a word that big. So many syllables. "I might have to sit out of hoops this season and everything."

"Thanks for your concern, Ian," I say. "You couldn't think about that *before* you went barreling after that deer earlier?"

"Will you back off me, Kendra?" he snaps. "What'd I ever do to you?"

"Called me a pathetic nerd, for one," I reply.

"God, you'll never let that one go, will you?" he says.

"Got my phone taken away from me, for another," I tell him. "Got me and your best friend lost in the woods. That's three. Should I keep going?"

Ian turns to PJ. "Dude, help me out here. You don't want me to take the hit for us getting lost, do you?"

"Right now, I just want to get home," says PJ, mopping sweat from his brow with his shirt.

"I'm just saying—"

"We know what you're saying, Ian," says PJ. He won't look at Ian, but his expression of fear has turned to one of anger. "I just don't care about it right now."

Ian stares at PJ, his eyes softening with hurt, then narrowing with rage. "Fine, whatever," he snaps. "Throw me under the bus. Thanks a ton, man." He turns and plods off through the woods, making as much noise as possible.

I walk next to PJ for a few minutes, and he says, softly, "It's really hard to argue with him."

"You two don't seem like likely friends," I observe.

He nods. "Our parents have been friends for a long time," he says. "And he's a really good guy most of the time. He just cares a lot about what people think of him. And I . . ." He sighs. "Being friends with me doesn't help people's opinions much. No one wants to be buddies with some weird film geek."

Maybe I'm unversed in movie fanaticism, but being an embarrassment—a freak, a loser—that rings a bell. Without understanding why, I reach out a hand and touch PJ's shoulder lightly. He looks up at me, bewildered, and then smiles. "Thanks for being on my side," he says. "I'm not really used to it."

This boy is your friend, somehow, Kendra. You can

analyze how it happened when you get home. For now, you've got to help him. If that means helping Ian by association, then fine. Start thinking for three.

We keep walking, and the sun keeps sinking. The shadows grow longer; the breezes seem chillier. For a while, we're silent, which allows me to make a mental tally of what's in my bag. We should eat soon—low blood sugar is terrible for outdoor activities. We have the granola bars, ramen . . . and that's it. Not a great assortment of food, but it should be enough to get us through the night. With some luck, we could also find some wild berries.

Remember from your reading, Kendra—are pinecones edible? Didn't Sondra from that French camping message board say that she cooked a pinecone once?

My uneasiness doesn't go anywhere but instead gets worse and worse, dragging my mind away from the task at hand and back to the stone wall, coated in rum, marked with that weird, incomprehensible symbol. While we walk on and on, I take out my notebook and stare at the drawing I made. It's an ornate cross, dotted with circles, frosted with swirls, adorned to be both welcoming and dangerous. Something about it being painted on the rum-covered stone wall in the middle of an uninhabited mountain range makes me feel increasingly anxious. It's as though I've overlooked a serious error that will return to ruin me later on.

"What're you reading?" asks PJ.

"Nothing," I lie. "Just some notes on which berries are edible."

"Good call," says PJ, nodding to himself, trying to play calm. "I could eat soon."

There's no point in telling them—my panic might rub off on PJ, and Ian will probably declare me insane.

Then a noise rings through the air, unlike any animal call we've heard. It's a low, sonorous moan that seems to bounce between the trees and pass over us in a wave. I watch dread creep over PJ's and Ian's faces.

"What was that?" asks PJ, looking up to me for reassurance.

"Flammulated owl," I fib, to him and myself. "They're common in this region."

He nods, but he knows I'm lying. His eyes ask me, *What are you* really *thinking?*

And with how scared my gut feels right now, I don't want to tell him.

CHAPTER SIX

PJ

I've got to be strong, for Kyra.

That's what I keep repeating in my head. *Kyra's out there. She's at home in bed in the blue sheets with the hippos on them, and she doesn't know why you're not reading her a story. She needs you to get back to camp and call home and read* Burly Bunny and the Thunderstorm *to her, because otherwise she'll have bad dreams.* That's all that gets me up the mountain.

We climb for what feels like miles, while the light fades and the shadows close in around us. The view of the sun disappearing behind the Bitterroot peaks should be beautiful, but we don't have any time to think about it, just to race against it.

Ian and Kendra are amazing. They make it look so easy. It's like Ian's body was built for the wild—skinny, muscular legs and arms, sharp hunter's face, and a sweaty mop of blond hair that never gets in his eyes once. My mom always says he's about to hit his "big growth spurt," and I can see it now; every time he stretches and climbs, he looks like he's about to rip out of his skin. He's so into being the hero, the pioneer, that he doesn't take the time to feel stupid, even when we're lost out in the middle of Nowhere, Montana.

And Kendra Wright's brilliant, even with us, with me. Before she opens her mouth, she stops, blinks, reviews the situation in her head, and thinks of the thing that will most encourage us to do what she wants, what she thinks will best get us out of here. More than that, though, she is trying to figure out what to do next. All that awkwardness is just her way of thinking things through. It's like she's the anti-Ian.

Between his hard head and her sharp mind, we're dragging ourselves farther and farther along. That noise, that horrible sound that Kendra claims was an owl, seems to follow us, along with the creepy stone wall and the huge disappearing deer.

Everything is terrifying out here. Every rock has a dark space underneath it that something probably lives in, and every pile of leaves looks like it has eyes somewhere inside it peering out at us. Even the trees start becoming a solid mass of shadows towering over us, reaching out with prickerlike branches, pulling us deeper into the wilderness. In horror movies, it's all set pieces—carefully placed branches, choreographed rocks, prerecorded animal noises. Out here it's random, wild. There's no control, no motivation.

I try to forget my fear, focus on the forest and the hike, but it's always there. Ian can outrun it and Kendra can outthink it, but I have nothing, just a lump in my throat. My backpack is full of a million different bug repellents and first-aid accessories, and a Burly Bunny book about not being scared of lightning, but none of those things can help us out here against a poisonous snake or a ravenous coyote.

Or the decayed bodies of the Pine City Dancers—no. I can't let my mind wander, can't let the fear overtake me. My hand fishes my camera out of my pocket, and it beeps alive. When the forest appears onscreen, I'm back on top, able to break free of all the fear that's bubbling up in my head.

"PJ, you should turn that off," says Kendra. I pan to her disapproving scowl. "We might need it later to help document landmarks on our hike. Keep us from walking in circles. Don't run down the battery."

There's truth to that, sadly. I hit the Power button, and the screen goes dead. Suddenly, all the agony of being out here comes flooding back into my skull and chest.

I'm not going to cry. I'm not going to have a panic attack. Not yet.

We find a flat spot that's more grass than leaves, and Kendra holds up a hand, telling us to stop. "Let's try to make a fire here," she says. "I have some Ramen noodles and a couple of granola bars in my backpack. We should eat."

"Does anyone know how to make a fire?" I ask, my voice cracking.

"I do," say Ian and Kendra at the same time, and then stare at each other dumbly.

"Trust me on this one," says Ian. "I know how to build a fire."

"Do you?" she asks. "Who taught you?"

"My dad. Dads teach their sons these things."

"Is that what this is about?" says Kendra, almost vibrating with anger. "Girls can't build fires?"

Ian finally wins because he just starts gathering stones and twigs without waiting for another argument. Kendra looks flabbergasted without something to do, something to make right. It gets painful to watch her looking so confused and awkward, so I say, "Want me to go get water for the noodles?"

"That'd be great," she says, folding her arms. "I'll study the map some more." It does the trick—she's in charge again. Besides, what else am I going to do?

The creek we stopped at before the wall extends up the mountain a few yards away, so I walk down to the edge with Kendra's canteen. The water rushing along the smooth stones makes a nice burbling noise that helps calm my nerves a little. Right now, I'm just relieved to not be stuck between those two opposing forces for a minute.

There's a tiny pool near me where the creek levels out, and I crouch down and dunk the canteen into the icy water. It lets loose a line of bubbles that stops when it's full, but I don't pull it out quite yet. Little fish swim around my fingers, sniffing at the canteen. One or two of them nudge my hand with slippery noses, and without thinking, I take out my camera and film them silently. The day's worry starts to disappear from my mind. I wonder about the fish. It must be strange, having a newcomer shove some big metal container into your home. What a funny idea, being a fish like these, spending your whole life in one little pool in a long creek. Maybe they change pools every year at some time, jumping upstream or letting the current take them down the mountainside. Maybe they're content to live in some small puddle—

Someone's here.

My eyes fly up to the forest as my breath gets yanked out of my chest. Gray woods and brown leaves surround me, the same as before only now backlit with the bright gold and reddish brown of oncoming dusk, but I can sense something, a new presence, off in the woods.

"Hello?" I call out. Nothing.

In the movies, the person who thinks they're being watched is almost always being watched. My mind's eye pans out into the trees, imagines a close-cropped shot from some bushes—me, kneeling by the creek—with heavy breathing over it. Now I'm eyeing every bush and burrow, wondering where the eyes are, from what angle this new presence is watching me.

But it's the curious people, who have to go wandering off to find out what's spying on them, who take a machete to the face. The people who get back to camp are the ones that survive. I screw the lid on the canteen, turn around, and retrace my steps quickly, eyes on my back the entire time.

When I return, Ian is trying too hard to kick a fire pit in the dirt with just his sneaker. He sweats and grunts with the effort, switching from toe to heel and back again. Kendra watches from a few feet off, her arms crossed, a smile on her face.

Poor Ian, wanting to kick and shove his way through everything. In a horror movie, he'd be the jock—the first to go. It's embarrassing to watch, so I find a decent-sized rock, kneel by the spot he's kicking, and start gouging the ground with the stone's edge.

"Here," I say. "Get the dirt broken up, then kick it aside. Can someone give me a stick?" Kendra hands me a thick twig, and I stab it into the ground and clear away the loosened soil. (I mean, I learned this from *Sleepaway Camp*, but still, c'mon, Ian.)

"Huh. Right." Ian wipes a sweaty clump of hair from his eyes. "It's good to see you're in survival mode, man." He looks at Kendra. "Why didn't you think of that?"

"I did," she mumbles, smiling meanly. "But you were doing so *well*."

He kneels to help sweep the dirt out of the hole. "We should be helping each other out here. This is the kind of situation that separates the wolves from the poodles."

Kendra and I share a little look, and it's obvious we're both thinking the same thing—*You've got to be kidding me.* I know that's not Ian talking; it's one of Coach Leider's stupid sayings repeated by someone who doesn't want to admit he's worried. Besides, Ian gets a lot of this jock wisdom stuff from his father. My dad says that Vince Buckley has "weird ideas about being a man." (Apparently, Ian's dad didn't even *play* sports in high school, just liked to hang around the locker room and talk a lot of game.)

As I help Ian push a circle of stones into the dirt and stack twigs for kindling, I decide that I'm neither a wolf nor a poodle nor a dog of any kind. I'm a little fish in one pool of a huge creek. But now I'm in a different pool. And I need to stay strong if I want to make my way upstream, back to my puddle, my house, my little sister.

Ian desperately tries to rub two twigs together but finally stops, shakes his head, and tosses them away. "Must be something wrong with the wood," he says.

Kendra picks the twigs up and tries it herself, and after a minute of rubbing, a wisp of smoke grows out of the pile of leaves, and pretty soon we have a little fire going.

"Good thing I got it warmed up for you," mumbles Ian. Kendra shoots me a look and rolls her eyes. We all take a moment to huddle around the fire like we're praying to it, hands out, eyes pinned to the small orange blaze.

After we all warm up a bit, Kendra stands and announces in this threatening tone, "I need to go to the bathroom." She points. "Over there."

"What, you think we're going to follow you or something?" Ian laughs.

Kendra's face flushes, and she storms off into the woods. The minute she's out of earshot, Ian looks at me and grins.

"Man, this is kind of crazy, isn't it?" he says. "Lost in the woods, left to fend for ourselves . . . we're learning more out here than anything we could back at camp!" He laughs again, a little too hard. I must make a face, because he switches tones. "You all right, man? You scared?"

"Yeah," I say with a shrug. Understatement of the century, but I have to stay strong. "Kind of. We just didn't plan for this is all. Aren't you?"

"Nah!" he says, just quick enough to let me know he means *yes*. "I mean, look, this isn't how I expected to spend my afternoon, but you have to roll with the punches. Sure, I'm a little, you know, *freaked out*, but scared? No way!" He nudges me with his elbow. "Maybe don't talk about this with Queen Brain, though. You know how girls get."

Weird ideas about being a man, my dad says. "My lips are sealed."

"You're not still ticked about me getting us lost, are you?" he says. "I mean, I know you think it was stupid and all, but it's not *totally* my fault, right?"

"You didn't force us to run after you," I offer. It's a weak response—it *was* stupid of us to follow that buck, and it *is* Ian's fault, and I *am* still upset, but saying that won't help anyone, especially Ian. That's how he works: everything about him rests on his confidence; make him feel uncool and he's useless. "We all got into this together."

Ian nods. "Exactly. We got into this together, so we have to get out of this together. If we get back, I promise I'll never go running off into the woods again." That *if* is a little open-ended for me, and I wrap my hands

74

around my knees and squeeze hard.

Kendra comes back, and Ian suddenly gets all official and hardcore again. "I better check the area," he says. "You never know what might creep up on us if we don't secure a perimeter." He crunches his way off into the woods, and Kendra walks over and sits down next to me.

"Stupid Ian," she mumbles. "The trip was going fine until he had to go chasing that deer. And I followed him, beyond all logic. PJ, what was I even thinking?"

This is how it will be until we're found, or we get back to the lodge. PJ Wilson, amateur therapist. But here I am. Because I know how to be a big brother.

"It'll be okay," I say. "You're doing really well."

After a pause, she says, "Don't tell Ian, but I'm actually kind of worried."

It's funny that they hate each other so much, because they're so similar. "This is a strange situation. None of us were prepared to go running blind into the woods—"

"That's not it," she whispers. "I *was* prepared. My directions were right, PJ, but they got us lost. My compass said we were facing north, but now it's reading west one minute and southeast the next. And I can't explain it, but since we passed the wall, I've just been . . . *unsettled*. About everything."

She looks up at me with big frightened eyes, and it sends chills across my skin. It's not just her. Deep inside, I know what she's feeling. Something's off about this neck of the woods. Looking back at it, maybe that wall wasn't meant to divide property.

Maybe it was meant to keep us out.

Ian comes out of the brush, and we both sit up with a start. "What?" he asks.

"Nothing," snaps Kendra, then stands and begins looking around. "Okay. My noodles are in one of those plastic cups. I guess we have to put the canteen over the fire until the water's boiling."

"Won't that ruin your canteen?" I ask.

She shrugs. "It's metal. Should be fine. Besides, what other options do we have?"

Good point. Kendra gets her backpack and digs around until she finds a small white cup rattling with uncooked noodles. She takes the canteen from me and slips a stick through the belt loop on the cap. Then she jams the other end of the stick in the ground, and voila, the canteen's suspended over the fire, the flames just out of reach of the wood.

We sit in silence, waiting for the watched canteen to boil, and the gravity of our situation begins washing over me in terrible waves. My hand rests on the lump in my pocket, and I know the way out, the one thing that will keep me from slipping into complete despair.

Both Ian and Kendra jump when the camera beeps, and stare dumbfounded at me as I lift it up to my eyes.

Suddenly, the whole scene is on my screen—Ian and Kendra around a campfire—and the cold strain in my head and chest begins to wear off.

"It's day forty-six of our hike," I say. "Ian Buckley, our perpetual protagonist, is joined by Kendra Wright, our new contender. Ian, what's going on?"

Kendra raises a shoulder and turns away from the camera. "Can you not . . . do that right now?" I'm feeling significantly better, but the anger is coming off them in waves.

"Things are looking pretty grim here, folks," I say. "We've just come upon a hidden store of food left here by the ancient Indian tribe the Kuppa Noodels."

"PJ." Pan over to Ian, his eyes looking tired and hard in the glowing square of my viewfinder. "Cut it out, man. Put the camera away."

"What's the point of getting lost in the woods if we can't document it?" I tell him.

"We're not in the mood for this," he says. "Another time."

"Wow, ladies and gentlemen, Ian is feeling a little antsy."

"Stop it, PJ," says Ian through gritted teeth. "Last warning."

We go silent again. The whole forest feels angry at me. The trees bear down on us; the blanket of brown leaves underneath me makes me want to scream. The only thing that's not pitted against me right now is the square screen on my camera.

"Tempers wear thin, viewers. What happens next, only time can tell—"

One minute, Ian's sitting cross-legged by the fire, the next he's on top of me, hand clenched around my camera, eyes wild behind his creased brow, teeth bared. He tries to yank the handheld away from me, but I pull back. The plastic creaks.

"Let go!" I scream. "You're going to break it!"

"Put down the camera!" he yells. "You're such a little creep!"

I put a foot on his shoulder and try to push him away from me. His big clammy hand slaps on my face and shoves me back.

"Shut up!" shouts Kendra.

"*You* shut up!" yells Ian back at her, and then he lets go of my face and my camera. I'm about to scream my head off at him and kick him in the shin when I notice Kendra's on her feet, crouched, eyes flickering from one direction to the other.

"I think I heard something," she whispers. "Listen." We go silent, and then I hear it—rustling leaves, one or two twigs cracking, and then a sound, sort of like a chirp, but not a bird's sound. Something weird.

Before I can utter my famous last words—*It was probably nothing*—an animal, some kind of big cat, slinks into view a few yards away. Its fur shoots out from its face in wild spikes, all of it covered in gray-brown stripes. It has a stumpy little torso and long legs. Its whole body moves like liquid. It spots us, freezes, and its big yellow eyes narrow. My hand immediately checks my camera to make sure Ian hasn't destroyed it in our scuffle. This could be great footage.

"That's a Canada lynx," whispers Kendra. "They usually only come out at night. Unless . . ." She blinks hard. "Unless they're hungry."

The animal lowers itself to the ground, front legs stretched out, and the low rumbling noise that comes out of its throat translates perfectly: *Look. Meat.*

Thirty seconds later, I realize that I'm running. Actually, all three of us are. Trees fly past us, firing sharp shafts of thick yellow sunset light between them, blinding us all the while. Kendra and Ian pant loudly next to me but never slow down; Kendra's backpack is open, and all of her stuff, her granola bars and field guide and map, come tumbling out onto the forest floor. There's no sound of the lynx, but with how swift and fearsome that thing looked, you probably don't even know it's there until there's a paw on your chest and the smell of blood in your face—

My foot hooks on something, and my whole body tenses and twists, defying gravity. My vision blurs, then explodes white, as my head thumps hard onto something cold and wet. My mouth opens, and a shriek comes bursting out.

"PJ!" yells Ian's voice from somewhere. Footsteps approach, and two sets of hands turn me over and shake me. My eyes open again, and I see Ian's and Kendra's faces peering down at me, outlined by the canopy of treetops.

"You okay, man?" asks Ian. His face is bright red. He wipes at watery eyes.

"I don't know," I moan. "What happened?"

"You caught your ankle on a root—" Kendra reaches her hand down, and my foot flares with pain. Looking down at the rest of me, I see my left ankle, swollen and red, a scratch on it. At first, it's small and angry but not that bad, and then a single bead of dark red forms on it and dribbles down to my heel.

My stomach whirls. My face feels damp and cold. Slowly, my head falls back into the leaf-covered grass. I groan, unable to calm down, stuck in a rush of panic.

"What do we do?" asks Ian.

"We need to go back," sighs Kendra. "We have to put out the fire."

"Are you out of your mind? There's a giant ferocious mountain lion back there!"

"There could be a forest fire. And it was a *lynx*."

"Our friend is hurt and you're worried about a forest fire?" he yells. "Is this Smokey the Bear's Happy

Fun Time? What about us? What are we going to do? If we stick with your plan, we'll end up like the Pine City Dancers out here—"

"Stop talking about the Pine City—"

That's when the tears finally come. Since we realized we were lost, I've done my best to force down the stone in my windpipe and the lava in my eyes, but now I just let it out, let my whole face curl up and gush, because between the red rage coming off my friends, the red pain radiating off of my ankle, and the biting red light of the setting sun, everything is irritated, angry, full of frustration. I know that there's no way we're getting home tonight, that Kyra's going to sleep without a bedtime story, and that we might be stuck out here forever and there's nothing we can do about it. Kendra's feelings were right—this place is horrible, full of terror, and tonight, it's having us for dinner. We're not wolves or poodles or little fish, we're insects, rabbits, *prey*.

We're dead meat.

CHAPTER SEVEN

Ian

Kendra wigs out on me. She won't let up on this forest fire routine, just keeps saying, "We have to put it out," over and over again. If you ask me, wild animals trump fires, and honestly, we barely had a flame back there, but she's crazy about it, "We *have to* put it out," emphasizing the *have to,* like it's not an option, which it totally is, but her weird superbrain is so wired with rules that it won't let her body keep moving until we put the fire out, so whenever I say anything, she comes back with, "You're just thinking about *yourself.* We *have* to put it out."

Finally, I just snap and yell, "Fine. I'll go."

"No," she says, "I should go. You might not suffocate it completely."

Like I can't put out a fire? "Look, someone needs to stay with PJ." Normally, PJ would try and be brave, say he's fine on his own, but he's useless right now, on the ground squeezing the scratch on his leg and making this little squeaking noise between his teeth. Total mess. "You stay here. I'll go take care of it."

For once, Kendra doesn't fight me, just nods and says, "If you're not back in five minutes, I'll come looking for you."

"I'll be back in five minutes."

"Try to grab any of the stuff we dropped," she says.

"Yeah, I'll try."

As I crunch back to our makeshift campsite, a prickle of excitement runs down my skin, 'cause yeah, maybe I ran from this weird lynx thing with the rest of 'em, but that was only because it surprised me. Now's my chance to see a wild animal close up, and not just any animal, either—a big one, a predator. Chipmunks and big bucks are all fun and games, but this is serious nature I'm up against. And wait, are lynxes, what are they called, scavengers? Maybe it could lead me to the Pine City Dancers. Here's hoping.

I hear a sound like a cough a few yards away, on the other side of the tree. Slowly, I peek my head out, and sure enough, there sits our campsite, lynx and all.

The lynx pads around the fire, pawing at bits of ramen that have spilled out of the plastic cup, and man, it is *funny* looking. A black spike of hair shoots off each ear like bug antennae. Its long legs move its stubby little body in a clumsy, swaying way, and when it sits, its shoulders seemed hunched over its fur-spiked face. All that plus the tiny eraser of a tail make it one of the dumbest-looking animals I've ever seen, something like a house cat, a lion, a monkey, and a rabbit mixed together. But even though it's not much higher than my thigh, and I could totally probably outrun it if I needed to, some part of me mixes enough fear with my excitement to hold me back. It's not that big, but this thing could use those big hindquarters to spring into the air and hit me pretty hard.

Then out of nowhere, this sharp knocking noise, kind of a *TOK TOK TOK*, rings out of the woods, and the lynx freezes, puts its head to the sky. Then it turns and bounds off into the woods, vanishing entirely after a few seconds.

I wait a little bit to make sure the coast is clear—also to keep my heart from exploding. When nothing else happens, I tiptoe toward our campsite, doing my best the whole time to ignore my shaking hands and dry, sandy mouth. I've never heard of bears or cougars or bigfoots making a noise like that knocking sound, but seeing as it scared away that lynx, my mind is coming up with craziness like you wouldn't believe, all sorts of monsters pouncing on me at once out of nowhere. It feels lame, thinking like this. Who am I, PJ?

Just like I said, the fire isn't even really going, barely smoking ashes, but it's still red enough in the center to burn a falling branch, so I kick dirt on it until it's dead, and then I kick some more dirt on it just because it feels good to trade in that cold fear for some hot anger. The canteen has been knocked to one side, but it's still full. On the way back to Kendra and PJ, I pick up the other things—the compass, the specimen jars, the granola bars—until I get to the creek, and I see something in the water, something mushy and flat—our map.

When I pick it up, the map crumbles into soaked pieces that slowly drift down the creek, leaving me with nothing but a sour taste in my mouth and a sick feeling in my gut.

Stupid Kendra, thinks she knows everything. Stupid PJ, gets in my face with his camera and then starts crying the minute he gets a boo-boo. They both act like I'm some jerk who can't do anything but run fast and yell. When things get crazy, though, *I'm* the guy who has to go *deal* with it. They think I'm so dumb, I'm not scared—*of course* I'm scared. That's what being tough is—being scared but doing something anyway.

When I get back, PJ's leg has stopped bleeding, and he's gone from sobbing to sniffling. Kendra is staring at something in her notebook, her eyes bugging out of her skull. When I'm only a few feet away, her head snaps up suddenly.

"What'd you find?"

"The specimen jars, the canteen, and the compass," I say, handing them off to her. "Oh, and the granola bars. Did anything stay in your bag?"

"Nothing, really." She kneels and pours some water from the canteen onto PJ's ankle, washing the blood away. He hisses, then dries the scratch with the hem of his sock. From his backpack, he pulls out a Band-Aid and applies it carefully to the tiny scratch, like it'll gush blood at any moment.

Of course, PJ brought Band-Aids. His parents probably stuffed them in his bag, afraid he'd get mauled by a sparrow.

"What about the map?" asks Kendra.

"It fell in the creek," I say. "It's in pieces. I couldn't save any of it."

PJ groans and shakes his head, but Kendra just shrugs. "Wasn't doing us much good anyway," she says.

"Did you guys hear that noise?" I ask. "The lynx was back there, and the sound scared him off."

"I guess," says Kendra. "It was probably a wood-pecker."

"Are you sure? It didn't sound like the wood-peckers I've heard, and I figure if it scared that lynx, it has to be pretty big—"

"Ian," says Kendra, in her hoity-toity please-shut-up tone, as if I don't understand that what I'm saying might upset PJ, who I've known my whole life. We're stuck out here together, people. Let's talk about what's going on.

"Well, sorry if I wanted to keep you informed," I say. "Did you hear when I said the lynx was still there? I risked my neck to prevent forest fires, and all I get is '*Ian*.'"

Kendra closes her eyes and drops her hands to her sides. "Thank you, Ian, for going back and putting the fire out."

"Thanks, Ian," says PJ, all raspy. At least he sounds honest about it.

"Whatever." Great, now I feel like a jerk for asking them to thank me. There's no winning here. "PJ, can you walk? Nothing broken, right?"

"Yeah," he says. Slowly, he climbs to his feet with Kendra at his side spotting him. He winces a little and sort of half hops on his twisted ankle (which, if you ask me, is all a big dramatic production; I've seen guys walk off sprains and twists *way* worse than that), but he gets up and does his best to smile through his limping.

"Okay, if you can walk, then we'll need to keep going."

"Wait," says Kendra. "Let's think about this."

"We don't have time to think," I bark, and she cringes

back from me. "All of your thinking has done absolutely squat for us so far. There is a lynx in the woods. We don't know where we are. The sun is five minutes from setting. We need to *do* something."

"Fine," she snaps, jumping to her feet. "Fine, let's go. We're going." She powers off ahead of us, leaving me to walk with PJ, who does his best not to hobble too much.

"What's her problem?" I ask him. "She needs to get with the program. You *both* do."

PJ laughs like it's not funny. "Now I have to ask—are you feeling all right?"

"I'm *fine*. Why?"

"Because you're being really mean. Even for you."

He—I—wow. It takes me a good ten seconds of deep breathing to calm down enough not to snatch him by the collar and shake him. PJ's right, I'm beyond angry; I'm furious. This isn't how a wolf behaves; wolves are cunning and quick and careful, not raging about every little thing. What's wrong with me?

"I dunno," I finally say to him. "Something's got me feeling really . . . crazy." PJ nods and then mumbles something I can't hear. "What was that?"

"I think it's the woods," he says softly, glancing around like the trees might be listening to him. "They're messing with us. I don't trust this place."

We walk about twenty yards behind Kendra for a

while, until she reaches a cleared area, lit red-orange, and she stops and stares west. When we reach her, we follow her gaze into the sunset, which, yeah, is just gorgeous. A blanket of misty white clouds hangs around the mountaintops in the distance, and the sun is a burning red wedge that sits in the middle of a million and one different shades of purple and pink sky, disappearing more and more every second until it's a tiny fiery dot, and then even that gets eaten up, swallowed by the clouds and the mountains. For the first time since we got here, I feel cold. While it was going on, the sunset was beautiful, but now it seems intense, like the mountain around us just ate all the light. And man, if these woods have been wild by day, wait until it gets dark. . . .

"I don't like those clouds," says Kendra, ruining the moment.

"Why?" I ask. "That sunset was beautiful. Are they not fluffy enough for you?"

She glares at me over her shoulder. "No," she says, "because they look like rain."

"But they're all misty and flat," says PJ, "not big or dark like storm clouds."

"Cumulonimbus, the big dark ones, they mean thunderstorms. But these flat cottony ones, nimbostratus clouds, can mean a prolonged rainstorm. More than that, they create a blanket of—"

"You're being paranoid," I say. "Relax. We'll see what happens."

Kendra spins and glares at me with this outraged face. "You're such a *jerk*, Ian Buckley," she yells, her voice going all high and echoing off the mountains. "One minute, you think I'm not getting upset enough; the next, I'm getting too upset. . . . It's like, like anything I do, you have to one-up me!"

"Maybe if you weren't always acting like a teacher, we wouldn't be panicking so much. It's all, *Think this out, these clouds look dangerous, they're nimbo-whatever,* blah blah blah. We're on a hike. If you hike in the rain, you get wet."

"Guys, really," says PJ, "this is getting us nowhere."

Kendra's cheeks go dark brown and she looks like she might explode, but then she closes her eyes, takes a deep breath, and says, "At least I can start a fire. It sounds like *my* dad taught me better than yours."

Ouch. My face feels really hot, and the air feels cold. I'm trying to stay cool, but I don't feel cool, just angry and hungry and embarrassed in front of my friend by a *girl*, a girl who almost broke my face in half once. "Well, if you could *read a map*, we wouldn't be in this mess."

"No, Ian, if your ADD-plagued jock brain hadn't sent you running off to try and tackle some deer, we wouldn't be in this mess," she shouts, throwing her arms wide. "Maybe I'm paranoid, or I'm freaking out, but that's because I'm a little busy trying to clean up after some *puerile dolt* who can't hold still for five seconds."

"Guys," says PJ, before I can tell Kendra to shut her stupid brainy mouth. "It's getting dark. How does this help us, in any way? Less yakking, more hiking."

He's right—the light from the sunset is already fading from pink to purple to navy blue, and the blanket of clouds is coming at us in a wave of soggy gray, and just like Kendra said, in the distance there's rain, a smear of shadow trailing down and behind the clouds like the tentacles of some big gross jellyfish. The woods up ahead don't look cool or inviting; they look dark, gnarled, and spooky, and they're getting spookier by the second. I keep telling myself that it's an adventure, that I'm still having fun, but it's getting harder to believe. It's like the mountain is enjoying this, like it won't let up on us.

Maybe PJ's right. Maybe it's this place.

Kendra snorts. "Fair enough. Maybe we can find a cave or something to spend the night in." PJ swallows hard at the idea of sleeping in a cave but nods along.

Then there's that noise again—*TOK TOK TOK*— and PJ and Kendra stop and raise their heads to the sky. It's louder now, and I can tell by the look on Kendra's face that it's no woodpecker, but she doesn't say anything, just tightens her mouth and moves forward.

PJ slowly pulls his camera out of his pocket, but then

he looks up at me, squeaks "Sorry," and puts it away.

"It's okay, dude," I say, "you can film this if you want." But he just shakes his head and shrugs. Poor guy. Guess I did attack him earlier.

Soon, everything is dark blue, and it's harder and harder to see the shafts of light between the trees. Every branch throws a weird, jagged shadow across my face, and every noise seems to come out of nowhere, like the darkness itself is moving around, following right behind us.

Then we hear it—the first slaps of water on the ground. An ice-cold drop hits me square in the forehead, and in a quick second, it's drizzling, then raining, then pouring, the darkening sky spitting waves of freezing water over us. There's a rumbling in the distance, and bolts of lightning cut across the sky, illuminating everything—PJ's panicked face, Kendra's soggy hair, the endless mountain around us—before plunging us back into even blacker shadows.

The storm changes the forest like *that*—there are no colors other than gray, black, and too-harsh lightning white. The trees all blend together into a rush of obstacles whizzing past us, getting in our way, slapping our faces with wet branches. The ground beneath us becomes this muddy mess, filling my sneakers with icy water and brown mud. Brambles grab at my socks, rocks bite my ankles, and the whole thing is like a nightmare, man, with the elements around us throwing picks and tackles in our path everywhere they can, closing in for the kill.

Suddenly, I'm thinking of the Pine City Dancers, how if there was ever a time for us to find a secret stash of rotting corpses, it would be now. On the third bolt of lightning, I can swear I see a corpse's face somewhere off between the trees, eyes bright, mouth screaming at me, and I can't help but cry out.

"What?" calls Kendra through the sound of the rain.

There's another flash of lightning, and it's gone. "Nothing," I say.

Gotta get with the program. Just a little rain. Gotta be a wolf.

We move faster, running, looking for some magical shelter that we don't know is there. Kendra desperately tries to cover her head with her hands, and PJ huddles into his arms, limping and whimpering. Our woodland adventure is officially becoming a total disaster. The trees get thicker, but their branches do nothing to cover us from the rain. PJ slips and falls facedown in the dirt, and Kendra and I have to haul him to his feet.

And for the first time, it hits me, with my face freezing and wet and my chest on fire, that we might *die* out here, and that it's my fault. The Wrights and the Wilsons will say they wish their kids had never met Ian Buckley, and Dennis Wilson will say that my parents raised an irresponsible son, and they'll find us out in the woods all huddled and pale, or worse, they won't, they'll never find us, and next year the sixth graders will tell the fifth graders about their first time at Homeroom Earth, how three kids vanished, and were never heard from ag—

Wait a second.

There. Between those trees.

Let this be real. Please, oh man, let this be real.

CHAPTER EIGHT

Kendra

The forest is a pitch-black labyrinth, and the icy, persistent rain is destroying both our peace of mind and whatever morale is left among us, and so in our panic we almost don't see our very salvation. It's Ian who freezes, runs backward, squints, and points. His finger guides us to a flat, shadowy shape that seems to come out of nowhere between the statuesque trees, but in that boxy silhouette, I make out a smaller square, crosshatched and shiny—a window. Before anything can be said, Ian darts over to the cabin, and we follow close behind. We rush around the side to find a small wooden porch and an unlocked door.

Inside, he flicks a switch on the wall, and a rumbling motor sounds out back, the air suddenly tinged with exhaust. As the generator shudders to life, light—beautiful electric light—streams through the cabin. There's one big room, wooden floor, wooden walls, and, thank the powers that be, a stone fireplace with a stack of logs next to it! Off to one side through a small door are a small kitchen and a bathroom. There is a sweet smell hanging in the air, like dirt and old fruit, but it's probably just stuffiness—the place is more dust and cobwebs than home. A few spiders and a centipede crawl around our feet and away from the light, sending PJ jumping, but I'm far too grateful to care. For the moment, this shelter has quelled my unexplainable unease. Normally, this place would be a hovel, but tonight, it's a palace.

You've done it. You're safe. Everything's all right, Kendra.

"I'll make a fire," says Ian.

"*I'll* make a fire," I counter. "You search for food and something to dry us off."

Ian runs into the kitchen and comes back with his arms full of useful things—blankets, towels, toilet paper, matches—but no food, no water. "The kitchen's got a lot of stuff in it, but nothing we can eat."

"We have those granola bars," rasps PJ. "Those should last us for now."

Through the haze of panic and relief, I remember

some of the camping tips I found online regarding fire preparation. I begin making small balls of toilet paper and placing them two inches apart under the logs in the fireplace. The sounds of the rain rumbling on the roof and the generator coughing out back calm me, help me focus. With a snap of a match, the whole thing goes up in a bright flare of flame. *Catch*, I think at the log, and fortunately, the brittle, dry wood ignites almost instantly. Soon, we're huddled in front of a warm fire, each of us dried off and wrapped in a quilt. Even through Ian's hardheadedness and PJ's panic, I see in their eyes what I feel: gratitude for being safe.

"How's the bathroom?" I ask.

"Don't ask," replies Ian with a shudder.

"Gross is better than nothing, I guess," says PJ.

"There's no sign of a phone, either," sighs Ian. "I don't like it here."

"It's shelter," I say. "There's heat and electricity. With the lights on, eventually someone will notice us out here."

"I just don't like it," says Ian. "A place like this in the middle of these mountains, that's not normal. And I don't like the smell. PJ, back me up here."

"I'm with Kendra," says PJ, rubbing at his eyes. "Anywhere I can sleep without having to worry about lynxes works for me."

Something about his voice sets off an alarm in my

chest. *Step it up, Kendra. Ian's all muscle and PJ's all nerves. You're the brain here. You have to think them through this.*

I take the remaining quilts and fold them into people-sized rectangles, then lay them out in front of the fire. Without having to be told, PJ crawls over to one of the blankets and wraps himself up in his own quilt. When Ian doesn't move, I spell it out: "Let's get some sleep, Ian. We'll think better in the morning."

Ian, of course, refuses to lie down but instead stands up, tosses off his quilt, and paces around the room, scratching his blond hair and glaring at everything.

"I don't like it," he reminds me. "There's, like, *no* furniture. And what kind of cabin doesn't have a phone? I don't like it. PJ, what were you saying about the woods—"

"God, Ian, *shut up and go to sleep,*" moans PJ from his blanket-bed. I want to hug him for it.

Ian keeps pacing and grumbling, so I lie down, hoping he'll follow suit. Immediately, fatigue drags my eyes shut and pulls me into near-instant sleep.

The noise—a loud clank—yanks me off my quilt and into a sitting position. There's no telling how long I've been unconscious; it's still night outside, but the fire has died down to a glowing mass of embers, and the rain has stopped. Outside, the generator still purrs. Next to me,

PJ turns over, mumbles something indistinguishable, and returns to his dream.

What really wakes me is Ian's hand on my shoulder, shaking me. *Great. He hasn't slept at all. He'll be fun tomorrow.*

"Where'd those matches go?" he whispers.

Stop. Take a deep breath. Now, think, Kendra. "Why?"

"I found something," he says.

Across the room, a trapdoor in the floor reveals a gaping black square. The offensive smell of the place has increased tenfold. Something about the open mouth in the floor unsettles me, just as the woods and the wall did earlier.

"Ian, you're crazy," I say in my most authoritative whisper. "Close that cellar and go to sleep."

"Just let me see those matches," he hisses back.

"It smells awful! There might be a dead animal down there."

"Or there might be a phone."

Ugh. It's a sad day when I have to admit that Ian Buckley has a point. I find the box of matches at my feet, and in a split second, Ian snatches it out of my hand and trundles down the basement stairs. There's the snap and smoke of a lit match, and then silence, flickering orange light coming from the edges of the hole in the floor.

"Well? What's down there?"

Ian's head pops out of the hole in the floor like a

prairie dog, a blank look in his eyes. "You need to see this."

An aversion to the disgusting—girly, I know—shudders through me. "Is it a dead animal?"

"No." He gulps, then exhales a slow, shaky breath. "I don't even know what this is. Maybe you can tell me."

My first reaction is to tell Ian to get out of the basement and go to bed, but now curiosity is gnawing at the back of my brain. I can't let him be the only person who looks at the fascinating find in the basement of the random cabin we've discovered in the mountains of Montana. True scholars and researchers don't ignore these kinds of opportunities; often, they lead to artifacts or treasure.

Slowly, as quietly as I can, I crawl from my blanket, take the box of matches from Ian, and carefully walk down the wooden steps leading into the cool, stuffy air of the basement. I strike a match, bathing the room in orange light.

At first glance, everything is typical—dirt floor, cobwebs, a couple of shelves, some wiring. "What's so cool about this?" I ask Ian over my shoulder. "It's a basement."

"The floor," he says. "Look at the floor."

My eyes travel downward, and I finally see the lines—lines of white paint or clay dragged across the dirt, meeting in the middle to form a . . . *sigil*. That's the word I'm looking for, a sigil, a religious symbol or inscription, just like the one that was drawn on the wall earlier. This one's made of weird jagged lines, like lightning bolts or tree branches with concentric circles spread out between them. My eyes follow the circles, one inside another, getting smaller and smaller, until I reach the center of the symbol, where a small pile of white sticks with a weird rock on top sits—

Oh no.

Not sticks. Bones. A pile of bones. And the rock on top is a skull, looking exactly like it would on a pirate flag or a punk rock T-shirt, grinning back at me like it's saying *You came to the wrong cabin, Kendra.*

Before I can stop myself, I cry out loudly and jump out of the basement, shuffling across the room on my backside and backing up against the wall of the cabin.

Okay, Kendra, deep breaths, don't hyperventilate, just calm down. You're fine. Everything's fine. There's just something awful going on here, that's all. Think around it.

"What's going on?" mumbles PJ, sitting up from his blanket and rubbing his eyes.

"There's a skull in the basement," says Ian.

"Oh," says PJ, and then, after waking up a bit more, says, "*WHAT?*"

Ian turns to me. His whole body is shaking. "Isn't that insane? Who do you think did that? Do you . . . do you think it's one of the Pine City Dancers?"

Think, Kendra, think. It's all you're good for.

"Crow Indian," I finally manage. "Looks very old. Probably hasn't been touched in . . . years. Decades. Maybe a century. So . . . probably not." *My word, Kendra, you're sounding incredibly intelligent. If only Mensa could hear you now.*

"There's still a *skull* in the *basement*, though," says PJ. "That's bad, I'd say. Bad enough that we ought to leave, right?"

My gut reaction is to agree with him, but my curiosity keeps me from fleeing. I light a second match and carefully ease down the stairs to the basement. Yes, without question, it's a skull, but as I stare at the winding lines of the symbol beneath it, something else on the dirt floor catches my eye, something small and square shaped and familiar. Against the tension flooding every nerve in my body, I dart down the stairs, snatch it up, and leap back into the safety of the illuminated cabin.

"What's that?" asks PJ, crawling over to where Ian and I sit.

It's a book, with *READ ME TO LIVE* screaming back at me from its cover. There's dirt, sap, and some sort of black paste I'd rather not think about smeared across the spine; the warning itself looks written in some kind of clay or red pencil which, I don't fail to notice, could be blood. I'm almost scared to open it, but I cast the fear out of my mind. Hopefully, this diary will inform us of where we are, why my directions have proved useless, and, just maybe, a way home.

The book opens with a sticky sound, and on the inside of the cover is a small note reading *The Diary of Deborah Palmer*. The first few pages are entirely normal diary entries:

March 16th—

Leonard was easier today, but kept calling Barry and Grace "hippos" because they'd gained a few pounds. "Plié, you hippos! Watch the feet, hippos!" Grace started crying and ran out. Not cool. Leonard keeps talking up this camping trip. We'll see if I even want to go.

March 23rd—

Chelsea wants us to go out and meet her new boyfriend after practice. If he's anything like the last guy, I could do without it. Bill's continuing plans for this outdoor trip. I know we argue sometimes, but haven't we bonded enough?

April 2nd—

Finally out in the Bitterroots. The scenery is beautiful, but I think Ralph and Charlie got us lost. They keep saying the map is wrong. Next time, we hire a guide.

April 3rd—

  Something got into our supplies last night, taking most of the food and some of our fire-starter logs. Everyone is blaming everyone else. Tempers are flaring. What is it about these woods that has us so on edge?

The stillness of the night around us sends shivers through my bones. Ian and PJ are huddled next to me, each one peering wide-eyed over one of my shoulders. My hands shake and my breath catches as I flip to the next page, both terrified of what is to come and unable to stop myself.

  If you are reading this, then it's too late. Even while I write, I can feel hungry eyes staring at me from the shadows. My only hope is that when you find my diary, you're able to use my story to find a way off this mountain.
  My name is Deborah Palmer, from Pine City, Montana. In April, I began a hiking trip in these mountains with my eleven friends as a group bonding exercise for our modern dance class.

A wave of biting cold hits me square in the chest. I look back at the boys, and their faces are openmouthed and ashen.

The Pine City Dancers.

"Oh my God," whispers PJ. "It's all true!"

"Those seventh graders weren't kidding," I whisper.

"Can we just take a moment," says Ian, looking from PJ to me, "and admit that I was right about this the whole time?"

"Shut up," I respond, and keep reading.

Almost immediately after setting out on our hike, we realized that something was wrong. Our compasses and electronic devices all stopped working. We could find none of the trails or landmarks that our guidebooks assured us would be there. We weren't that worried at first—we had enough food, equipment, and time that we could get lost for a day or two and eventually find our way back to the road.

It wasn't until we passed the stone wall that we noticed we weren't alone. Someone—no, something—was following us. Eventually, we all admitted that we felt a presence in the woods, something spying on us from up in the trees and behind the rocks. Leonard kept claiming he heard voices on the wind, and Ellie would scream and point at eyes she said she saw off in the underbrush, glittering out at her. On top of that, the weather turned on us almost overnight.

One minute, it was pouring; the next, it was sweltering. That night, we slept poorly, and in the morning we found our tents torn and our supplies ransacked. We began fighting. We didn't trust one another anymore.

When we found the old woman in her cabin up the mountain, we thought she would help us, maybe even give us shelter from the bitter weather. Instead, she screamed bloody murder, ordered us to go back to wherever we came from. The cabin was full of what looked like tools for witchcraft—bones, feathers, boiling pots, dark symbols. The men snapped, and Leonard and Bill almost attacked her. The woman ran off, screaming that we'd "be sorry." At the time, we were too ecstatic to have the cabin to care. A fireplace, a bathroom, a generator, a roof over our heads, these were all we could think about. Everyone calmed down—we thought it was all over.

The first night in the cabin, Bill said he saw someone peering in the window, smiling at us. He was convinced it was the old woman and ran out in the dark after her, cursing and screaming. An hour later, he came stumbling back, his face a bloody mess, his body broken and torn. He said three words—"They're out there"—and collapsed.

"So . . . is that Bill's skull?" whispers PJ, his teeth chattering in fear.

"What I want to know," says Ian, his voice quivering, "is who was out there."

As if on cue, a moan, husky and dry like the one we heard earlier, rings out through the woods. All three of our heads snap up, and while I can't speak for the boys, a fearful feeling spreads over me, pumping ice water through my heart. Then there's another moan, and another, and soon a chorus of soft, sad moaning can be heard distinctly outside the cabin, moving slowly in our direction.

"This place is haunted," whispers PJ, his voice cracking. "There are ghosts out in the woods. The evil spirits, like it says in the diary—"

"There's no such thing as ghosts," I hear myself say.

Outside, twigs crunch. Ian goes to the window, and I jump to my feet and join him. The clouds have parted, and the bony light of the moon paints everything a cold, luminous blue.

Through the woods, silhouettes move slowly toward us, marching on two legs. My heart leaps, and relief washes over me.

"People!" I yelp. "We're saved!"

"Wait," warns Ian.

"The school must have sent a rescue team!" I yell at PJ. "See? There's no need to panic—"

"Kendra," says Ian, his face drained of all color, "I . . . don't think that's a rescue team." He points out the window, his hand shaking. Outside, the silhouettes have come through the trees, the moonlight falling on their faces.

Immediately, my stomach cramps up, and my breath disappears.

There are six of them that I can see—hunched, slumped figures, faces gray and unmoving, eyes glassy and white set in deep black sockets, like stepping stones in the middle of dark, stagnant pools. Each one of them looks old, but too old, with dried skin stretched tight over gnarled bones and yellow teeth protruding from pulled-back lips. They wear hiking gear that's been torn to shreds, smeared with dirt and filth. The smell that comes off them is sickening, and I have to cover my nose and mouth to even stand being at the window.

They move forward through the underbrush with slow, deliberate steps, crashing through sticker bushes and around trees like they barely notice them, hands outstretched in grasping gnarled claws. With each step, a deep wailing moan comes out of their open mouths, which is even worse when I realize that their chests don't move, their lips don't quiver, their nostrils don't flare or twitch, *they aren't breathing*.

One of them raises its head, and where its eyes should be are two empty, bottomless holes. It opens its mouth, and between the rotten teeth sprouting from behind its black crusty lips, it lets out a deep, sorrowful cry.

"They're . . . dead," murmurs Ian, as if reading my mind. "They *are* ghosts."

"No," I whisper through my quivering lips and fluttering breath, "not ghosts . . ."

Not ghosts. There's no such thing as ghosts, and anyway, ghosts don't come stalking through the woods at you, at least not in the literature I've read. Ghosts are phosphorescent and can fly and come out of paintings or cellars.

These are . . . something else. The stumbling, the shriveled faces . . . it's on the tip of my tongue. Living dead, walking dead . . . my mind strains, exhausted, angry. What's the word I'm looking for—

"Zombies."

CHAPTER NINE

PJ

Ian and Kendra turn around and stare at me like fish, eyes wide, mouths open. Finally, Kendra chokes out, "Excuse me?"

"Zombies," I repeat. I can't really see through the window over Kendra's huge hair, but what I catch—stumbling figures, outstretched arms, deep moaning, the sudden spike in my heart rate and breathing—all points to zombies.

Kendra's mouth snaps open and shut a few times before she declares, "That's ridiculous."

"I don't know," says Ian, "I mean . . ."

I come up behind Ian, and my skin crawls. My

stomach churns. I know I'm right. Look at them.

Only a handful of them are close enough to see in the moonlight, but off in the trees there are more, slouching into view like the shadows just coughed them up. The visible ones are horrible, bony grayish-green things wrapped in ruined hiking clothes, flannel and boots and fur-collared jackets. Their arms reach stiffly out straight ahead, their fingers clasping and unclasping. The throaty moans have gone from soft and creepy to overwhelming, a great big chorus of hungry death rattles. The closer they get, the more violent they sound, going from sighing to moaning to snarling and growling.

My hands nearly tear my pocket open trying to yank my camera out. It's a race against time—can I film this before I start having a full-on panic attack?—and I win, pulling up my handheld and holding down the Record button hard. Ian and Kendra jump at the beep and then stare wide-eyed into the glowing screen as I zoom in on one of them, a skinny woman with wide white eyes and not much left in the way of lips. The pounding in my head and chest die away, my breathing slows, and I can focus on things for the first time since we were attacked by the lynx.

"We've come across some strange creatures," I whisper into the camera, "which appear to be . . . we're pretty sure they're . . ." It's like the woman, the *thing*, hears me, because those white eyes turn and focus right on the lens of my camera. Her yellow teeth part, and she lets out a harsh rasping growl. "They're zombies," I say. "No question. I'm filming a zombie."

"They're not . . . that's a *ridiculous* word," whispers Kendra between sharp breaths.

"What do we do?" Ian shouts, his hands tearing through his hair.

I pan over the crowd of zombies, taking in the sheer number of them. There are definitely more than six, more like fourteen or fifteen that I can see. Not all of them are in the same state of decay—some are just gray skinned with sunken eyes, while others are almost like walking bones wrapped in yellowish canvas—but they're all dusty, dry, covered in cobwebs, leaves, dirt, the kind of stuff you pick up when you drag yourself through the woods all day.

"God, it's just like the movies," I whisper to myself. "This is like *Night of the Living Dead* redux."

"Oh man, that's it!" says Ian, grinning like an idiot at Kendra, then at me. "This kid knows what's going on! He's an expert! PJ, tell us about zombies!"

"Huh?" I ask, not really paying attention. Whoa, look at that one. How's it moaning without a lower jaw?

"Come on, PJ, help us out!" Ian jumps in front of my lens, forcing me to look up at his sweaty face. "You've watched all those scary movies. What do we need to know?"

Reciting things about movies—this I can do. My mind is a blur of black-and-white stills, of wide angles and worm's-eye-view shots and bad old film posters with blood-dripping font on the title, but through it all I manage to grab the vital information and spit it out.

"Zombies are walking dead people," I say. "They come back from the grave because of . . . radiation. Or space dust. Or black magic, or a virus. It depends on the movie." What else, what else? It's hard to concentrate with Ian taking up my shot. "They're mindless, but they're strong, and come in serious numbers, so it's tough to fight them off. Usually, it's easier to outrun them."

"What do they want?" asks Ian.

"They want to eat us," I say, and I can see the fear spread across his face (got it on camera, too—fantastic). "They're cannibals—no, not cannibals; they're not human so it's not really cannibalism, but they . . . they devour people alive. Wait, or is it brains? Sometimes they only eat the brains. But usually in those movies, they yell 'Brains' a lot, and these ones aren't. At least not yet."

"I think we can safely say that both options are problematic!" shouts Kendra.

Ian shakes his head like he's forcing the idea out of his mind. "How do we stop them?"

"Shoot them in the head," I say. A line from the movies themselves comes to mind: "Destroy the brain, kill the ghoul."

"Okay," says Ian. He steps back with his face bunched in contemplation, like he needs room to think. "We . . . don't have guns. Maybe if we hit them really hard. Does that work?"

"I don't know—I can't remember—"

"Guys!" gasps Kendra from the window. "They're getting closer!"

I push Ian aside and keep filming out of the window. She's right. For slow-moving creatures, they're gaining ground surprisingly quickly. That's how it always is in the movies—you think you're safe, and then they're right on top of you.

Up close, we can see every wrinkle in their mottled skin, every white grub writhing in their matted hair. As I pan across the approaching crowd, each individual corpse stands out disgustingly in the harsh eye of the camera, their horrible features incredibly detailed. A large muscular zombie moans at us, and when he turns his head, the light from the windows reveals that half of his face has rotted away. One skinny zombie in a scout-master outfit has a huge antique camera hanging from his neck, the lens cracked.

This never crossed my mind when I woke up this morning. The list my parents gave me has a million things on it, and none of them say, *Whatever you do, don't get eaten by corpses.*

"What do we do?" says Kendra, her voice sharp with

panic. "We can't— They're going to— *What do we do?*"

Ian stands at the window scratching his head so hard he might hit skull, saying, "Uuuuh, *uuuuh*" over and over again. The whole army-of-the-dead thing has wiped his mind clean.

The more I stare out at these creatures, the more bad movies come back to me. Ian's right, I've done my homework here. Maybe I was paying more attention to the camera work in *Citizen Kane* than the zombie behavior in *Tombs of the Blind Dead*, but if anyone's an expert on our current predicament, it's me.

"They'll beat the door down if we don't act fast," I say, spouting everything, anything I can remember from the movies. "They don't have any powers, like vampires or whatever, but they just keep coming, and they have strength in numbers."

"Vampires aren't real—" starts Kendra, shaking her head.

"*We know, okay?!*" yells Ian. "*None of this is real! That doesn't matter! Whatever's out there is coming for us! We need to do something, ANYTHING!*"

Wow, is this how I sound when I'm having an episode?

I'm expecting Kendra to flip out, but she just nods, blinks, nods harder. "What do we have that we can use to barricade the door? What about in the kitchen?"

Ian darts in and out of the room. "There's a chair we

could jam the knob with. But nothing heavy. No fridge."

"You get the chair," she says. "Are there *any* weapons here?"

My brain spits up an image from one of the movies—a lone warrior waving a burning bundle of sticks at a zombie, the creature cowering in fear. "Kendra, can you make us a torch with some of that firewood?"

"Maybe," she says. "We need something flammable, though."

"There's some bug spray in my bag," I call out, "and some gauze. Wrap the gauze around one end of some wood, soak it, and set it on fire."

"You brought gauze?" asks Ian as he shoves the back of a small metal chair under the knob of the door.

"My parents were worried I might get cut or scraped during—"

A slapping sound sends us all a foot into the air and my camera flying out of my hands, clattering across the floor. Our eyes flick toward the window. A zombie—old, withered, bones covered with a tight draping of greenish rot—stares hungrily back at us. He pounds a feeble hand against the glass and hisses between his yellow teeth. He looks too weak, too wasted away, to break the glass, but he's smaller than the others. The big one with half a face could easily smash his way through that window.

That's when the fear takes me, prickles my veins, splashes cold water in my face, fires that familiar tightness through my chest and throat. Because before, these creatures were footage—footage from a late-night spook flick maybe, but *just* footage, not real without lighting and set and special effects. And now, there's one right outside the window, trying to beat its way in. It's like the lynx, only worse. It's an army of lynxes, and they can't be killed, not like normal creatures.

"We'll talk later," Ian says.

"Totally," I choke out.

Kendra wraps a white bulb of bandages around one end of a piece of firewood and then hits it with bug spray until it's soaked. She shoves the one end into the fire, and with a *whumph* it goes up, creating a rippling flame that gives off black smoke that stings my eyes and nostrils. I dive for my camera, hoping that maybe if I turn it back on, start filming this, it'll all become a movie again and I won't feel like I'm drowning in a freezing ocean—

There's a knock at the door, no, not a knock, a pound. Then it's joined by another, and another, and soon there's a constant drumbeat of fists slamming against the wooden door. The window is full of faces, sunken eyed and yellow toothed, twisted in rage. Slowly, the doorknob wiggles, and the chair makes an ugly scraping noise against the floor as the door pushes in inch by inch. Hands, gray and dirty, make their way around the edges, poking into the cabin.

"Here they come!" screams Ian.

Ian and I put our backs against the door, shoving hard. The gray fingers catch between the door and the wall, but there are no cries of pain, just more hungry moaning. The heels of my sneakers dig hard into the floor, but our barricade isn't working. Every pounding hand sends a shudder down my back.

For a second, the whole thing goes quiet in my head, and everything seems still, surreal, like it's not really happening. There's Kendra Wright, Queen Brain, waving a torch at the window like some Transylvanian villager; there's Ian, my best friend, screaming something I can't really hear as he puts his shoulder into the door; there's the cabin, full of light, literally vibrating with the pressure of dozens of dead hands. It's a dream. Has to be. I mean, stuck in a cabin in the woods, attacked by zombies—what an obvious nightmare. Something this horrible can't be real. In a second, someone will say my name, and I'll wake up on the bus to find out we've only just arrived at Homeroom Earth, and all of this will be forgotten in an instant—

Glass shatters, and masses of frantic hands come reaching in through the window, grasping at Kendra. She waves the torch at them, but they don't seem to notice, even when the flame glances on their skin and smokes it black. The chair wedged under the doorknob digs trenches into the floor with each shove and pound.

This is no dream. This isn't a horror movie; it's a

horror reality. I'm here. And so are they.

"What are we going to do *now*?" shouts Kendra. She's resorted to stabbing the lit end of the torch into the wriggling hands over and over.

"PJ!" screams Ian. "If you have any clue what to do next, now's the time!" An arm has snaked its way around the edge of the door, the hand clawing at Ian's T-shirt. He wriggles out of its grip just as a pair of demon eyes appears at the crack between the door and the wall.

I scan the room and land on the square of darkness in the floor. "The cellar!" I shout. "Get in the cellar! We can hide down there!"

"There's a skull in the cellar!" Ian responds.

"But it's not moving!" I yell. "They won't be able to find us down there!"

I'm not much of a fighter, but I know a thing or two about running away.

Kendra grabs her backpack and leaps down into the cellar, and somehow I mange to hobble down the stairs without twisting my ankle any further, and yes, there's the skull they mentioned on top of a pile of bones, in the middle of some weird witchy design, lit orange by Kendra's torch. That's the least of our worries right now. Ian comes flying down last, grabbing the edge of the trapdoor and yanking it shut with a dusty, echoing BOOM.

And now it's us three, huddled together around the

light of the noxious-smelling torch, making the room flicker like an old film reel. Our only company is the human skull in the middle of an evil symbol, staring up at us with hollow eyes and a toothy grin, laughing at what should be a goofy Halloween story but instead is life or death.

"Quiet," whispers Kendra.

Above, there's the muffled thump of eager hands, and then, slowly, the beating stops. The occasional creak, the crackle of the torch, is all we hear.

"Do you think they know we're down here?" whispers Ian.

"They saw us," Kendra mumbles. "They must have." The words shoot electricity through my heart, down my arms and hands.

"Maybe their eyes don't work well," he says.

"Some of them don't even *have* eyes," whispers Kendra.

A boom makes us jump, followed by a clatter over our heads—the chair flying across the room.

A sickening scrape shakes the ceiling over us—the door being shoved open.

Something not quite like a person lets out a long, sad moan.

Quiet.

Then, *thump. Thump. Thump.* Footsteps, heavy, slow, enter the room, sending tiny showers of dust floating down from the floorboards over our heads. My hand covers my mouth instinctively—no sneezing, no coughing, not now. Each step sounds like the ticking of a clock counting down our doom. Behind the first set of feet, more footsteps follow, just as heavy, just as deliberate. Forget how many of them I could see out in those woods—between the number of feet and my imagination, there are hundreds up there, thousands, a million hungry monsters.

A moan, raspy but powerful, cuts through the silence. My arms feel pinched, and I look down to see Ian clutching one, Kendra the other, with both hands. Normally, it would hurt, maybe even leave a bruise, but my body is so tense right now that I can barely register any pain, not even in my messed-up ankle. Every inch of me is cold and numb. I don't think I'm breathing.

Finally, we hear the feet move over the trapdoor, and all three of us exhale a little. The picture my mind was painting—the square of light opening, withered hands pulling at the door, a set of milky eyes and dirt-covered teeth appearing in our view—melts away.

The footsteps stop. Stillness like this is impossible; anyone, no matter how poised, shifts their weight or moves their feet around a little, but these things don't. The quiet takes forever, and with each second, I grow a little more hopeful. Maybe they'll leave. Maybe they are that dumb, that they think we've just disappeared.

Maybe they're blind, and they never saw us in the first place.

I don't know. This is my first day as a zombie expert, so I'm playing this by ear.

"I think," says Ian, very softly, "I think we're okay down here."

There's a shuffle and another moan.

Directly behind us.

Kendra whips the torch around, and there, climbing out of the dirt floor of the cellar, is a chubby man in a bloodstained T-shirt, the gaping hole in his cheek revealing a line of white molars. He rises out of the ground, pieces of dirt falling out of his hair and mouth, until he's fully on his feet.

I try to come up with a plan, but when I open my mouth, horror pulsates up into my throat, and I scream, "WE'RE ALL GONNA DIE!"

His clouded eyes fix on us, and the thing stretches his filthy hands out, grasping at our faces. He opens his mouth, but any snarl or moan he might make is lost in the deafening scream that comes out of Kendra.

CHAPTER TEN

Ian

The dirt floor of the cellar behind us rises, then crumbles apart, and there, climbing out of the ground, is *another* zombie.

Another one. Outside the cabin, down in the basement—they're everywhere.

PJ shouts and sputters; without his camera, he's lost all composure.

"Now what?" yelps Kendra.

That's a fair question.

"Fight!" I yell, snatching the torch from Kendra's hand and waving it right in front of the zombie. For a second, it works, the creature backs away from us with his arms held up to block his face, and I figure, *Yeah, we're saved, we can fight 'em off with a bunch of homemade torches and our wits to guide us—*

Then the thing reaches out with a moan and just wraps his hand around the burning end of the torch, like it was nothing. There's a sizzle and a smell like burned hair, and the light goes out.

And then a cold hand lightly scrapes my face, and I just *lose it*.

"RUN!" I scream, and then I'm up the stairs and throwing the trapdoor open.

Too bad the cabin's full of zombies. In the light, they're even grosser than they were outside, like something out of the worst nightmare I've ever had. Their skin is gray and wrinkled, yanked tight over their bones and chipped away. Their mouths are black, full of dirt and bugs. They're missing body parts, ears and eyes and the occasional nose, but their cuts and wounds don't bleed, just sit open and gooey and *black*.

And the smell, man, I can't even describe it, like a roadkill sandwich with rotten lettuce and toilet sauce on sourdough. With every slow, stupid movement, mossy dirt and wriggling worms fall off of their bodies and tumble onto the floor. And even though some of them don't have eyes, it's obvious by the sudden simultaneous moan that comes out of them that they all see us just fine.

All at once, they reach out for us, twisted hands at the ends of stiff arms. "We're out of here!" I scream.

We bolt past the forest of outstretched claws and out the door, Kendra hot on my heels, PJ sort of limping and skipping, the army of hands only grazing my hair and clothes. The light of the cabin disappears as we're charging out into the woods again, only now there are more zombies, ones who haven't seen us before, whose faces twist hungrily as three fat entrees come barreling out at them.

"This way!" I shout, hooking around the side of the cabin and running full throttle, putting as much distance between the moaning mass of dead people and us as humanly possible.

"We're heading back the way we came!" shrieks Kendra.

"I don't care!" I yell back. "As long as it's away from all of them!"

"I'm with Ian!" PJ agrees.

Run, little poodle, says a voice in my head that I still can't shut up, that eats away at all my wolfish courage. I try to respond that even wolves have to retreat from a fight sometimes, but I know I'm just being soft on myself. I'm not running because it's the right strategy. This feeling burning through my arms and legs isn't hot blood; it's plain old fear.

We run for what seems like years, crawling over

rocks, squeezing between trees, gaining ground however we can. The rain starts up again, this time more mist than downpour, but enough to soak our clothes and make every breath a wet soggy hassle. After a while, even my chest burns enough that I need to stop, and when I turn around, I see Kendra and PJ a good thirty yards behind me. Both of them are doing their best to catch their breath and keep up; PJ's doubled over, his hands on his knees. I turn around and jog back to them, still keeping my eyes out for another wave of stumbling shadows.

"Everything all right?" I ask.

"Yeah," pants Kendra, "just . . . need . . . a . . . moment. . . ."

"PJ?"

PJ answers by puking his guts out. A granola bar and what's left of his Homeroom Earth lunch go everywhere. It's gross, but not that bad compared to, you know, everything else. Kendra reaches out a hand and starts rubbing his back the way your mom's supposed to.

"Sorry," he says between spitting.

"It's okay," says Kendra. "Hold on." She digs through her backpack and finds her canteen. PJ swishes his mouth out and then takes a deep drink from it. Kendra wipes the rim off and takes a sip herself before passing it to me. "We've got to stay hydrated."

"And not get our brains eaten," says PJ.

I can't help but laugh, even though I'm not feeling very amused. Must be my nerves. You can't blame me.

My whole body shakes, no matter how hard I try to keep it still. When I focus on one part of it and will it to stop, another part of me starts quivering. When I focus on it all, I feel like I'm going to straight-up cry. If Coach could see me now—just another shivering little poodle. If I get eaten tonight, I deserve it.

"We need to keep moving," I stutter, mostly because it's the only thing I can think of doing that'll stop the nervous chill going through my body.

"Shelter," whispers Kendra. "Somewhere to catch our breaths. Hide."

We stumble forward, even less sure of our direction than we were earlier, only it's like there is no earlier, no home base or woods or mountain. The whole day we just went through, and the day to come, don't even exist. There's just the woods in front of us and the things we're running from.

Finally, we find a huge rock jutting out of the side of the mountain with a little hollow under it, almost a cave but not quite, and the three of us huddle underneath it. Less reassuring than finding a cabin with electricity and a fireplace, but definitely better than finding out the cabin was host to a living dead convention.

Kendra nudges my hand with her canteen until I

take it and have a drink, and then I'm thirsty like whoa, and she has to nudge me again to keep me from pounding the whole thing.

We're silent for a little while longer. Kendra, of course, has to be the one to speak up, again. "We should figure out what happened just now."

"What do you mean?" PJ asks. "I'm pretty sure we were attacked by zombies."

She shakes her head. "No. Those . . . aren't real. It has to be . . . something else."

"Like what?"

"Maybe . . ." She goes quiet, staring off into the woods, and then launches into "Maybe there was some kind of viral outbreak, a chemical weapons accident, or something. There's some kind of government facility up here, and they spilled a toxic agent that makes human beings deranged and hostile. The people who lived in the cabin got sick, and they attacked us after returning home and finding us there."

"You said yourself no one lives up around here," I reply. "And anyway, did they cart their furniture along with them when this phantom chemical spill happened?"

"That's not—"

"Plus, that was a lot of people to be living in just that cabin."

"Granted—"

"Sick people don't walk around with missing body

parts," mumbles PJ, looking up from his ankle. "You need eyes to see, no matter how bad your cold is. Honestly, with what was written in that diary, zombies sound more believable than that."

Kendra pinches her brow. "Okay. Maybe . . . maybe they weren't there at all. Maybe we had some kind of group hallucination due to a . . . a chemical spill, something in our food, and we just *saw* . . . those things. Maybe we're exhausted, and it's affecting—"

"Yeah," says PJ rather sarcastically, "I *hallucinated* the dead guy in the basement."

"I'm just trying to come up with a logical explanation." She sighs, throwing her hands up. "Okay? I'm trying to think of a way all this could happen within the realm of possibility. Sorry if that's offending you two!"

Silence. We're all so beat. It's not even Kendra's fault that her brainy explanations are total baloney; at least she's trying. In my head, I weigh our options. So Kendra is right, it's insane to think those were zombies that attacked us, because she's also right, zombies don't exist; they're one of those things you come across strictly in bad scary movies and first-person shooter video games.

There are rules you learn in real life, and two of the most important ones are, first, that monsters like vampires and werewolves and zombies aren't real, and second, that dead things stay dead. The second one's a pretty big rule, too, one that you learn early on as a kid: there's alive and dead, and dead means no moving, no talking, no nothing. So this is insane, because it's breaking that rule, and suddenly I feel like, I don't know, like PJ without his camera, like all bets are off and I can't win.

And I haven't forgotten that this is all my fault. Well, mostly my fault. Obviously, I didn't put the zombies here, but I did lead us to them, or them to us, or whatever, and if you think about it, the real bad guy here is Michael McDermott's stupid asthma, making me move to Ms. Brandt's activity group, which meant I had to take that stupid wildflower class, which meant I was willing to run headfirst after anything that wasn't boring enough to make me want to go right back home.

But technically, yeah, this is my bad, so the zombies must be nature's way of calling me on breaking the rules and running off into the woods. I break the rules; nature breaks the rules. I disobey Professor Randy; the dead come back to life and try to eat us.

The rock outcropping is pretty lousy shelter, only blocking about 60 percent of the rain blowing at us. My clothes begin soaking all the way through. A rattling noise perks my ears, and when I look over, I see Kendra's lips vibrating. It's her teeth.

"It's really cold up here," PJ shudders, and Kendra and I both nod hard.

Between the camera addict and the library resident, there's not much meat or muscle, and the temperature must be killer. With no idea what time it is, no clue how far we ran from the cabin and the blankets inside, there's only one way I can think of that will keep us all warm, and I'm not happy about it, but we're in a pretty rough situation here, what with the cold and the zombies.

"Here," I say, scooting over and pressing myself next to Kendra. PJ gets the idea and crawls over onto her other side, and the three of us huddle together in a little clump, trying to pass some warmth from one person to another. Of course I'm not *thrilled* about having to cuddle with my buddy and a girl I don't especially like, but we get warmer instantly, and hey, Kendra's poofy hair is sort of pillowy, and it smells nice.

When I lean my head into it, I feel my eyelids getting heavier right away. Some time must pass, 'cause the rain lets up, and for a second, in the quiet forest, pressed against my friends, it's almost nice out here. The moon gives everything a pretty blue-white color, and the air is silent, without even the sound of crickets interrupting this little moment of rest we've got going.

"If they *are*, you know," says Kendra, finally, "how do we get rid of them?"

"In *Night of the Living Dead*, you have to hunt them down with guns," says PJ. "That usually involves getting the police together and sending out a search party."

"Yeah, but is that the movie that said they were afraid of fire?" I ask. "So maybe the movie lied."

"Right," says PJ.

"In ghost stories, people come back from the dead because of unfinished business," says Kendra. "We could try talking to them. To see if they can tell us what's wrong. Maybe they were reaching out to us for help."

"Okay," says PJ. "*You* go talk to them."

We all laugh. We could use a laugh right now.

"But if they're . . . *infected*, in some way," she continues, "by a disease, or by radiation, like you said, PJ, then we'll probably just have to . . ." She doesn't finish the sentence, but PJ and I meet eyes, and we both understand what she can't say, because it's disgusting and horrible.

We huddle closer.

My eyes close, and the woods drift in and out of focus. Kendra keeps talking about disease control and quarantine, but I'm barely here, slipping off toward sleep, imagining my parents at home, happy to see me, Coach Leider throwing an arm over my shoulder and welcoming me back, PJ's parents thanking me for keeping him alive. My eyes crack open and I glance at PJ, my buddy from birth, looking sad and wiped out in the shadow of the rock ledge.

Poor guy. It's been an insane day for him. For all of us, I guess.

PJ looks over at me, and then his eyes go huge, and

he screams bloody murder.

The zombie is just over my shoulder, bending down so she can snatch me in her rotting claw, so close that I can see her flaking black lips, her sunken dark-gray cheeks, her matted hair, her filthy red fur-collared jacket, her fanny pack bulging with dirt and leaves. One of her legs is twisted painfully—I think I see a bone sticking out of it, *yecch*—and she claws at the rock around us, trying to stay standing as she lunges forward and grasps at me.

The three of us go scurrying out from under our rock, slipping and sliding in the wet dirt beneath us, but the zombie's no better, and she slips on her own broken leg and falls face-first into the mud. I leap back up and grab PJ's arm with one hand and Kendra's with the other, and we three manage to climb back to our feet just as the zombie regains her footing and comes at us again.

"We've got to run!" I shout at my friends, dodging a claw by only a few inches.

"There's nowhere *to* run!" shrieks PJ. "They're everywhere! They're—"

The zombie lurches forward, and her hand wraps around PJ's shoulder, but she slips on her broken leg again, and with this *awful* ripping noise, the hand comes free, so that she goes staggering in the mud but PJ is left screaming at this severed hand clutching his shirt.

"Get it off!" he yelps. "Get it off get it off get it off—" I grab the hand with both of mine, but when I yank it from PJ's sleeve, the whole thing comes apart in a dusty, gooey mess in my grip, small finger bones falling out of the powdery gunk and tumbling to the ground beneath us.

"Oh my *God*," moans PJ, his face turning green.

The zombie stumbles into a nearby tree, the trunk creaking as she leans against it, and then with a howl, she lunges toward us—and then stops. Her teeth snap, her arms snatch at the air, and her feet slide in the mud as she tries to walk, but something keeps her from gaining ground.

"Look," says Kendra, "around her neck!"

There's some kind of rope attached to her neck, one of those lanyards you hang whistles and glasses and stuff from; it's caught in one of the branches of the dead tree she stumbled into. With every lurch forward, the rope tightens, and the whole tree shakes.

Wait. Hold on. The creaking, the bending. The tree the zombie is caught on is like her—dead, rotten, like the one we found in the woods earlier.

Oh man, I have an idea.

"Hold on!" I shout to Kendra, then circle around to the other side of the dead tree. I take a few steps back and then bodycheck the trunk as hard as I can. Nothing.

I go again, the bark biting my shoulder through my

shirt as I push with all my might. There's a creak, but nothing else. Then, I hear a grunt next to me, and I see Kendra putting her shoulder into the tree, too, then PJ, and now we're doing a sweaty and desperate imitation of our tree-dropping routine from earlier, only now there's a living corpse turning back toward us and stumbling forward with her arms spread open and her mouth gaping wide.

"One . . . two . . . three!" I yell, and the three of us clench our eyes shut, put our backs into it, and heave.

Come on, come on, do it, do it, *break, BREAK*—

There's that sound, that sharp crack that echoes through the whole forest, and then the dead tree begins moving with our shoulders. The zombie's head lifts up to stare at the oncoming tree trunk, and for a second I see a look on her face, like a lightbulb just went off over her head—*uh-oh*—before the tree comes crashing down on her with a BOOM.

CHAPTER ELEVEN

Kendra

Field research requires dynamic rationality. All the greats—Jane Goodall, Amelia Earhart—took the time to be brilliant before rushing into action. And part of being brilliant is being able to comprehend any situation. If one *must* leap into the fray, one's mind must be experienced enough to think its way through even the most unbelievable or upsetting scenario. Up until now, I assumed my own mind was just such a versatile muscle.

This, though, I . . . I just don't know.

The echoing crash of the fallen tree rings in my ears over and over again, until I take a few long, deep breaths and realize that the echoing boom is actually my heart beating against my rib cage. My brain and body feel cold and hot in uncontrollable waves, no matter how many times I tell myself that it's over, the threat is gone. My mind's words fall on deaf ears. The scene at my feet seems too horrific to think past.

Out of the corner of my eye, I see Ian's chest rising and falling, and PJ drops to one knee. There is a tree on the ground in front of me, dead and dusty, recently felled. There is the spiny trunk, a mass of upright splinters. And sprouting out from under the fallen tree, like the feet of the Wicked Witch of the East, is the hand of what I'm supposed to believe is a . . . a murderous walking dead person.

And maybe it's the ludicrousness of thinking such a thing, or the sheer horror of it, or my complete inability to *calm down, Kendra*, but I'm . . . having a hard time grasping any of this.

If Mom is right about following my gut, then yes, there's an evil living corpse underneath this tree. My gut is certain of that. My head, though, refuses to wrap itself around the idea.

"Is it dead?" pants Ian. "I mean, dead-dead. Dead*er*. Dead as in—"

"Yes," I state firmly, if only to quiet the frantic look in his eyes. "You crushed it."

"I wish we could just go home," mumbles PJ.

"W-w-we better get out of here," stammers Ian.

"The other ones probably heard that. We need to leave, right now."

He's right. That's a good idea, Kendra. Remember when you had those? Stop thinking about the terrible thing under the tree. Stop staring at the pale, filthy hand at the end of the fur-lined sleeve. You've seen enough.

But no, I can't let it go that easily. There has to be a clue, an explanation. Don't leave quite yet—look. There, next to her hand. It's square, it's shiny, it's what was tied around her neck, what leashed her to the dead tree.

"What are you doing?" yells Ian while I crouch down and grab the thin laminated square. Yes. It's a badge, an ID of some kind, dangling out from under the fragile bark of the dead tree, just between the telltale hand and an ever-growing pool of black viscous fluid. My hand darts out, tugs hard, and yanks it free before the dreadful arm can leap back to un-life and snap my bones in an icy grip.

"What is it?" asks PJ, wobbling back to his feet. The two boys close in around my shoulders as I catch the square in a patch of moonlight coming between the trees.

"It's some sort of identification card," I tell them as I use my sleeve to wipe at the dirt covering it. "Hikers wear these around their necks. It's like dog tags for soldiers."

"In case they ever die up here on the mountain,"

quivers PJ, saying what my mind has been trying to ignore.

The film of black filth smears away from the front of the ID, and a girl stares back at us, the smiling, fresh-faced version of the creature that just attacked us, with long brown hair and a small button nose. The name next to her head reads—

"Deborah Palmer," I say, despair settling on me like a heavy, damp cloud, "the girl who wrote the diary."

"Whoa, you mean the zombies are the *Pine City Dancers*?" asks Ian.

All I can do is nod.

"The Pine City Dancers are back from the grave, trying to eat us," mutters PJ.

"Kendra, do you still have that diary?" Ian questions.

My hand darts through my bag until it feels soft, sodden pages squeeze together. Somehow, through the panic, I remembered to toss it in here. "Yes," I say through a sigh of relief. "Let's examine—"

"No," says PJ. "We have to get out of here first. They're probably already on their way."

Still a good idea, Kendra. But stop, breathe, think— maybe this time, you shouldn't wander aimlessly. North? No, you probably can't find it right now without sun to watch a stick's shadow by, and it's too dark to look for moss or cobwebs on the side of a tree. For all you know, north could take you right back to the cabin.

Look at the facts. What are you trying to do? Avoid a threat. What are that threat's natural qualities? Slow moving, unbalanced, uncoordinated, strong but not terribly hardy. It walks unstoppably, has considerable physical strength, and shows resilience to pain, but it's basically mindless.

"Let's head uphill" is my final answer. "It'll be a harder climb for them, and it'll give us the higher ground, so we can see them in time if they find us."

"That sounds good," says Ian. "PJ, can your ankle take some climbing?"

"I'll manage," grumbles PJ.

The rain has died down, but the forest is slick with mud, and our uphill trajectory is steadily treacherous. PJ's the first to take a spill, his bad ankle causing him to go clawing for the ground, but only a few minutes later, I feel the earth slip out from under me as my sneaker squeaks on a patch of moss, and then I'm facedown in the dirt. Ian helps us up, but five minutes later, he takes a spill of his own, catching his foot in a small burrow and nearly smashing his knee on a rock. From there on out, we proceed slowly, carefully finding our footing along the mossy mountainside and making sure that PJ can keep up with Ian and me.

PJ's limp grows more pronounced with every minute, but he's doing his best to cover it, supporting himself against the nearest tree and looking away whenever he puts too much pressure on his bad ankle and has to grunt with pain. Ian prattles the occasional tidbit about the terrain—"Careful here, there's a hole there, watch that tree root"—and I make sure to point out nearby landmarks in case we need to retrace our steps, but PJ is completely silent, lost in an ever-present scowl of concentration on his foot.

"Sorry I'm slowing you down," he says after a while.

"It's fine, man," says Ian, slapping him lightly on the arm. "Take your time. As long as you're faster than the zombies, you'll be okay."

PJ nods, and then a strange little smile crosses his face. He lets his injured leg go limp and drags it along the forest floor. His hands jut out stiffly in front of him, and he lets out a breathy moan that's far too accurate an impression of the ones we just heard.

"They're coming to get you, Deborah," he moans. When Ian gasps and takes a step back, PJ glances at us with a tired expression of amusement and says, "Too soon?"

As exhausted as I am, I can't help but laugh a little at our meek friend trying to buck us up. Ian joins in, still a little shocked by PJ's mimicry. The response seems to put some warmth in PJ's face and makes him climb a little faster.

In the ground in front of us opens a deep ravine, its edges dotted with twisted almost-trees bending their long branches down into the muck-filled pit below. When we reach the precipice, we all sit down to catch our breaths. Past the ravine, the mountain slopes up sharply, and the leaf-covered ground gives way to stony terrain that looks wet, loose, and treacherous.

Observing it, I fret about our progress from here on, especially given our injured party. The descent down into the ravine is more than ten feet. We'll have to find a way around it or slowly help each other down, but even then, the steep-sloping mountain beyond it will be a hard climb.

You've been lucky so far, Kendra, only dealing with leafy forests with plenty of trees. From here on out, you've got a real mountain to deal with.

"What do you think turned the Pine City Dancers into zombies?" asks Ian.

"Again, it's not certain they are . . . those," I tell him. "They're probably just lost. Maybe this witch woman they mentioned poisoned their food and water, drugged them."

"In the movies, it's almost always bites." We turn to PJ, who sits with his ankle in his hand, staring intently into it, his face cast in shadow. "It's spread like a fast-acting virus. If they bite you and don't manage to eat you alive, the bite gets infected, and then it kills you. Soon after that, you come back."

"You're saying that this mountain had zombies on

it before the Pine City Dancers showed up?" Ian asks.

"It makes sense, in a weird way," says PJ. "It looked like there were more than twelve of them. Maybe those first few who got taken came back as zombies and got to their friends. Kendra, what else does the diary say?"

I fish the sodden journal from my bag and reopen it to Deborah Palmer's testimony. Now that I know her fate, the words come a bit easier:

> *It wasn't long before Bill passed away in our arms. Looking back, I wish we'd figured out a way to get him to the road, made some kind of a sled or backpack to haul him along in, but we were scared and had no idea what to do, so we buried him in the one place that felt safe—the dirt floor of the cellar.*

"Really?" says Ian, throwing up his arms. "You couldn't have read that *one paragraph* before we went down into the basement with Bill the zombie?"

"Dude," says PJ sternly.

Ian snaps his mouth shut and nods. "Right, sorry. What's done is done and all that. Keep reading."

> *Suddenly, the cabin was no longer our beacon of hope but a morbid prison. Grace and Chelsea said they saw someone peeking into the*

windows, and more than once we all heard what sounded like footsteps on the roof. We barely got any sleep, lying in a pile by the fireplace. When morning came, a fight broke out over whether to stay put and hope for a rescue or head back into the woods. We finally decided to keep going, if only to be somewhere where poor Bill wasn't. We headed down the slope, determined to make it back home by nightfall. It didn't work, of course—the mountain seemed to be endless, and we walked for miles, until the sun set and we had to set up camp.

That was a couple of days ago, when there were eleven of us left.

There are only three of us—me, Leonard, and Grace. The others have simply vanished—we would bed down at night, and in the morning they'd be gone, leaving some sort of telltale item behind, a hat torn to shreds, a guidebook smeared with mud. This morning, all we found outside of Chelsea's tent were finger marks in the dirt, like she'd clawed at the ground while something dragged her away. We're out of food, and we're too tired to keep walking. Grace won't stop crying. Leonard seems crazy, bursting into bouts of angry laughter, saying he needs to destroy the entire forest, burn it to the ground. He says

he's seen some of our friends walking off in the
distance, only it's not them, just things that look
like them, something inside of their bodies. The
forest feels more hostile every day, and the things
haunting it, whatever they might be, seem to be
closing in.

If you're reading this, there may be hope
for you yet. You need to find a way out of this
horrible wilderness. The old woman we chased
from her cabin might still be out there. If you can
find her, force her to lead you back, and tell the
outside world our story.

My hand aches from writing this, and
my pencil is a tiny stub. Grace says she hears
something. The sun is going down, and I have to
help prepare the bonfire for

"For?" asks PJ.

"That's all she wrote," I tell him.

We sit in silence, shudders coursing up and down my spine. Dealing with Ian and PJ has been tough enough, but fighting with a dozen of your friends while trying to outrun something you can't see . . . it must have been brutal on her.

This poor, frightened woman. These poor lost souls.

Still, a nagging confusion buzzes in the back of my mind. Where could this witch woman have gotten to? If Deborah got attacked out in the woods while writing this journal, how did it end up in the basement of the cabin, sitting next to that skull? None of this makes sense yet. There's something here that none of us is seeing.

"Anything else?" says Ian, catching me off guard. He stands behind me, staring down at the diary in my hands. "Maybe there's another clue, something about getting us out of here or destroying the zombies."

"No," I tell him, "just the diary."

"Are you sure?" asks Ian. "Keep looking. See if there's anything else about this old mountain woman."

I flip a few pages forward, blank, blank, blank, and then—

"Whoa," says Ian, pointing to the next written page. "That's different."

PJ sidles over and peers at the paper. "What do you think this is supposed to be?"

"I'm . . . unsure," I reply.

The next few pages of the book appear to be written by a different author, someone less hurried. There's a drawing, a detailed sketch of a dream catcher, one of the circular nets used by the Native Americans to capture good dreams, though this one looks like it was made to lure in night terrors. The strings running through it form a shape not unlike the one painted on the stone wall, and among them are sewn in what appear to be teeth. All around it is a series of strange, foreign symbols that could be Arabic or Cyrillic, but are definitely not from any alphabet I know.

Something about this part of the diary sends a vibration up through my body. The script, the drawings, they're all done by a surer author than the scribbled confession of the Pine City dancer; and like the wall and the woods and the cabin, there's a feeling of *wrong* that goes along with them, a sort of . . . *inauspicious* association (four, a bit of a stretch, though).

On the page after that, though, there's something useful. The author, whoever he or she may be, has drawn a rudimentary map, a big triangular peak representing the mountain, and on it I can see landmarks, including a detailed miniature stone wall, evil sigil and all, and a tiny cabin, beneath which is a sigil with a skull at its center. A little ways up is another place, decorated with a crosslike sigil in the middle of a circle, with a miniature dream catcher over it. At the very top of the mountain, right below the point, appears to be a cave with a figure in front of it, a hunched stick figure with wispy hair. A thick black line runs up the triangle, connecting all the landmarks. There's more writing around it, all done in the same odd script, but try as I may—*remember when Sorin from Romania tried to teach you the Cyrillic alphabet online, Kendra, remember*—I can't decipher it.

When I show it to the boys, they perk up, if only

slightly. "Beats no map at all, I guess," PJ says, sighing.

"What do we think this is?" Ian points to the cross-circle, the landmark we haven't reached yet.

"Unsure," I say. "It has to be important, though, seeing as it has this dream catcher over it. So far these symbols have been found only in the places we've run into something strange. The wall, the cabin, they've all had symbols like this on or in them. It must all tie together with the . . . creatures. What it *does* mean, though"—I feel my heart swell and my voice go tight and high with excitement—"is that if we can trace our way back to the cabin, we can find our way to whatever trail this is"—I trace the center line on the map from the peak of the mountain downward—"and presumably make it back to Homeroom Earth."

Ian nods, his eyes glowing with the prospect of getting home. "Awesome. So." He looks around us and shrugs. "I guess we need to figure out a plan, huh?"

"Kendra?" asks PJ, looking hopefully at me. "Any ideas?"

Excellent—with PJ referring to me, Ian will probably follow suit, and so our plans won't constitute "Run!" or "Go after it!" or other amazing Buckley family remedies. *Now, it's time to think, Kendra, to work your muscle of choice. Sort out the information you've been given, use it to build and back up an argument, aaand . . . postulate!*

"Our goal is to either escape those things," I say,

"or find a way to destroy them. To achieve that goal, we need to analyze what we know about them and come up with a strategy. First, we believe these creatures to be linked to this old woman—"

"Zombies," says Ian, eyes wide and accusatory.

"Let's call them 'creatures' for now," I say. "I'm not sure I'm comfortable with that word yet."

"No," says Ian, jabbing out a hand, *"zombies."*

"Look, Ian, I understand that you believe that's what attacked us; it's just that maybe there's a more reasonable explanation—"

Before I can finish, he grabs me by the shoulders and spins me around rudely. I'm about to protest when I see shapes off in the distance, slowly staggering our way.

CHAPTER TWELVE

PJ

They're here.

It's hopeless. They've found us. It doesn't matter how, whether it was the sound of the tree crushing their sister or some kind of undead sixth sense that tells them where warm meat is. Those white eyes shine out of the shadows and fix on us, and then the moaning starts, the grasping, the stench of rotting flesh. They crunch through the underbrush, marching in our direction one sickening foot after another. No matter what we do, no matter how far we run, they know where we are, and they find us.

My ankle hurts so much. It's like my heart is beating inside of it.

Any hope I had from seeing Kendra's map is swallowed up by the horizon of lifeless gazes, black rotting mouths, and dirt-caked hands. The entire forest shakes in a chorus of hungry gasps that builds into a single sorrowful moan. There may have only been twelve Pine City Dancers, but there are definitely more than that here, some gray faced and fresh, some withered and ancient, all moving forward with the same blind drive.

"Right," says Kendra in a low voice, "I see."

"They're going to catch up to us if we rest in one place for too long," says Ian. "If we stay on the go, we should be able to outrun them."

"I don't know how much more I can climb," I admit.

"If we're lucky," says Kendra after a moment of staring into the oncoming horde, "we won't have to."

She points to our new map of the mountain, so scribbled and basic that it might as well be one of the treasure maps Ian and I used to draw when we were little. Her finger traces the central line running up the mountain, the one that connects to all the other landmarks on the map, and that we're hoping and praying is some sort of road back home.

"If we get past this ravine and hike uphill for another quarter mile, we should hit this central path. We could follow it downhill." She looks over the edge of the small gorge in front of us. "This will be a good obstacle to put between us and them, too."

"But they might reach *us* before we reach the path," I say, the crunch of dead feet behind me the only thing I can hear. "This map isn't exactly . . . exact."

"It's our best bet," she says. "This is all we have."

That's our strategy now. "Our best bet." "All we've got." "This or nothing."

We climb to our feet, myself a little slower than the other two. My legs ache, and my muscles are sore, and I can't put any weight on my ankle without it exploding in unspeakable pain. My face must speak for me, because Ian comes up next to me and puts a hand on my shoulder.

"You gonna be okay, PJ?" he whispers. "Maybe you should lose the backpack."

"No," I say. "I'm fine. I'll be okay." My backpack's cargo is precious. I can't lose Kyra's book. Getting home and reading Kyra her bedtime story is my goal. I need it. "It's okay, I'll keep up."

The slope down into the ravine isn't a *straight* drop, but it's about fifteen feet of incredibly steep loose earth, and it ends in a brown-rainwater-filled pit. Kendra goes first, easing herself down the edge of the ravine hand over hand on a series of overhanging branches and well-placed rocks, and then carefully hopping around the pit in the bottom.

When she's safely down, she calls up, "Ian, help lower PJ. I'll ease him down from here."

"Okay, man, here we go," says Ian, grabbing my one hand in both of his and digging in his heels. My whole body shakes as I take my first step backward down the edge of the ravine. Slowly, Ian shuffles forward and I take baby hops backward, wincing any time pressure is put on my ankle. Staring straight ahead, I see Ian, cheeks puffed and red, lowering me down into a hole, a dozen hungry figures swaying a ways behind him.

"I've got him," says a voice from behind me, and two thin hands wrap around my waist. "PJ, push off the edge with your good foot on 'now.' Three, two, one, *now*!"

Ian's hands unclamp from mine, my working foot presses against the sloping dirt, and Kendra yanks me backward. For a moment, I'm in midair, with no control over my own movement, and total panic seizes me, jabs at my heart and eyes like a cold needle. Then, I land on my butt, Kendra falling next to me, narrowly missing the blackish puddle. The ground kicks me in the tailbone but feels good and solid underfoot (or underbutt).

"You okay?" I ask Kendra.

"Fine," she says, stretching her back with a pained face.

"Can you guys spot me while I lower myself down—" There's a crunch and a moan, and Ian's head whips behind him, and suddenly he comes screaming over the edge of the ravine, arms and legs spinning in the air, mouth open in a stunned yelp. He manages to land crouched on his feet directly in the puddle before us, sending streaks of mud flying through the air, spattering on our faces and clothes, leaving Ian brown and filthy from the knees and elbows down.

At the edge of the ravine stands one of the zombies in a torn flannel, gray filthy hands shaking at his side, green-gray face twisted in a ravenous sneer of blind hunger. The moonlight gleams off his dead white eyes. His gore-streaked mouth opens and lets out a desperate moan. Off in the distance, more moans respond to his, and a mad dance of shadows runs through the night as the ravenous crowd begins catching up with him.

My fingers instinctively scramble for the camera in my pocket, but Ian and Kendra yank me to my feet before I can get the shot.

"Sorry about the mud," says Ian.

"At least you got down," I say. "Besides, Kendra's right—now we have time to climb while they find their way around the drop—"

There's a gray blur, a sickening splat, another splash of mud and filth. We all cry out and leap back from the giant puddle, fright still stabbing me in the chest.

No more than two seconds after it lands, the zombie climbs up on his hands and knees and comes at us. His face, now drenched with muck, seems to be melting, the flesh hanging in great loose gobs off his decayed skull.

We all scream and backpedal as he jabs out a bloated hand at us, but then there's another blur, and another zombie comes falling face-first on top of the first one. There's a crunch and pop of bone, and then the second zombie sits up, sees us, and reaches out his hands. At the edge of the ravine, a third one puts out his boot into thin air and steps forward.

It's raining zombies.

"They're like lemmings going over the edge of a cliff," yells Kendra, backing away from the growing heap of writhing corpses. "They're just so stupid."

"But they feel no pain," says Ian. "They'll be on their feet again any second!" We turn to the rocky uphill in front of us to the tune of crashing bodies.

After the ravine, the ground gets much steeper, and the soft, wet forest floor is replaced with jagged stones in rocky moss-eaten earth. I hobble and curse and do everything in my power not to scream every time I put the slightest amount of pressure on my ankle. Before, the woods were rough but manageable, and now they're an obstacle course, and every loose stone is a trip wire, sending me sprawling to my knees and leaving my friends to try to steady me. Over and over, Kendra and Ian walk ahead, stop, and waste precious time doubling back to help me. Sweat pours down my face. My working ankle throbs. My chest hurts when I breathe.

And soon, the sound of stumbling groans dies out

155

in the background. The zombies are back on their feet. And they're gaining on us.

No matter how hard I hop, I look back and there they are, stiff shapes in the distance, growing bigger before my eyes. They come from all sides, from behind every tree, their faces only able to express blind hunger or twisted rage as they lurch diligently along. Soon, I can hear every snarl and footstep behind us, can sense their slow-moving presence at my back, can almost feel their cold, bony hands scraping at my skin. It's hopeless. Our doom seems pretty unavoidable.

My foot meets a patch of moss, and I stumble into a puddle of mud. Ian and Kendra run over and help me to my feet.

Kendra pulls one of my arms over her shoulder. "We can carry him for a while, right?"

"Right," agrees Ian, but the dark rings around his eyes and the grimace on his face tell me he's flagging. He grunts with fatigue as he gets under my other arm and hoists me up. When he looks over his other shoulder, the gasp that comes out of him tells me that the dead are getting a little close for comfort.

We walk like this for only a couple of yards, the two of them supporting me, me pedaling along with my good foot, but we're slowing down, and now we can't climb over any useful obstacles, rocks and ledges that would help throw off the zombies behind us. Instead, the undead's lack of pain or weariness just makes them superior hikers.

When I look back, I see the buttons on their flannel jackets, the buckles on their belts, and the blackish rotting patches on their faces and necks, the yellow crusts on their lips and eyelids. Even the ones with the messed-up legs, the draggers and hobblers, are moving faster than us.

"It shouldn't be much farther," grunts Kendra.

"I think I see something up ahead," says Ian.

A web of brambles and interwoven sticker bushes tears at my pants as we burst through the underbrush and come upon a jagged wall of rocks, stretching up some thirty feet, creating a craggy scar between the trees of the forest. Ivy and briars slither out from every crevice. Multiple jagged boulders seem strategically placed all up the wall, giving it multiple smaller ledges throughout. It probably wouldn't be the worst climb in the world—if my ankle wasn't horribly sprained.

"The map didn't mention this," groans Kendra, her eyes scanning up and down the cliff face.

"We can do this," says Ian, taking it in and mapping it out in his head. "See, these rocks aren't that big, and the vines growing out of here make decent ropes."

"I think those are poison ivy," Kendra bellows.

"Then our hands will itch!" yells Ian. Behind us, the moaning grows, and his face gets more and more panicked. "They can't *fall* up a mountain. This is a *real* obstacle. And right now, it's our best bet—"

"You two keep saying that!" I shout. Something hard and heavy rises up from the pit of my stomach and fills my throat. My eyes burn. My head blurs. It's hard to breathe. "We put a ravine between us and them, they fall down it! We put an hour of uphill hiking between us, they scale it! We're done for! It's *over*!"

"We *can* do this," says Ian, and then he looks at me, his face hard and pale. "PJ, *you* can do this. I know you can. You've got to try. Otherwise—"

Before he can keep trying to convince me, the decision is made for us: from behind a nearby tree stomps a zombie, a tall one in a torn peacoat and a red stocking cap, pus-colored teeth gnashing beneath a bushy gray mustache. His milky eyes settle on the three of us, and those hands come up as he stumbles stiffly toward us, moaning and clawing at the air.

The first rock is slimy and cold beneath my belly as we scramble up onto it. Ian and Kendra immediately launch up onto the second one before I can even get back on my feet, hanging like mountain climbers from big hairy strings of ivy. I manage to climb up onto the next rock outcropping just as the zombie comes crashing into the first one; I'm halfway up when icy fingertips glance on my ankle, and then my good foot shoves me up the next two before I know what's happening. Without even trying, I'm halfway up the wall. Maybe Ian's right. Maybe I can do this.

Below us, they come spilling out of the woods, hungry moans rising out of breathless throats. The mustached ghoul stares straight up the rock wall at me, raising his hands over his head. His mouth chews open and closed, black goo smacking between crusty chapped lips, and his eyes, white with death, never leave mine. The other zombies have caught up with him, and I can see them now, gathering at the bottom of the cliff—the skinny woman in pink spandex, swaying in her ballet shoes as she tiptoes en pointe toward us; a wiry black woman missing most of her lips and one of her eyes, old flesh drawn tight over her face and neck; Bill from the basement, chubby and slow, his torn cheek leaking black scum; the big guy with no shirt, his half face crawling with maggots, his eyes mean looking under his sloping brow. Each one is individually revolting, but as they pile up below us, they amass into an indistinguishable crowd of upraised hands that sends shudders up and down every sinew in my body.

But for once, Ian and Kendra are right—the crowds of undead crash against the wall of boulders, building in number but never attempting to climb.

"Come on, PJ!" yells Kendra, some twelve feet up. I look up the rockface to see the two of them overhead, peering down from a jagged stone ledge impatiently. It's only a really hard jump and some climbing ahead, but with the throbbing in my ankle and the weakness in my arms, it might as well be the entire mountain.

Maybe, I tell myself, *maybe I can just wait it out here. Maybe help will come, and someone with a rope will pull me up—*

"PJ, you need to climb!" screams Ian. "Grab that vine and hoist yourself up. I'm going to hang over the edge and grab your arm."

"I don't think I can do it," I try to say, but really sob.

"You're wrong!" he calls back. "I *know* you, man! For someone as strong as you, this is *nothing*!" He dangles his torso over the edge, Kendra kneeling behind him and grabbing his ankles, and stretches his muddy hands out toward me.

A few feet below his hands hangs the vine he's talking about, a furry stretch of ivy wrapped across the next big rock ledge. I jump as hard as my good foot will allow and feel my hand close around it. With one strong yank, I pull myself up toward Ian, stretching my hand up to his, his smiling face dripping with sweat, outlined by the cloudy night sky—

And then there's a snap, and the vine breaks.

Ian's face goes wide with fear. I fall, slam into the rock below me, roll, fall again, totally weightless, and then my chest hits something hard, my fingers tighten around something cold, and I swing in the air, my feet dangling in open space.

I hang from the edge of the second rock up, my heels only inches away from the rippling ocean of the dead beneath me. The moaning gets louder and more excited; the decayed fingers claw at the air. Sobs send spit and snot and tears coursing down my face. Every time I breathe in, a sharp pain shoots through my back. Somewhere far off, I can hear Ian and Kendra screaming my name, but it's drowned out by the throbbing of blood in my ears, the wails shaking out of my own mouth, and the slobbering horde beneath me.

It's not so bad, I tell myself as my fingers begin to slide down the rock, *being eaten alive by zombies. At least your parents will know you did something exciting on your trip. And hey, maybe Dad and Ian's father will finally bond over this tragedy. And when they find your body, Kyra will hear that you had her book with you, and will know that even during his gory murder, her brother never forgot his promise to read her a bedtime story. Besides, this is a dramatic death, the way they would do it in a movie. No hospital beds, no car accidents, just good ol' devoured by a wave of hungry ghouls. Maybe Mom will start a cinematography scholarship named after you. Could be worse.*

My fingers slide down the smooth wet rock face until I'm holding on by the very tips. A cold, steely hand closes around my ankle and lazily pulls me downward.

TOK TOK TOK TOK.

The cold hand releases my leg just as another snatches me by the back of the neck and yanks me to the ground. All around me, the zombies lie on their backs or fall to their knees, writhing in agony, their hands clapped on their ears, their eyes whirling in rage.

My savior stands next to me, rigid and tall, wrapped from head to foot in tattered rags, two polished sticks gripped in his hands like clubs. His face is covered, but his eyes are visible through the shadows of his hood, and in them, I see color, light, movement—enough to tell me that my new friend has a pulse.

The female zombie in the spandex lunges for the newcomer with a cry, but the skinny figure holds the sticks over his head and whacks them together. *TOK TOK TOK*, the spandex zombie is on the ground, desperately clawing at her ears.

Note to self: Get myself a couple of those.

"Oh my God, thank you!" I cry out to my savior. "Thank you so much—"

The newcomer shoves me forward, pointing with one of his sticks to a narrow hole in the ground near the base of the cliff, barely bigger than an animal burrow.

"I don't understand," I shout. "What's in there?"

"*You are,*" growls a voice from beneath the rags, and his hands seize me, lift me off my feet, and stuff me into the pitch-black burrow, sending me tumbling into darkness.

The tunnel is large, tall enough for me to stand up in, though I have to hunch a little to keep thick tree roots from smacking me in the head as I hurry along behind my guide. He holdsall, smoky lantern at the end of one of his polished clubs, its tiny candle providing only a flicker of light for me to follow blindly, overwhelming darkness pulling at us from every direction.

He darts through the shadows and I stumble behind him for ages, my feet colliding with insects, roots, even the bones of small animals. My elbows bang against the walls, and my knees scrape on rocks every time I fall down.

"Please help me!" I call out in the echoing blackness, and my guide grabs me by the arm and yanks me forward. It's hard to tell direction down here, but sometimes I think we're heading up, climbing our way through the mountain in tiny underground steps.

Finally, a circle of light appears faintly in the distance, then grows larger and larger, until we push through a wall of underbrush and out into the open, fresh air, cool and beautiful against my face and in my dusty lungs. We stand before a stone cave, black and ominous, in the center of a rocky clearing, trees bordering the gray rock floor on all sides. A small bonfire flickers in the center of the clearing. Without a word, the figure flings me to the ground, and I climb to my feet shakily, doing my best not to put pressure on my ankle or puke again.

When I stand up and observe my surroundings, the night sky overwhelms me. We must be near the peak of the mountain, because the view from the clearing is breathtaking, stretching out for miles around us. The woods rise and fall between gaping crevasses and swooping valleys, all of it lit creepily by twinkling stars and a bone-white moon. For a few seconds, all I can do is take in the expansiveness of the mountain, blue with moonlight, other peaks off in the distance topped off by the occasional low-hanging cloud.

Wait a second.

Mountain peak, stone cave. The diary that Kendra found had a map of all this.

Which means my new friend isn't a he—

"Now," says the gravelly voice behind me, "if you don't mind . . ."

She stands over me, cracking her bony knuckles. The ragged hood around her head is pulled away, revealing a slim, wrinkled face outlined by a rat's nest of tangled hair. With the light of the fire behind her, all I can see is a shadowed silhouette, but her eyes, hard and shiny, stare out cruelly from the darkness that surrounds her, pulling the breath right out of my lungs. She raises her lantern near them, throwing twisted shadows on her withered face and sending twinkling firelight off of the blacks of her eyes.

". . . you can explain to me what you're doing on my mountain."

My lips try to form words, but her eyes shake me, make me feel dizzy and sick, and before I can answer, everything swirls into blackness, and my legs go out from under me.

CHAPTER THIRTEEN

Ian

"Quiet," whispers Kendra. "They're leaving."

Behind me, moaning and footsteps fade away into the forest. For the longest time, I can't look, since a picture of PJ's strained face sliding into a crowd of zombies sits in my stomach like a cold, hard rock. Thirty seconds ago, Kendra had to hold me down to keep me from going over the edge and down to him, and as soon as the noises fade away, and despite the curdling going on in my guts, I turn around, peek my head over the edge, and survey the damage.

One last zombie, a hiker with long gray hair who looks like he's made of beef jerky, stands at the bottom of the cliff and raises his eyeless head in the air, like he smells something not right. For a moment, I figure we're toast, and my fingers hurt from gripping the stone beneath us, but then he turns away from us and crunches out of sight.

Kendra and I breathe a little sigh of relief as the last of the silhouettes and moans disappear in the distance, but we wait another five minutes before even thinking about getting up. That last attack taught us something: these things may be slow and dumb, but they don't give up easily. If we run around making noise and one of them even glimpses us, we'll be surrounded in no time.

And they'll do . . . whatever they did to PJ. Whatever made that weird knocking noise.

PJ. Oh, PJ, man, what do I tell your family?

While I'm feeling wiped and depressed, Kendra's all nervous energy. "First things first," she says, running her hands through her puffball hair nervously. "We ought to secure a perimeter. Make sure for certain that we're alone out here. Right?" I shrug. "Fine. Then, let's go see if PJ's still there, and we'll . . . deal with that. Got it?" That one I can't even shrug about. After a while, she continues, "Then we need to eat, rest, reconsider our options, and in the morning, we can figure out how to get off this mountain. Right? Does that sound good?"

"Whatever."

"No, not whatever, Ian. That's the plan. Please let me know you understand."

"Whatever."

She grabs my shoulder and gets up in my face. I look away from her, but she moves her head to keep her eyes focused on mine. "Ian, this isn't— We need to—" She stops midsentence, lets her hands fall at her sides. Watching it hit her makes everything worse, and my eyes burn so hard I have to rub at them, which just makes me feel totally lame for crying in front of a girl.

My mind can't get past it, though. When I get home— I mean, *if* I get home—I'll have to explain to the Wilsons that I let their son, my friend, die. I couldn't help him when he needed me most. After the tears stop and I can keep my eyes open for more than a millisecond, Kendra's sitting next to me, her hands in her lap, staring straight ahead.

"I'm very sorry, Ian," she says. "Truly, I am. This must be really hard for you. I . . . cannot even imagine."

"I should've gone down there," I say through a sob. "I could've done something."

"No, you couldn't have," she says.

"Yes, I could've!" I sob. "I could've fought them off, or pulled him up, or—" I can't even finish, I'm crying so hard. Just the thought of how he must have felt, the fear that must have gone through him as he slid down among those moaning monsters, gets me going all over again, shivering and bawling and totally losing my grip.

Kendra slides over next to me and puts an arm around my shoulder. She doesn't say anything, but every time I sob, she squeezes a little harder. Maybe it should feel lame, being babied by Queen Brain, but it doesn't;, it's just nice to have someone here.

"Look. Ian," she says, patting my shoulder awkwardly, like she read about how to comfort someone in a book once. "PJ was hurt. He slipped, and the vine broke. You did everything you could to save him. It's not your fault. You did what you had to do." She runs out of one-liners and finally says, "I could've gone after him, too."

"He wasn't your friend."

"Yes, he was," she says softly. "Maybe I only knew him for a little while, but . . ." She sniffs, then wipes her glasses on her shirt. "Nevertheless. If we don't come up with a plan, he will have died for nothing. For his sake, we need to get off this mountain and tell everyone what happened here. Can we agree on that? Let's honor PJ by making the best use of the time we have."

I nod, finally. Sitting here feeling sorry for myself only gives the living dead a greater chance at rediscovering our position. Maybe that wouldn't be such a bad thing, though. Maybe I deserve it. Here's Kendra trying to put together a strategy, and here's Ian Buckley, crying like a baby. One wolf, and me, what, not even a poodle, a cockroach, pond scum, dirt.

No. Can't think like that; have to keep going. PJ would have wanted me to.

I wipe my nose, shake her arm off my shoulder, and climb to my feet. "Okay."

"If you like, I can take care of PJ," says Kendra. "You can check out the perimeter."

"No," I say quickly. "I'll handle PJ. You do the rounds."

"You don't have to do that, Ian."

"I want to."

I really don't *want to*, but I *ought to*, if only so no one else has to see what happened to him. Some things you have to take care of yourself.

Kendra picks up a big, jagged rock—"Just in case," she whispers, swinging it down in a smashy-smashy motion—and heads off into the woods. Slowly, I turn around and shimmy my way down each of the big rock outcroppings that make up the cliff ledge we just climbed, all cold and clammy beneath me. Each step downward makes my stomach knot up a little more— that's the vine that snapped and sent PJ falling to his death, that's a quarter that fell out of my pocket while I hung by my feet and failed to pull my friend to safety. The closer I get to the bottom, the less my body wants to move, knowing what it'll see, or worse, not knowing it. What if the sight is more twisted than I could ever imagine? My poor, brave friend.

My feet finally press into the slippery forest floor, crunching twigs and leaves underfoot, and I turn to see . . . nothing.

Wait, what?

I mean, there's a hat at my feet, one of those big square-edged hats with the fuzzy earmuff things on the side, meant for a hiker or hunter. I knock it over with my foot and see dirt and black crud smeared on the inside—definitely belonged to a zombie. But I scan the area, and other than the hat, the place is totally clear. No blood, no guts, no skeleton with PJ's head. Just a hat, some rustled leaves, a bunch of slimy zombie footprints. Even PJ's backpack is missing.

And they didn't take him, I know that much. The zombies wandered off into the woods like they usually do, no screaming PJ under their arms or PJ nuggets running down their chins. I heard him scream and figured that was it, but come on, Buckley, you know PJ, he screams like a girl when he stubs a toe. Getting eaten by zombies, he would've been going off like a car alarm.

So where is he? His ankle was twisted pretty bad, so there's no way he ran out of here. I look into the trees— did he scale a tree?—but there's no sight of him. What about the zombies—why'd they wander off? Did he just disappear? PJ, man, *where are you*?

My foot knocks something out of the leaves, something that clatters against the ground. PJ's little flip video camera that he got for Christmas.

I pick it up and press the Play button. The screen glows white for a moment, and then there's a green flash, heavy breathing, and a shaky landscape, something coming into focus—the buck, *my* buck, all twelve points of him, me crouching in front of him.

"Look at that," says PJ's voice, buzzing out of the tiny speaker. "Got him on camera." There's a flash, and then it's us in the woods, first me and then Kendra, telling PJ off for being a pain in the neck.

"Tempers wear thin, viewers. What happens next, only time can tell—" Then I come flying at him, and it's all static. Another flicker, and there's PJ whispering, Kendra crying out, and there's a zombie, Deborah, the one I dropped the tree on, stumbling toward the cabin, then looking right out of the camera and into my eyes, and letting out this vicious snarl that gives me a feeling like huge fat worms burrowing through my whole body. On the camera, I yell his name—"PJ!" One last flicker of white, and then all black.

My poor friend. His last piece of footage. All that's left.

"Thank you so much!"

Wait. Something's up. The camera is on, but the screen stays black. Muffled, I hear PJ's voice, then that noise, the *whack-whack-whack* noise, sounding out. There are screams, grunts, shuffles, another set of noises, and suddenly the screen comes back alive, tumbling to the ground, and there's PJ's body being dragged by the nape of his neck by a hooded figure. The stranger yanks him offscreen, toward the cliff.

"I . . . don't understand, what's in there?"

"*You are.*" Then, PJ's screams seem to fade and echo off into nowhere.

My head feels like it's going to explode. I can't get the pieces to fit—PJ got saved by someone and put, what, in between the rocks of the ledge? I run over to the flat rock wall, pushing and scraping against the cold rocks, sweating my face off as I try to find a door or a secret passage or a—

Cold air blows against my ankle from the wall. I look down to see a gaping black hole where the wall meets the ground.

A tunnel.

On my hands and knees, I peer in, and the cool air blowing in my face is like the hand of an angel. PJ must have survived.

"Ian?" Above me, Kendra shimmies down the last rock ledge and drops to the ground. I barely notice her due to the epic rush of relief washing over me right now. "Are you okay? Did you . . . find him?"

"He's not here!" I shove the camera into her face,

laughing and crying at once. "He made it out! You need to see this!"

Kendra watches the video with those wide bookworm eyes. As the camera beeps off, she looks up at me, and I point her to the tunnel. She kneels down and pushes her face to the narrow entrance, and when she feels the cold air on her face, she leaps to her feet and grabs me by the shoulders, laughing and screaming, "He made it! He made it!" over and over.

Then she yanks me in and hugs me really hard, which I'm not sure how I feel about, but I'm so happy PJ's not dead that I hug her back and don't care.

Once we've had our little celebration, we both kneel down by the entrance of the tunnel and check it out. We can't see anything in the total darkness, so I reach my arm in up to the shoulder and don't feel a thing.

"That and the draft suggest it goes on for a while," says Kendra.

"We could go in," I suggest, that spark of adventure doing its best to jump-start my muscles. "We could feel our way around."

"If we had a light, I might chance it," she says, "but there could be endless tunnels down there, each of them going on for miles."

"True," I tell her. "Starving to death in the dark seems worse than getting attacked by zombies."

"At least we can run from zom—*attackers*," she says,

correcting herself. "We don't even know who saved PJ. Maybe they've set booby traps down there."

"All right," I say, "the tunnel's out. What do we do next?"

She blinks, and then heaves a breath. "We sleep."

"What! Forget that—let's *go!*"

"Hold on. I know what you're thinking—"

"Someone has PJ, Kendra!" I yell, or try to yell, but my body is running on fumes and excitement at this point. "It could be that witch the diary mentioned, or a bunch of cannibal rednecks, or some kind of . . . of megazombie, that digs burrows and prefers takeout! How can you sleep at a time like this?"

"Ian, I'm so tired," she says. "And you are too, by the looks of it. We've barely eaten, and barely slept. Think about it: if that person risked their life to save PJ, they probably aren't doing it just for fun. PJ will most likely be alive in the morning, and until then, we need to rest up."

"I almost let him die, Kendra."

"If you don't get any sleep, he's as good as dead," she says in a voice that makes me believe her. "We'll collapse up on that mountain. We'll get hurt, or worse, we'll run back into . . . them." She stretches out her arms in front of her and moans halfheartedly.

As she talks, I feel the last eighteen hours weighing on me. My hands hang at the ends of my arms like anchors. My eyelids feel like steel shutters. This is how the zombies must feel all the time—limp, used up, in need of one desperate thing.

"But where?" I ask her. "What if the zombies come back?"

She blinks, and looks up as though a lightbulb appears over her head. "We can set up some noise-making devices," she says. "One of my internet contacts described it to me. Basic traps that make enough sound to wake you up if they're jostled. They keep intruding animals from getting too close to you. We'll even put one over the tunnel entrance, in case our mystery guest returns."

It's a flimsy idea, but I'm way too exhausted to complain. We go to work collecting dry leaves, strong sticks, and heavy rocks. Kendra creates a neatly stacked pile of rocks at the base of the stone wall, then uses the stick to prop up a single heavy stone. Somehow, it works, and the stone stays up. "If someone knocks the stick to the side, the rock falls," she says. "The sound of the pile below it being crushed should wake us. And if we pile dry leaves, they'll crunch loudly if anyone steps on them. Maybe put some twigs beneath them."

"Okay," I tell her, my stomach growling. On to the good stuff. "Are there any granola bars left?"

"There are two . . . but." Her face goes superserious. "But we need more than that. And I have an idea. But you've got to have an open mind about this, okay?"

"Do I even want to know?"

"Well," she says, "I've been gathering specimens from our journey so far in a couple of jars. And I have peanuts and coffee beans from the stone wall. Those will provide us a little protein. But . . . look, the easiest way to get protein is by eating meat."

"You want us to go hunting?"

"Not exactly . . . another great way to get protein is eating insects. Lots of tribes in the rain forest eat bugs. And . . . I do have those termites from the dead tree."

"You want us to eat termites."

"I don't *want* us to do anything," she snaps. "But we don't have many options."

Find a pile of human bones in the basement. Get chased by dead people. Almost lose your best friend to zombies; instead lose him to some tunnel-digging forest creature. And now, for a bedtime snack . . .

Why not?

Kendra pulls the jar out of her pocket. At the bottom is a thin layer of peanuts and coffee beans, and all over them are termites, so white they're almost see-through, crawling over each other. Just the thought of their little bodies in my mouth makes me want to puke my guts out, but I can't because my guts are completely empty. I'm starving, and beggars can't be choosers, so . . .

"All right," I hear myself say, "let's eat."

She unscrews the lid and holds it upside down. Three

big, fat, pale termites cling to it, shaking, like they know what's coming.

"You first," she says.

"Why me first?"

"Because . . . because you're a boy," she says. "Maybe this is sexist, but you've probably eaten bugs before."

It's like she knows about that worm when I was five. I was just *curious*.

"Okay," I say, and pinch one of the white antlike bodies between my fingers, its head and legs wriggling, and you know what, this isn't the *worst* thing in the world; this is what wolves do, they *survive*, and moments like this are what separate the wolves from the poodles, so it's time for Ian Buckley to man up and face the—

Crunch.

Oh God, it's *awful*. Every leg moves the *entire time* it's in my mouth. There's this flash of a sweet jelly flavor, almost pineapple-y, and then it's layers of bug shell stuck in my teeth and twitching legs on the back of my tongue.

"Well?"

"Delicious," I choke out. "Your turn."

She takes her termite and pops it fearlessly into her mouth, then grimaces at me. "It's *horrible*," she gurgles. "You *lied* to me!"

"Gotcha," I say, and then reach for another termite.

CHAPTER FOURTEEN

Kendra

We are going to see a movie, PJ and Ian and I, in a theater in the side of a forest-covered mountain. We hold hands as we hike to the theater, as though we've always been good friends. Coach Leider, resplendent in a camouflage tuxedo, takes our tickets, and we buy popcorn and soda from a wrinkled old woman whose hair covers her face. There's only one other person in the theater, a thin man in a black suit with his back to us. I cannot see his face. Once we're seated, the screen flutters to life, displaying a twelve-point buck, then Ian and me getting angry; and it soon becomes clear to me that we are watching the video from PJ's handheld camera.

But when I turn to PJ to ask him how he's projecting his footage onto the big screen, his eyes are gone, his face is gray, and when I say his name, he snarls at me with a mouth full of termites and reaches out for me with cold, stiff hands—

My body reels, my fingers dig into the dirt beneath me. Someone screams. I decide it must be me.

There's light. It's cool out. Everything is wet.

Wait, stop. Take a deep breath, Kendra. You just had a bad dream. Count to ten, and exhale. Now look around.

Morning. Sunlight, gray from the overcast sky, illuminates the scene. I lie next to Ian at the base of a big oak tree with a low-hanging bottom branch that covers us like a canopy, the soft, dangling leaves splitting the light into a million white dots at my feet. Around us are poorly constructed noise-making traps, dried leaves stacked precariously for maximum crunch, rocks suspended over piles of smaller rocks. They look foolish in the harsh light of day, though they seemed expertly constructed last night. In fact, the whole forest appears benign without shadow and moonlight draped over it. The tree branches covering us shudder lightly with a mountain breeze, feathery wings that last night seemed like grasping claws. The air hangs with a refreshing mistiness that would've seemed clammy and creepy a few hours ago.

My foot rattles something—my specimen jars.

My belly gurgles. Blecch.

If last night's dinner doesn't earn me some kind of research cred, then I am at a loss. Ian and I are probably two of the few people this side of the Congo who know how bad an aftertaste termites have. Still, I feel better with the nutrition they gave me. Going to bed on a full stomach, no matter how scarce and repellent the food was, did us some good. As I rub my eyes and stretch, I feel renewed.

Ian mumbles something in his sleep and rolls over. When he's not conscious, he's almost cute—pet cute, not boy cute. There is nowhere for all that arm and leg to go, and so he bunches it up into his chest. Of course, I have to ruin everything by waking him up.

"Ian?" His eyes crack, blink, and then he leaps up to his feet, his back to the tree, gasping for air. "Relax, *calm down*, Ian, it's Kendra. We're okay."

"Sorry," he pants. "Long night."

"The longest of my life."

He lowers himself back to the ground and rubs the sleep from his eyes. I pass him the remaining water—the rest of my purification tablets must have fallen out when we ran from the lynx—and he chugs it gratefully. He stretches and groans, mumbling about how tree roots make lousy pillows. We share a granola bar, the sugar and carbohydrates energizing us further. Then I open Deborah

Palmer's diary to the map page and outline a plan.

"I still think we have to find this central path," I tell him, tracing the thick black line with my finger. "We'll have to climb this rockface again, but I think that's doable."

"But where are we heading?" asks Ian. "And what about the zombies?"

"The . . . creatures will have to be avoided, or dealt with however possible," I say. "As for finding PJ, I think it's pretty clear from the diary and the map that this old mountain woman or someone related to her took him. We've got to reach her hideout."

Ian nods, but then he frowns and rubs his forehead. "No, hold up. That person in the video didn't look like an old woman. I've never heard about witches living in underground tunnels."

"Maybe this woman has some kind of henchman," I say. "In folklore, witches use dwarfs and hunchbacks as familiars—"

"What else does the diary say?" he says. "Can I see it?"

"You wouldn't understand it. It's in another language—even I can't read it."

"Let me take a look at it."

Don't do it, Kendra. Ian Buckley comes across as the boy who handles library books and peanut butter sandwiches at the same time. This is a boy who once tried to put the class hamster in his mouth to "see what would hap-pen." Maybe a compromise will placate him. "Why don't I take it out, and we'll look at it together?"

He laughs and shakes his head. "I'm not six years old," he says. "I'll be really careful."

Against my strongest gut feelings, I take the diary from my backpack and hold it toward Ian. He snatches our precious clue out of my hand and flips through it errantly, leafing through the final pages until he reaches the section with the drawings and the strange writing, at which point his eyes grow wide. "Whoa. This is . . . different."

"Exactly. I don't recognize it as any alphabet I've ever seen."

"Yeah, me neither." He stares into the pages intensely. "Huh."

Once again, Kendra, it's up to you. Go over the facts: Corpselike creatures attacked you in a cabin. A book found in said cabin contains a first-person account of supernatural forces and an evil woman of some kind. The book then changes into a series of strange drawings seemingly designed by a different hand. Last night, a stranger saved your friend from certain death, which argues against said stranger being an old woman, so maybe there's another variable, maybe this is one of the Pine City Dancers who survived and learned to fend for him- or herself out in the wild.

"This one letter that looks like a backward *R* comes up a lot," says Ian.

Think, Kendra. You want to do field research, fine, but eating termites is only half the job. What are you not seeing here?

"And this one that's like a backward *E*."

Come on, Kendra.

"And this one that's like a backward *S*."

. . . oh.

Kendra, you fool. Today, Ian Buckley beat you at a mind game. You should be ashamed of yourself.

"Hey!" says Ian when I take the book away from him, study the last pages, and yes, see the pattern.

"Do you have a mirror?"

Ian looks dumbfounded. "Why would I have a mirror?"

"I need a reflective surface."

"Uh . . ." Something in his mind finally snaps into place, and he points at the book with a childish smile. "Oh, cool, I get it now! Uh, *uh*, water! Water's reflective, right?" He runs off into the woods for about a hundred yards, stops, raises his nose into the air, and then darts in a different direction, calling for me to follow.

"You can't actually smell the water, can you?" I yell.

"What, you can't smell it?" he yells back.

Ian finally stops and points. At the base of the rock wall sits small pool, a puddle bordering on becoming a pond, being fed by some kind of tiny rivulet burbling out from underneath the stones.

I open the book and lean carefully over the water, my fingers tight on the pages so as not to drop it and seal our fate. The scribbling on either side of the dream catcher drawing reflects back at me in perfectly good English:

Follow the marked path
Find the web of dreams
Reach the witch's lair
Burn the wicked totem
Destroy her evil power
Break down the walls
Set us free

"How about that?" says Ian. "You were right."

Actually, you *were right*, I refuse to say. "Deborah must have written this backward, just in case it fell into the wrong hands," I tell him.

"Makes sense," says Ian. "Mountain folk probably aren't big on secret codes."

"This proves, though, that if this witch took PJ, then we need to get him back soon, and that if we can, we need to free the Pine City Dancers from her power." I flip to the next page and study the map. "If this is the marked path, it should still be at the top of the wall. Ready to climb?"

"You sure about this?" he says. "You had trouble reading the last map. No offense."

The comment . . . stings, but I let it slide. "That map had hundreds of trails on it and we couldn't find any of them," I reason. "This has one."

"Good call," he says.

Climbing up the levels of the rock wall in front of us is harder without the motivation of a crowd of hungry attackers, but we make do—I give Ian a leg up on my shoulders, he helps pull me up; we repeat on the next rock level. In no time, we've reached the top, a cool breeze blowing through my hair. As I brush myself off, Ian turns and looks out onto the forest below us.

"At least we get a nice view from up h—" His arm snags mine and yanks me to the ground. "Get down. Now."

"Ow! Ian, that hurt!"

"Look," he says, pointing. "You can *see them*."

In the distance, there's a break in the canopy of trees, and in it sits the cabin, the lights still glowing inside, the generator humming faintly. And at its edges stand a smattering of figures lurching aimlessly around the porch, shoulders hunched, legs stiff.

"They're still hanging around the cabin," says Ian. "Some of them must be *that* slow, huh?"

"No," I tell him. "They were on us in full force last

night. They must have gone back there. It attracts them for some reason."

We watch the stiff silhouettes hobble around the clearing for a few minutes, and I think of how strange and wonderful a research opportunity this is. Shane, the boy from Queens from the forum at ravenousminds.org, would love this—he's into all that punk rock morbidity (mental note: make *morbidity* a vocab word).

Memories of last night come flying back to me. Fascinating or not, those things were trying to kill us. "Let's forge ahead," I tell Ian. He nods, and we leave.

By day, the hike is easier. The sun is barely there through the blanket of low-level stratus clouds, but being able to see anything is much better than last night's near-complete lack of visibility. The closer we get to the path, the more the mountain sinks beneath the forest, the ground turning into jagged rocks fuzzy with moss and dangerously loose layers of fallen brown pine needles. Quiet rows of gray-brown trees stretch off endlessly around us, but as we climb farther, the grappling gray branches and fresh spring leaves of the deciduous trees are replaced with sturdy evergreens that don't creak or sway but loom like columns in some massive maze.

All is silent except for our footsteps. No birds squawk; no insects chatter. At first, the lack of noise is nice and lets me consider our rescue plans, but soon it becomes maddening. No sounds, no signs of life—it's just us and, somewhere off where we can't see, *them*. The thought makes my teeth chatter and my skin prickle.

Ian always finds his way, though, brushing past sticker bushes and clambering over slippery stones. He's probably *ideating* (there's four) some kind of action-movie story for himself, and I suppose with a kidnapped friend and a horde of ravenous creatures stalking us, it's not too far from the truth. His face is streaked with dirt, and his sneakers are coated in a scummy film of muck, but none of it fazes him.

The never-ending silence of the woods wears on my nerves. My eyes settle on Ian, and I think of my dad— *Make some friends! Have an adventure!*

Well, Kendra, you've been given Ian Buckley. No greater adventure than becoming friends with him.

Think. You two must have something in common.

"I can't wait to get home," I say.

"I. Hear. *That*," moans Ian, rubbing his eyes. "I was all psyched for this trip, but after this, I doubt I'll ever go camping again. I keep thinking about the first thing I'm going to do when I get home."

"And that is?"

"*Cheeseburger*," he says, his hands gripping a phantom burger before his eyes. "Cheddar, lettuce, tomato, loads of ketchup. Undecided on bacon. It's not going to know what hit it. You?"

I close my eyes and let my mind wander to my ultimate fantasy at the moment: "Hot shower" is what comes out. "For maybe an hour. Maybe more. Then my laptop. But shower first."

"Good answer," he says. "I think real food beats a shower for me. Gotta get the taste of termites out of my mouth."

I consider offering him the remaining granola bar, but something off in the woods catches my eye, a blotch of red in the expanse of green and gray, and when I close in on it, my mind immediately leaps back to the past week's studying.

"Here," I say, grasping a red segmented droplet and tossing it to Ian. "These are wild red raspberries. They're still not ripe yet, but they're flavorful. They should do the trick." I pop one in my mouth and it's sweet, juicy, if a little bitter. Its tartness is a jump start, waking me up a little bit more.

"Oh man, these are amazing," he says through a mouthful of berry. "Did you remember those jars with the termites in 'em?"

We empty the remaining termites out of one jar—we now have plenty of food without resorting to entomophagy (*it could never be a vocab word, Kendra; when else would you use it?*)—and fill it with raspberries.

"How do you know all this camping stuff?" he asks me as we hike and snack.

"I took out a book on Montana wildlife last week," I say. "I wanted to be prepared for this trip."

"Huh!" he says, a perplexed look crossing his face. "I didn't even *think* to do that. I sort of figured I'd get here and . . . get into it. Learn it firsthand."

"That's sort of your MO, isn't it?" He looks up at me quizzically. "Modus operandi. Your . . . main way of . . . doing things."

"Yeah, I guess." He laughs. "Leap before you look. Guess that's kind of *inauspicious* of me, right?"

"That's not what *inauspicious* means," I tell him.

"Didn't you call me that earlier?"

"I called you *puerile*," I say. "That means childish. *Inauspicious* means menacing or unlucky. You were puerile. The cabin was inauspicious." Without warning, I blurt out, "I assign myself vocabulary words on a weekly basis. My goal is to use each one five times a week."

WOW, Kendra. You have never told anyone that before. What on earth made you say it now, here, to Ian Buckley of all people?

Ian nods as though he understands. "Cool."

Still, my cheeks burn with mortification. "What do you expect—I'm a 'pathetic nerd,' right?"

"What do you—*oh.*" He looks away from me. "When I . . . That was just a stupid thing I said. I never meant for that to be a big deal."

How do you respond to that, Kendra? "Well . . . surprise! It was!" I say, sort of laughing.

"Right, but did you really have to bash me with a textbook?" he gripes. "That seems harsh. It hurt a lot."

"You called me a *pathetic nerd*, Ian," I say. "Has anyone ever called you *pathetic* before? It hurts, too."

He gets this look on his face—now he's hurt and confused, like the very idea of the word is painful. "You're right," he says. "I guess that must feel pretty awful. I'm sorry."

We're silent again, and part of me is glad, glad that maybe Ian Buckley has learned something today, but another part of me is sad for losing the conversation, guilty for going after him at a time like this. I almost had my second friend in two days.

Change topics, Kendra. Get back to the problems at hand.

"I've been thinking," I say. "According to PJ, there seem to be two different ideas about the creatures attacking us, if they are what he *believes* they are. Either they're magic creatures, servants for some kind of witch doctor, or science creatures, dead bodies reanimated by a virus, ambient radiation, or some other form of scientific anomaly."

"That's one of your vocabulary words, huh? Anomaly."

Keep it simple, Kendra. "Last month, yes. It means

something that's not as it should be. Something wrong or weird."

"Gotcha."

"Now, if these creatures are science creatures"—there is still no way I am saying that idiotic z-word—"then there has to be a scientific cause for this condition. Maybe someone's been using this mountain as a toxic waste dump, or there's a special moss that grows here. That means that whoever saved PJ is definitely on our side and most likely doesn't want to hurt him. If they're magical creatures, it implies that the person who rescued him is their master and needs PJ for some reason."

"Like?"

This idea still doesn't sit right with me, because *magic isn't real*. "Unsure. But if he or she saved PJ from his or her own henchmen, I can only assume it wasn't with PJ's best intentions at heart."

Ian gulps and nods. "Let's hope they're not magic zombies," he says. "Look. I think this might be the path up ahead. . . ."

The woods stop suddenly, and we stand in the middle of a wide pounded-dirt road trailing off both up and down the mountain. Unlike the woods that seem to have no end, the mountain is perfectly framed in this vista, from its peak to its foothills. We've gained ground, apparently, as the hillside sits far down below us. And there, at the bottom of the mountain, is a gray winding line, almost invisible beneath the trees—a paved road.

If we followed this trail down, we might be able to escape, find a car, get back to Homeroom Earth, leave this place behind.

"Kendra?" Ian stands behind me, pointing up to the peak, where a line of smoke dances into the sky. "We're heading that way. See? There's a fire."

The downhill climb would be so much easier, and it would mean our safety. For all we know, PJ is already doomed. Berries or no, I am so tired, so hungry.

"Maybe—"

"No." Ian's voice is scary. His face is alive with outrage. "I know what you're thinking. I know this sucks. But you couldn't do that." He narrows his eyes. "Could you?"

"Ian . . . maybe if we got the authorities, there's a better chance of finding him."

"How many hours will that take?" he snaps. "In that time, PJ could be dead! You're not worried about saving him; you just want to go home!"

He's caught you red-handed, Kendra. Try to outthink him. "It's only logical—"

"Don't *do* that!" he screams. His voice echoes off the mountains, and a bone-chilling moan rings out in response. He doesn't notice. "Maybe I didn't read a book about these mountains, and maybe sports is cooler to me than studying, but I'm no idiot! I know what you're doing! What happened to PJ being your friend, too? When'd it become okay to abandon someone, just because it *makes sense*?"

My mouth opens, but my arguments all fall apart when they reach my tongue. Finally, I come up with "I'm just . . . so tired, Ian."

"Wow," he says, his voice quivering. "Never mind, guess I was wrong about you. Go home, get some sleep." He turns and begins stomping uphill toward the mountain peak.

My eyes fly from one direction to the other—paved road, mountain peak, back again. It'd be so easy. There'd be a shower, my mom, my phone, my laptop, my life—

And he'd be right about you, Kendra. You'd be that kind of friend.

"Ian, wait!" I yell, jogging after Ian. He stops and looks at me over his shoulder, visibly trying not to smile.

CHAPTER FIFTEEN

PJ

As my eyes crack open, I think, *It's cold in here. Mom should turn up the heat.* Then a dull moan rings in my ears, and you bet I'm awake.

When I'm done scrambling against a wall and hugging my knees to my chest, I realize that I'm alone—the moaning isn't a zombie moan but something softer and more natural. Everything's dark, but light streams in from somewhere, casting everything in dim gray. To my back is cold stone, and somewhere I hear the sound of dripping water. A cave. I'm in a cave.

As my eyes adjust to the dim light, the outlines of shapes around me come into focus—wicker furniture, stacks of linens, framed pictures leaning against the walls. Beneath me, a musty mattress covers the stone floor. Someone's using this cave as a home, or at least a storage locker. A breeze ruffles my hair, and the moaning increases.

It's the wind, just the wind. No need to cough up your heart.

The smell of smoke and food drifts into the cave, and my stomach growls. Barely thinking about it, I climb to my feet and stumble toward the day.

Outside, it's cold and crisp, just damp enough to be biting but not so much to make me shiver. The rocky clearing is bordered on all sides by walls of dark pines, and across from the mouth of the cave, I can see the whole mountain range, an ocean of green hills folding into each other. From here, the other mountains look so close, great peaks reaching into the air, some furry with trees, other stony peaks showing like rocky bald spots. The sky's mottled gray clouds look painfully close to the tops of the mountains, but the two never quite meet.

The pop of a bonfire draws my eye back down to the clearing, and the old woman. She sits on a wooden stool before a small fire, hunched over Kyra's picture book with a look of intense concern on her skinny face. Her body is wiry, a scarecrow dressed in a filthy jean jacket, fatigues, army boots. Her hair flies in gray tangles down the back of her head. Her skin is a deep earthy brown, and her hands look hard, like they're made of wood.

She scares me, not like the zombies but like the lynx—like she's a wild creature ready to snap me up at any moment. When the diary said there was an old woman on the mountain, I imagined a fat old crone with a boiling cauldron and a wart on her nose. This woman looks more like a coal miner.

My breath catches in my lungs, and my hand goes flying into my pocket, but it's empty. My camera must have fallen out while I was being saved from the zombies. There's nothing separating me from this horrible woman—

Her eyes meet mine, and she gives me a yellow-toothed smile. She motions to a stool across the fire from her, on which sits a plate of eggs, bacon, and toast. Like in a cartoon, the smell snakes over and drags me by the collar, puts the fork and plate in my hand, sits me down on the stool, and—

Now wait a second. I should know better than this. This is a witch, a woman who cursed a dozen poor modern dancers to their doom a year ago. This is Scary Movies for Beginners stuff. You never want to take anything that's offered you—poisoned apples, monkey's paws, puzzle boxes. When people do this in the movies, you laugh at them for being so dumb.

"What is this?" I ask.

"Breakfast," she says. Her voice is like stone and leather. "Eat it."

"What's in it?"

"Breakfast, mostly," she says. "Eat it."

"Did one of your zombies make this?"

She snorts. "That's cute, *my* zombies. Eat it or don't."

With those options, what else can I do? Everything's delicious, but I barely taste it. A long night of near-death experiences works up an appetite. The old woman watches me the whole time, her eyes following my every bite.

"Thank you," I say, licking bacon grease from my fingers.

She grunts, then holds up Kyra's book and taps the cover. "What's his deal?"

"Who?"

"Him. The guy."

". . . Burly Bunny?"

"Right."

"You want to know about Burly Bunny?"

Her eyes narrow. "I asked, didn't I?"

"He's a bunny. . . . He ate a radioactive carrot that makes him superstrong, but he's clumsy and he breaks things because he doesn't know his own strength. It's a book for five-year-olds."

"Gotcha," she mumbles. "Felt like I missed some backstory."

Okay. . . . "It's my little sister's book."

"Kyra?"

Her name is like an electric shock. "What?"

"You kept saying that in your sleep," says the woman. "Kyra. She your sister?"

"Yeah. I was supposed to read her a bedtime story yesterday, before we got lost."

She hangs on me with those pale hazel eyes and says, "Just the three of you, huh?"

If this is anything like the movies, I'm either okay or about to die. "Yes."

She nods. "Good. I was worried you might've been a big group that got split up." Then her face turns angry; all her wrinkles come out at once. "You didn't think to stop at the wall? The girl even picked up some of the peanuts, for crying out loud."

"How long have you been watching us?"

"Long enough."

It all makes sense now. All the missteps and confusion we went through weren't accidental; they were planned. "You did all this to us, didn't you? You . . . you tricked us somehow. You led us here, to be eaten by your zombie minions!"

She shakes her head. "There you go again, *my zombies*. I've got no love for those walking piles of meat. And a zombie's got no love for anything but pain and death."

"But you're a witch, aren't you?"

"Not quite." She leans forward, squinting at me.

"Where's all this coming from? Seems like you have an awful lot of ideas about me."

"We . . . we found a diary," I tell her. "In the cabin. In the basement."

She spits and shakes her head. "That's not a good thing. Whose diary was it?"

"This girl, Deborah Palmer . . . she came after us later, as a zombie. And we . . . killed her."

In seconds, she's on her feet, over the bonfire, grabbing my collar with one of those industrial-strength hands. "You killed one?!" she shouts. "How? Which one? What'd you do to it? You sure it was dead? *Speak*, boy."

"A girl—broken leg, furry jacket! Deborah! She had her ID hanging around her neck! We dropped a dead tree on her! It crushed her!"

"Hrm." The old woman drops me, and I go falling on my butt and scooting away from her. "I guess crushing them works. I gotta remember that. Anything that destroys them completely, smashes the spinal cord. But if the tree's not heavy enough . . ." She looks over at me. "It takes some backbone, killing a zombie. I'm impressed." She holds out a bony hand. "O'Dea Foree, at your service."

"PJ Wilson," I say, shaking it.

"Your name's PJ?" she says, then shrugs. "Takes all kinds, I guess. How's your ankle?"

Whoa—I barely noticed it when I woke up. "It's . . . still a little stiff."

"Let me see." She leans over and wraps a hard hand around my ankle, and suddenly there's a buzzing coldness that comes out of her grip, reaches deep into the joint, and vibrates the pain away. She begins mumbling a steady line of hushed gibberish under her breath, then stops suddenly, lets go of my ankle, and sits back down. "Now try it."

There's no stiffness, no ache. It even feels stronger than before. My lips quiver so hard, I can barely speak. "What was that?"

"Amateur's magic," she said. "I put a salve on it last night, and it seems to have worked—"

"Okay, wait." I scoot my stool back away from her and hold up my hands. My ankle's still buzzing, my head is swimming, and my stomach's churning. It's all too much. "I'm sorry, what's going on here? There are walking dead people, and you say they're not yours, but you *are* a witch, and . . . please. I just need an explanation."

She's quiet for a moment, then looks away from me. "It's the land," she says. "Believe it or not, you and your friends wandered onto one of the worst places on earth."

"Oh, trust me," I say, "I believe it."

"There are bad spots in the world, see," she says. "They get rotten, like a bruise on an apple. That's what happened here. Way I heard it, there was a settlement on this very mountain, mostly escaped slaves, some Crow Indians. They thought that the altitude would keep away the law—no cop wanted to climb this high. They didn't really have neighbors, so who would rat them out? But one night, a runaway slave making his way here got caught and had the truth tortured out of him. The next day, a council member from one of the nearby towns— odd fellow, not quite right in the head—rounded up a couple of slave trackers and went for a hike."

"And he caught the slaves?"

She chuckles darkly. "Nice try. No, he ordered the trackers to destroy the settlement. And they did. Burned it to the ground and killed every man, woman, and child who lived here."

The words make the hairs on my arms stand on end. "That's horrible."

"Yes it is," she murmurs. "And when something that horrible happens somewhere, it seeps into the earth, affects the karma of the place. You know what karma is, right?"

"It's like luck?"

"Sort of. It's like the soul of a place, the energy running through all living things. That's why I'm here. I'm a Warden, see. You know what that is, right?"

"Someone who protects wildlife?"

"Again, sort of. We're a different kind of Warden. We keep the dark forces from getting out into the world at large. I was basically born to be Warden here. My blood's a good mix for magic—Appalachian mountain folk, Crow Indian, and just a bit of Haitian slave. I have some voodoo priestess, some medicine woman, and yeah, some good ol' American witch."

"What do you do, brew potions in cauldrons? Commit animal sacrifices?"

"Nah, that's all Shakespeare," she says. "It's sigils, mostly. Don't know that word, do you?" Her hand darts into the bonfire's ashes, and then she finger-paints a black design on the gray stone, a cross marked with circles like the one we found in the basement of the cabin. "They're symbols with power to them. Spreading food's good, too—the darkness is always hungry. Rum and nuts for the voodoo gods. And of course we have totems, which are the real important things. They're objects we create that control the flow of energy to keep things balanced. Indians around here used totem poles, but I've always preferred dream catchers myself."

My mind flashes back to the drawing of the dream catcher in Deborah's diary, but I keep my mouth shut—I still don't know if this woman can be trusted. "Is that why you live in a cave?" I ask. "To be close to the earth?"

"What? No," she says. "I live in a cave because a bunch of college kids forced me out of my house at gunpoint."

"What?"

"Oh yeah," she said. "Last year, bunch of kids in spandex and leg warmers. They showed up, saw all my Warden's gear, and flipped out. Pulled a gun on me. Said *I* was the reason they were lost, just like you did. *I* made the weather go bad, made the forest swallow them up. They chased me out of my house. When I came back the next day, they were gone . . . though not for long."

From somewhere off in the trees a sorrowful moan echoes up the mountain. My blood turns frosty, and I climb to my feet, but O'Dea holds up a hand.

"Far off," she says. "They'll never come around here. That's why I put that bone totem in the cabin's basement—it's a beacon. Draws them like flies, keeps 'em away from up here. As long as no one messes with my magic, we're fine."

Something in her voice makes me believe her. I sit back down, and after a moment, she continues.

"You ever hear stories about whole towns just disappearing? It's always a Warden issue, a Warden passing away suddenly or being chased out of town by people who don't know any better. Next thing you know, everyone feels like they're being followed or watched. Everyone gets roaring mad at each other. If they're lucky, they escape the cursed land, usually with a Warden's help. If they're not, they die. And then they come back."

"Zombies."

"You got it," she says. "When evil forces find a vessel, they use it. It's not pretty or smart, but it doesn't feel pain, just cold hate and hunger; and while coffee and peanuts and rum feed the earth, the walking dead only hunger for one thing—fresh meat. They'll eat anything and anyone they catch. There's nothing human about 'em except for their bodies, and those are far from saving. A few days later, I was still cleaning up the mess in my cabin when I heard that moan in the forest, and I knew they were lost. I grabbed what furniture I could and hauled it up here, piece by piece, and then got to work."

"Whose skull was that in the basement?" I ask her with a shudder.

"Bird-watcher, crushed by a falling branch," she says. "The woods got him, and he came back the next day. He wandered off a cliff chasing a rabbit two days later, and it killed him again. Wardens aren't allowed to kill zombies ourselves, see—interference isn't allowed. I figured that poor sap's bones would be powerful enough to create a beacon. That's why they came after you when you kids entered the cabin. You basically flicked the light, and the moths came running to see what was up."

"Are you sure it's a curse? Couldn't this just be a disease, or some kind of . . . mutation?"

O'Dea shrugs. "No one knows. There was a Warden in Russia who tried to find a cure—she thought it was a *fungus*, if you can believe that. There's always a Warden who thinks that science is the answer. March of progress! Yeah, well, there's *something* marching out there. Besides, virus, curse, science, magic—it still means the dead walk the earth. Only two things are certain—one, they're real hard to kill, and two, you're a goner if they get you. One bite, one scratch, and after a few hours, the breath just gets pulled right out of your chest. A few minutes after that, you stand back up and go after the nearest thing with flesh on its bones."

A wide-angle shot flies through my mind—Ian, toothmarks on his arm, on the ground, his eyes closed. Kendra's holding him, crying. And then Ian's eyes crack open, and he begins to sit up, and Kendra screams—

"My friends are still out there," I tell her, urgency flaring up in me. All this information has been so fascinating, I haven't been thinking about my friends. "We need to find them before the zombies do."

The old woman nods, then stands up and marches into her cave. When she returns, she has two sticks in her hand, short thick pieces of wood carved with strange symbols. "You like them? Carved them myself. They saved your life. Watch."

She raises the sticks over her head and hits them together three times—*TOK TOK TOK*—and from the woods around us comes rustling, hissing, snorting, crackling, and from far off another low, sad moan.

"Totem sticks. Best magic weapons around, flameless and bloodless. Lots of big predators are scared of the noise. To the living dead, it's like a boot to the brain."

A smile creeps over my face—this is just too cool. "Can you make me a pair?"

"Won't do you much good," she says. "No offense. It's a Warden thing. *You* whack these things together, it'll be loud, but it won't have any power. What I can do is use these to keep you safe and get you to the path. It's a hiker's trail with some sigils protecting it, goes all the way down the mountain."

"Well, let's get going!"

"Wait," she says. She lets out a sharp whistle from between her teeth, and a sparrow darts out of the forest and flutters into her cupped hands. The sight sends prickles down my arm, like something from a surreal version of *Snow White*, but she treats it like it's no big deal. She brings it to her ear and listens intently.

"Sounds like your friends might not need our help," she says, tossing the bird into the wind. "They just found the path themselves. They're on their way."

CHAPTER SIXTEEN

Ian

We've walked for hours, but the path goes on and on, getting spookier with every step. The trees on either side of us are carved with symbols a lot like the stuff we saw on the stone wall and down in the basement, and it's freaking me out, man. They aren't cool climbing trees any longer, just big solid poles that block us in on either side. There hasn't been a bird or squirrel for miles, not even a grasshopper, just the trees, the path, Kendra, and me. At points, the path gets so narrow that the branches create a canopy over us, and I feel like a kid in a fairy tale wandering down some dark scary tunnel. There are wolves here—not wolves the way Coach Leider thinks of them, but big bad wolves, wolves with rotting flesh and eyes full of wriggling worms.

But the map was right—we can see all the way up the mountain, and the smoke cloud up at the very top gets closer with every step. So, yeah, my legs are killing me, my eyes feel like raisins, and I'd let a zombie bite me if he gave me a cheeseburger—I've decided I'm pro-bacon—but we're getting there.

For all we know, PJ's up there watching some horrible old hag light a fire under the pot he's bathing in.

Kendra's rattling off endless wilderness survival tactics, like if she impresses me with her knowledge of nature, I'll forget that she almost left PJ to die. So far, I haven't forgotten.

"Want to know how to find north?" she says excitedly.

"Whatever," I say.

"Hold on," she says, and breaks a twig off one of the trees, sticks it in the ground, and marks its shadow. "We have to wait about fifteen minutes for the shadow to move."

"We don't have time for that," I tell her. Sure, it's cool, but I'm still ticked at her. You trust someone for one second, figure they're going to do the right thing, and then they poodle out on you. Not acceptable.

Every couple of minutes, when my foot hits a hard

rock or my calves start burning, I wonder why this is happening. In all of PJ's favorite movies—why, oh why, didn't I take PJ up on all those invitations to come over and watch a movie?—gross and scary things happen to people who deserve it: drunk teenagers making out in their car or stupid rednecks driving around looking for trouble. So why us three? I'm a good person, right? Maybe I'm a lousy friend, I'll own up to that, but I'm just an average kid who wanted to play basketball and get a picture of a big deer.

And what does the universe reward me with? Flesh-eating zombies. That's what.

Okay, maybe I'm getting a little nuts, but it's not my fault. To try to get me back on her side, Kendra won't stop talking about owls. For forty-five minutes straight, just . . . owls.

". . . because in certain African and Native American societies, owls are considered harbingers of dark magic," says Kendra, to me, I guess, "which makes sense in a weird way. We Westerners think the big eyes in the small head means wisdom, but it *does* sort of look like a skull. Maybe these cultures think wise people cause death and destruction. *There's* an idea! But in a lot of traditional folklore, they're *funerary* birds, which means they carry souls from the land of the living to the land of the dead. That's different from being harbingers of death and destruction."

Do crazy people know they're crazy while they're talking crazy?

"Hmm, but maybe . . . This is interesting: owls are *nocturnal* animals, which means they only come out at night—"

"I actually know what *nocturnal* means."

"Maybe the reason these cultures consider owls evil beings, or not evil, *funerary*, is because they come out at night, and in those cultures night holds a lot more danger than it does in Western culture, what with our long traditions of electric bulbs and gas lamps. That's a fascinating idea, isn't it?" She looks back at me with this totally stoked *Eureka!* expression, and then it drops like a sack of bricks. "I'm boring you."

"It's cool."

"I'm sorry," she says. "I just figured, the berries, the termites . . . so far, my knowledge has really kept us alive!"

"Not sure every little fact about owls is going to help us."

She nods, still looking downtrodden. "You're right, I shouldn't . . . talk much." Maybe she is a betrayer, but I feel lousy shutting down her rambling. "Most of my friends are internet friends, so I . . ."

"Never get to *actually* talk to anyone."

"Yes." She stares up the mountain, her eyes following the faint indent of the path through the trees. "Let's talk about something else."

"Sure," I say, "let's talk about how we're going to save PJ."

She clasps her hands in front of her and twists them like a mad scientist. "Good point. First, we need to get past this mountain woman and her creatures."

"*Her* creatures?" I ask. "So you believe they're magic."

She sucks on her lower lip. "I believe that two things happened to PJ here in the woods—attacked by creatures and captured by someone—so they're most likely connected. It doesn't *have* to be magic. But we know they're stupid creatures, and easily distractable, so I figured that's what we need to do, act as bait. That way one of us can sneak around and find PJ." She gulps. "So what I was thinking was, you provide a distraction while I attempt to get PJ away from the old woman and investigate our surroundings. Maybe I can find a clue as to how to get us home."

Whoa whoa whoa, this plan sounds a little uneven on the danger spectrum. "Why do I have to play bait for the zombies?"

"Because . . . you're faster," she says. "Remember that game against Monroeville, when you spun around that tall kid with the terrible acne and snatched the ball right out from in front of him?"

Wow, Queen Brain goes to my games? Of course I remember that one; the kid fouled me three seconds later and wasn't called on it, and Coach nearly got thrown out for flipping out at the ref. Great game. Ugh, now Kendra's got dirt on me. Can't go soft on her, though. "Yeah. So?"

"So I can't do that," she says. "I have bad knees. There's this disease, Osgood-Schlatter's, that makes your knees weak and can cause serious—"

"I *know* what that is. I play basketball."

"Right, well, I can't pivot well or jump on one foot, things like that. And we need that kind of agility when it comes to avoiding these creatures."

Something tells me I'm getting played here—*oh, Ian, you're so fast and strong, do me a favor and get in harm's way*—but the last thing we need is someone taking a sharp turn, popping their knee, and lying there wincing while the dead close in around them. It just sucks that Queen Brain's smart enough to know how to get me to go along with whatever she says, even though *I'm* smart enough to know what she's doing, which makes me wonder if she's smart enough to know that I know, but whatever, now I have a headache and there are only so many hours in the day before we get eaten. Take one for the team. It's what a good wolf does, I guess.

"Fine," I say, "but this had better not end with me getting my brains eaten."

"Trust me, this will work."

We must both be attuned to the same weird *uh-oh*

frequency, because the crack of a stick suddenly makes me tense and cold. Kendra grabs my arm with a kung-fu grip. We dart into the trees on one side of the path. For a second, I hold back, like if we leave the path it might disappear forever, but I know something's wrong—we both do—and in the past twenty-four hours I've learned to trust my instincts. We find a large cedar and duck behind it. Any other time, I'd feel a little weird about how hard our shoulders are pressing together, but it's all fear right now, man, no time for anything else.

"I don't see anything," she whispers.

I peek around my side of the tree. Same old path, same old trees on the other side. "Yeah. Maybe it was just a deer or something."

"Probably," she whispers. "We are somewhat high-strung, after all, so— Oh, no, wait." She grimaces. "There they are."

Another peek and I see them, stumbling between the trees on the other side of the path. Their faces hang in the shadows of the woods, grayish ovals with sad, drooping mouths and shining white eyes. It's hard to tell how many of them there are, because for every face peering directly out of the trees, it looks like there are two or three behind them, staring blankly at us—

"IAN!" screams Kendra, and I look up to see a bearded zombie in torn pants come shuffling right freakin' toward us, his gray arms scraping at the air and his mouth open in a dusty growl. We yelp and jump out from behind our cedar, scrambling back into the path. From the other side of the woods, we hear the zombies begin moaning and snarling and snapping their yellow teeth. I look for the nearest rock, stick, anything that we could use to fight them off. The path is all pounded down, though, and scratch as I may, there's just no way to dig out anything usable—

Kendra grabs my shoulder and shakes it. "Ian," she pants, "what's going on?"

The zombie coming after us in the woods stands at the edge where the forest meets the path, moaning and crying as he claws his hands out at us. Behind him, more are coming at the usual slow-mo pace, but the few that have caught up with him also stop at the edge of the path. On the other side of the woods, they're doing the same thing, crying out in hunger, snatching out their rotten hands in the hopes of grabbing us, but never crossing the threshold of the woods, never setting foot on the flat pounded dirt.

"I think . . . they can't come onto the path," I tell her, getting back on my feet. I take a couple steps forward, right up to the bearded zombie; I can see every wrinkle in his dried gray skin, every fly crawling along his cracked lips. The stench I won't even go into. But for all his moaning, hissing, and grasping at me, he can't leave the woods.

"It's gotta be these," I tell her, pointing to the symbols carved into the tree trunks along the path. "If they are magic zombies, like you said, these have to create some kind of force field or something." The eyeless zombie with the heavy camera around his neck appears between two pines and starts snapping at me with his rancid teeth, but his face never once crosses the line of trees. This close, I can see every inch of him, down to the yellow crusts in the corners of his eyes.

"Isn't that right, big guy? You and your buddies can't follow us onto the path, can you? Who's a trapped little zombie, huh?"

"Please don't patronize the monsters," says Kendra, but that smart-kid curiosity gets the best of her, and she wanders up next to me and peers at the zombies like they are zoo animals. "You're right. Look at this one. He's dying to eat us"—Kendra extends a shaky hand, and the camera zombie's jaws begin clicking faster and harder—"but he can't. Fascinating. These sigils are protective." She turns back toward me, motioning out into the trees. "Maybe we could copy some down and use them for—"

Her arm must break the barrier, because the camera zombie grabs it with his skeletal hand and pulls hard. Kendra shrieks, and I grab her by the waist and yank her back toward me. There's a pop and the zombie arm comes unattached. Once we're back on the path, it drops from her arm and falls to pieces with a little cloud of dust.

"You okay?" I ask her. As the spots in my eyes stop sparkling, I realize what I'm doing and take my arms from around her. "Sorry, just trying to help, didn't mean to grab you too hard—"

"It's okay," she breathes. "Now we know what happens if they enter the path." She kicks the bone dust at her feet and smiles nervously at the zombie. "Bad creature," she says with a little laugh. Then her smile drops, and she bites her lip and shudders. "That was . . . really . . ."

"It's okay," I tell her, "I'm here." Then I remember that I'm angry at her, and I step back, brush myself off, and keep walking. "Just stay inside the path, okay? And try to keep up."

We walk and they follow, never tearing those big white eyes and deep black sockets away from us. At first, I figure it's no problem—yeah, their faces are disgusting and their moaning sends chills through parts of my bones I didn't know I had, but they stay outside of the path; everyone's happy until we reach the witch's cave and find PJ. Right?

Wrong.

Twenty minutes in, I think I'm going totally bananas. The whole time, they flank us, dead faces staring back at us from out of the woods. The smell travels with them like a great big stinky green cloud, and my nostrils burn, my stomach groans, and my brain feels too tight, like someone overtwisted a screw in it. Kendra tries to talk about owls again, but she's drowned out by the crunching footsteps and hungry moans coming from both sides of us. Every time I look up to admire the woods or talk to her, there are zombie eyes, coldly floating in the shadowy background, sizing me up for dinner.

The more we walk, the louder they moan, the more it annoys me, the worse it smells, the less I can take it, until finally, my foot hits a rock and I snap, and before I can stop myself, I grab it and chuck it with all my might, and it crunches into the forehead of a skinny walking corpse, who drops to his knees in a dusty pile.

"There!" I scream. "You like that? Shut up and leave us alone!"

"Ian, stop," says Kendra, grabbing my shoulder, but I don't listen, I *can't* listen, it's like I'm entirely beyond calming down.

I start grabbing anything I can find at my feet, pebbles, pinecones, bits of grass, and hurling them at the line of gray empty faces, but nothing works. The pebbles bounce off, the dirt flies in their eyes and mouths, and they don't so much as flinch. The one with the rock in his head is back on his feet, moaning even louder, like the stone in his half-caved skull is making him hungrier. Kendra finally grabs my arm and shouts at me when I take off my shoe and cock it back. When I look at her, she stares at me with these wet, scared eyes, and I start breathing hard and fast, and the whole time, they keep moaning, biting, clawing at the air. There's no scaring them, hurting them, convincing them.

"At least now we know getting them in the head doesn't do anything," says Kendra, trying to help. "You've furthered our knowledge of how we can combat these—"

"We need to get out of here," I tell her. "If we don't, I might have a nervous breakdown."

She nods hard. "I know. Wait a second. . . ." She fishes the diary out of her backpack and flips to the map. Her finger lands on the third landmark up, a little cross with a tiny dream catcher drawn over it. "If we started out where the cabin is, we should be getting close to this place here. If it's protected by the same power that's keeping them from setting foot on the path, it might be a good place to hide out for a bit and see if they leave."

"They always find us," I tell her, trying not to sound as crazy as I feel. "How do we escape them?"

She glares at the horde in the woods, hate in her eyes. "They're slow," she says, "and stupid. If we jog, we should be able to outrun them. Do you have the energy?"

Not really, but whatever it takes to get us away from the moaning. I start running without giving her a response, and Kendra follows close behind. The zombies baby step after us, but we're kids and they're corpses, so they eat our dust, which feels amazing.

Our exit is hard to miss, even from a hundred yards away—there are all these trees carved with symbols that look like someone went crazy midway through drawing a math problem, and then bam, two of them are painted all over with white circles. Between the two is a narrow trail that cuts through the forest. Kendra puts her hand to one of the trees and peels it back with a sticky sound.

"Rum," she says.

Looking at the trail, I see that the grass is heavy with nuts and coffee beans. No matter what's at the end of this trail, it's been guarded from any zombie attack.

We walk down the narrow path, trail mix crunching beneath our feet, trees brushing our shoulders on either side. Branches lean in around us, and we have to stay crouched and sure-footed to not catch our clothes on them. It's a creepy little hiking trail, and I'm still pretty on edge after my little PJ moment back there, but there's no sign of the zombie horde, which is enough to turn down the pressure on my exhausted brain at least a few notches.

"There's something up ahead," says Kendra.

The trail ends at a wide clearing, the grass underfoot brown and superdead, the trees on all sides leafless and scary, their bark peeling and their branches jagged and clawlike, leaning in over us. All through the clearing are piles of rocks, perfectly stacked, each one painted white and surrounded by circles of white paint, radiating in rings on the grass. Something about the place, the rock piles, the awful trees, the white paint, it all gives off that weird feeling, like what I felt in the cabin last night or in the woods before that when I was freaking out at Kendra. Something in the air bothers me like crazy, like bugs crawling over my body.

"Where are we?" I mumble.

"It's a graveyard," whispers Kendra, running her hands through her hair and shivering. "An Indian burial ground. These piles of stones are grave markers."

"Great," I say, "more dead people."

My eyes follow the lines of white paint leading off each grave as they all come together in the center of the clearing at one extra-large rock pile, on top of which sits something new but familiar.

"Look," I tell Kendra. Quickly, I tiptoe between the grave markers, doing my best not to step on any of the white lines connecting them, until I'm next to the little stone platform. On top of it sits a circle of wood, strung in its middle with strings, feathers, beads, bones—the dream catcher, the one from the diary.

"Check it out," I tell her, "we found it!"

"Found what?" she asks.

I grab the dream catcher in my hand and lift it up

for her to see. "Remember, from the diary—" But no way, man, I can't even finish my sentence, something's up. My hand buzzes and my whole body tingles, like the dream catcher is electrified.

"Ian, put that down!" shouts Kendra. "We don't know what it does!" I try to respond, but I can't, because just as the dream catcher stops Tasering my hand, the ground starts rumbling beneath my feet.

CHAPTER SEVENTEEN

Kendra

If I'm going to admit the existence of magic, some parameters need to be established. First, if magic *does* exist, it's *probably* just some kind of energy current that we don't have a name for. It's science we haven't gotten to yet. Next, magic, like any system, must have rules that govern it. No ordered system exists without some boundaries, and magic can be no different. Finally, if magic does exist, then we must be able to affect it in some way.

Just because I'm beginning to maybe, *somewhat* believe that we're in a supernatural situation here does not mean I believe in fate or destiny or space aliens building the pyramids or any of that nonsense. I have facts here, cold hard facts. Walking corpses that don't die. Secret messages about dark forces traveling the woods we're currently trapped in. An Indian burial ground with a dream catcher in it, a dream catcher that appears in a piece of text written by a dead, or re-dead, zom—

See, for example, that is still an unacceptable word in my mind. But I have facts. So fine, we're dealing with magic. It's believable, in this situation. During certain adventures, being rational only hinders progress, so one must accept the unexplainable.

Now, if I'm right and we can affect the system of magic around us, the question is whether or not we should. For example, if there is a magical totem sitting on a platform that appears to have been *specifically built* to seat it, perhaps we shouldn't errantly pick it up. Sadly, Ian Buckley is not one for scientific consideration, so he waves the dream catcher over his head like a trophy, and almost immediately the forest floor beneath us starts shaking.

One after another, the neatly stacked grave markers tumble to the ground. The dirt underneath them seems to swell and billow outward, and then the earth itself grows limbs, skinny black arms with wiry claws at the ends of them. Then the hands grab onto the grass and pull, and the ground shakes harder as larger shapes haul themselves out of the black earth beneath the grave sites.

To call these Indian dead "corpses" wouldn't be quite right—without eyes, faces, muscles, or clothes, they're no more than rot-covered skeletons, grayish bones held together by putrid filth, tattered shrouds, and writhing masses of night crawlers. But somehow, without any bodies to speak of, they pull themselves out of the ground, cough up blackened clouds of dust, and climb unsteadily to their feet, letting loose a wave of unspeakable stench that burns my nostrils.

At first, they simply rise, standing on two legs but otherwise lifeless. But one of them turns its skull toward me, and though it can't see, hear, or smell me, it knows I'm there. The others, seven in total, raise their hands for me and begin stumbling slowly forward. My mouth goes dry, my hands twitch at my side, and my legs freeze up, unable to move as the skeletons close in. . . .

"Kendra!" Ian calls out to me from across the graveyard. He whips the dream catcher like a Frisbee, and it spins through the air over the rotten skeleton heads. Somehow, through my distress, I manage to catch it. The skeletons all hiss at it, their bony hands becoming gnarled claws, but Ian is working his arm, throwing fallen grave stones like they were baseballs and doing pretty well at it. The Indian dead are even less balanced and coordinated than the zombies, and every rock to the face sends them sprawling backward and falling to the ground.

Once they're all struggling to regain their footing, Ian sprints across the burial ground.

"Time to go," he shouts, grabbing my arm as he darts past me, and without a word I let him drag me, moving as fast as my legs can carry me down the narrow trail back toward the path.

We burst back onto the pounded dirt road, gasping for breath, happy to be out of the cemetery and back on the path to PJ. But then I see something that yanks a shriek out of my mouth. With our removal of the totem, the rules appear to have changed. Drastically.

The path is no longer safe, but instead is full of creatures making their way slowly up the hill. For a moment, they stare at us dumbly, as though they're surprised we still exist, and then they begin a new round of wild moaning and outstretched hands, closing in. Behind us, we hear crunching footsteps along the trail.

Corpses in front. Skeletons bringing up the rear.

My mind feels like a classroom after the last bell, swiftly empty. My heart feels like it's being dropped down a long, dark hole.

The creature with the bushy mustache comes closing in on us, and before I can think of swatting his outstretched hand, I hold up the dream catcher in front of me, brandishing it like a shield in my shaking hands.

The dream catcher seems to tingle in my grip as though momentarily charged, and the zombie recoils, hands clawing at the air in front of the dream catcher but never touching it, backing away, *afraid* of the totem.

"Whoa," says Ian. "They don't like that."

"Like a cross for vampires," I say.

"I thought vampires weren't real," he mumbles.

"Shut up," I tell him.

I inch forward; the walking corpse backs farther away. The brawny man with the half face stumbles up beside me, but I whirl at him with the dream catcher, and *yes*, he cries out and pulls back as though it were red-hot.

"Come on," I say, and slowly, Ian and I inch our way up the path, away from the oncoming horde.

They crowd in on all sides, the circle of string, wood, and bone the only thing standing between us and certain death. Ian huddles next to me yelling out directions—"Three o'clock! Eleven o'clock! Right behind us!"—and I pivot, forcing the dream catcher in the face of any shuffling cadaver that gets too close for comfort, my terror turning into excitement with every frightened moan.

Through the web of strings, I can see every pockmark and blue collapsed vein in their dead faces, every shudder of their jaws and clench of their brows. A chill rushes down my spine at the whole ordeal. In their faces isn't simply disgusting decay or pure malevolence; it's a lack of life, the absence of a spark behind those eyes. Of everything about these monsters, that shakes me the most—there is literally not a single thought in those heads, no rationale, no humanity whatsoever, just instinct, rage, and hunger.

Right then and there, I promise myself to destroy this witch's power and set these pitiful creatures free from this prison. She'll pay for what she did to these poor people.

Finally, we break through the mass of decaying bodies and retake the high ground, the entire shambling horde a few yards behind us at all times. The Indian skeletons have lurched onto the path and joined the corpses; for a moment, I hope that some sort of combat will ensue, with corpses and skeletons taking care of each other, but the restless Native American dead pay no attention to the Pine City Dancers and vice versa. Instead they blend into a walking mass of death, their eyes focused on the dream catcher now rather than us. This must be the totem that Deborah mentioned in her diary, the web we must break to set these creatures free.

"Let's get moving," I say, and at once we turn and sprint up the path, leaving the lumbering horde to follow us at their slow and steady pace. Under my arm, the dream catcher feels heavy, still humming with whatever unnatural power it contains.

The peak grows in the distance, then vanishes beneath the horizon, meaning we're probably close. Around us, the looming trees begin to thin out, and the murky overcast sky reappears, now over huge swaths of tall grass and claustrophobic swarms of sticker bushes. A cold breeze ruffles my hair, and on it is the smell of smoke. We can't be far now.

The witch's cave sneaks up on us, so we don't know we've arrived until we stumble out into the open clearing around it and have to scramble back into the forest. Ian and I crouch behind a fallen tree and carefully peek out at our aggressor, sitting before a tiny fire with her head raised, as though she's smelling the air. She's skinny and sharp instead of withered or *corpulent* (a good word from two weeks ago), and she's wearing pants and a jacket instead of a tattered dress and pointed hat, but her slapdash frizzy haircut and the way she prods the fire with a stick suggest to me that she's the witch we're looking for. Plus, she's the only living person we've seen since we got lost, so it only makes sense. Facts, people.

"Where's PJ?" says Ian, clenching his hands over and over, frantic to get moving. "What if she doesn't have him? What if she killed him and ate him? What if she's already turned him into one of those things out there—"

"He's probably in the cave," I whisper.

Perhaps Ian's right, perhaps we're too late, but admitting that will only send him running at this woman, bellowing at the top of his lungs, and every time Ian does something without thinking, it results in tragedy. Rational thought is essential here. "Here's what I'm thinking—you run into the woods and start making noise, rustling bushes. Try a fake animal call or two. While she's distracted looking for you, I'll run in and get PJ. Once he's safe, I'm going to threaten her so she'll help us get home."

"Threaten her? What're you going to do, beat her up?"

I hold up the dream catcher. "Something tells me she'll give us everything we want and more if I threaten to destroy this." Ian gulps and stares into the woods, obviously worried. "What's wrong?"

"What if the noises I'm making attract the zombies?" he says, motioning back toward the woods and the creatures on our tail.

"You'll have to outrun them. If things get too hairy, climb a tree, and I'll meet you there with the dream catcher to chase them away. That work?"

Ian nods and then kneels down and starts retying his sneakers. Once he's ready, he softly says, "Look, if something happens and I don't . . . make it out of this, just tell my mom that I spent my last moments trying to look after PJ, like she told me to, okay?"

"You'll be fine," I say. "Should I tell your dad anything?"

He snorts. "That I was running?" Then he hops to his feet, stretches a little, and trots off into the woods. The wait is painstaking, even if it's probably only a few minutes. Then, across the clearing, a large shrub rustles back and forth. It's time.

The witch leaps to her feet and yanks two heavy brown clubs, somewhere between bats and drumsticks, from the back of her jeans. She approaches the sound crouched, sticks raised over her head. Another bush rustles a few feet away, and something chirps. The witch whips around, sticks poised. Her eyes dart back and forth, confused but ready.

A few more feet away, something moos.

Really, Ian? Of all the sounds . . .

The witch turns toward the mooing but lowers her sticks—she can tell something is up. She keeps her head down and her shoulders hunched, ready for the attack.

Wait for it, Kendra. . . . A few more steps away, and she'll be too far to—

A chorus of moans floats out of the woods, and Ian yells, "Whoa!"

The sticks go up again, and she rings out the sound from earlier—*TOK TOK TOK*. The moaning turns to shrieks of pain.

Now. She's distracted. One chance. Save the day.

In three quick leaps, I reach the bonfire, hold the dream catcher over my head, and shout, "FREEZE!"

The witch woman spins around, mouth curled into a snarl, brandishing her sticks at me with her wiry arms. Closer, I can see sigils carved into the sticks, like the ones we've seen all over the woods. There's no longer a doubt in my mind that this is our culprit.

"One false move," I tell her, "and I drop it into the fire."

Her eyes settle on the dream catcher, and her face loses a shade of color. Panic grips the air. "Trust me, girl," she says, "you don't want to do that."

"Where is my friend?"

"First, put it down."

"I want my friend," I say, hard and clear, "and we want safe passage off this mountain. Give me those or your precious totem burns."

"Don't go making threats at me, sweetie," snaps the witch, pointing at the dream catcher with one of her sticks. "What you got there is dangerous. Stupid enough that you took it from where it rested, but you have *no idea* how bad things'll get if you burn it. Put it down on the ground, and we can talk. I've been expecting you."

"I don't see my friend."

"I am trying to *save your life*—"

"HELP!" comes a shout from the woods. In the background, excited moaning and feral snarls grow louder and louder. "Kendra, they're here! A little backup would be nice!" shouts Ian's voice.

"Trying to save your buddy's life, too," she says, nodding over her shoulder. "Removing that totem, bringing those *things* to my home, all that I can handle. But if you burn that dream catcher—"

"Bring me my friend," I yell at her, "or so help me—"

"Kendra?"

PJ stands at the mouth of the cave, eyes bugging out of his skull. His gaze goes from the witch to the woods to me and back again, and his lips quiver in confusion.

"There he is," says the old woman, "safe and sound. Now give me what you got there, or else—"

Ian sprints into the clearing, his face sweaty and sheet white. "They're out there," he stutters. He points at a slimy handprint on his leg. "One of 'em almost had me. *Really* could've used that backup."

"Ian?" gasps PJ. "Wait, what do you mean, *they're* out there?"

As he says it, the creatures begin to appear around the edge of the clearing, moaning in excitement as they approach the witch.

"Oh my God, guys, what have you done?" shrieks PJ, backing toward the cave.

"Give it here, girl!" shouts the witch.

Ian's yelling, the witch is yelling, PJ's screaming, the horde around us is moaning, but through it all, my mind is clear. I can't trust this woman. She could destroy us. She could smash me in the face with one of those carved sticks, crush my skull, feed me to the ring of monsters around us.

My eyes dart to one of the creatures coming slowly toward me, his dry eyeless face contorted in pain and hunger. My mind flashes back to the zombies on the path, huddling away from the dream catcher, caught in a place worse than death.

SET US FREE, the diary said.

My hand opens, and the dream catcher falls into the fire, bursting into flames.

"NO!" shriek the witch and PJ at once.

No?

The creatures freeze in their steady march toward us. The moaning stops at once. For a second, all is silent, save the popping of the dream catcher as the fire turns it black.

Then, as one, the dead start screaming.

CHAPTER EIGHTEEN

PJ

Before I can explain that I don't need any saving, Kendra lets the dream catcher drop into the flames, and all hell breaks loose.

The circle of zombies around us begins screaming, thrashing their undead bodies around, clawing at their skulls. The sound is horrible, like ripping metal mixed with white noise and microphone feedback. My hands slap to my ears, trying to block out the racket.

The first one to pull itself together is a man, shriveled and long-haired, and something's definitely up. The blank look on his face is gone, and instead he wears a furious snarl of rage. He grunts at O'Dea and then does something none of us expect—he runs. It's not a sprint, but for how fast these things normally move, he's an Olympic gold medalist. The zombie barrels across the clearing, straight past the rest of us, and disappears off into the woods. One by one, the other zombies do the same, scrambling to their feet and booking it into the forest. The ones with bent and broken legs do sort of a power hobble, but even they are gone almost instantly.

O'Dea screams, "No!" and rushes one of the marching corpses with her totem sticks raised over her head like clubs, but the zombie dodges her attack and knocks her off her feet with a hard swing of his arm. The big guy with the half face is the last to go, and he even stops at the edge of the forest and growls at us over his shoulder before vanishing into the woods with a loud crunch of sticks and leaves.

The clearing goes quiet. O'Dea lies on the ground, a hand over her face. When I look at Kendra, she's shaking, staring at her hand where the dream catcher once rested.

"You okay?" I ask her.

"I think so." She blinks and puts the hand to her forehead. "Did it work?"

"Did what work?"

"I was trying to save you. From the witch."

"She's not a witch; she's a Warden. It's like a nature warden, only with magic." Kendra blinks at me, so I go

236

the *Wizard of Oz* route. "She's a good witch, not a bad witch."

"Oh. Good witch. But. But in the diary—"

"Turns out the Pine City Dancers were a bunch of jerks," I say. She gapes and blinks faster, clueless, so I pat her on the back and say, "I appreciate being saved, though. Real sweet of you. Technically, you did the right thing."

"Did I?" she asks. "I did. It was a logical assumption. There's no way I made things worse, right?" Here's where I don't say anything. "Right?"

"Man, did you see those zombies go?" says Ian. "That was *nuts*. They were just, like, whoosh, we're *outta here*. That's not normal, is it?"

O'Dea stands back up and mutters a string of curse words under her breath. She dashes from one part of the clearing to another, squinting at the ground and the trees, then cursing louder and moving on. It goes on for about five minutes before Ian says, "So this is the witch, right? What's her deal?"

"Guys, this is O'Dea. O'Dea, these are my friends Ian and Kendra. O'Dea's a Warden, which means she keeps cursed places like this mountain in check, because apparently, when people die here, it fills them up with bad karma and reanimates them as hungry zombies."

Ian says, "Oh," and scratches his head. "So . . . we're good?"

"I'm not sure about that," I tell him.

O'Dea crouches near a wet footprint at the edge of the clearing and then slowly rises to her feet. "Nothing," she says, her hands balling up into quivering fists.

"What's that, O'Dea?" I ask.

"NOTHING!" O'Dea whirls around and leaps at Kendra, shoving her panicked grimace right into Queen Brain's face. "Not even a fingernail, a scrap of flesh, a strand of hair! I'm back to square one! Do you have *any idea* how hard it was to get all the pieces of that seal? *Do you?* Months and months of following those walking pimples, plucking and dashing, inspecting footprints, nonstop painstaking work—*and you burned it up*!"

Kendra blinks for what seems like forever, and finally says, "Seal?"

"You think I built that thing for fun?" shrieks the witch, clenching her hands up by her face, like it's taking every ounce of her energy not to choke Kendra. "You ever tried to sew with zombie hair? You ever handle human fingernails day in, day out? That there's a *seal*, darling. The wall, the bones in my cabin, all those piles of rocks in the old cemetery, they were all *carefully laid*, and they had *that*"—she points at the fire—"holding 'em together. All those spells, those symbols, all the rum and peanuts in the world, aren't gonna do *squat* now, because you broke the seal! You set them free!"

My stomach sinks. They're free. They're off the

238

mountain. Of course they were running—they wanted to get away from us before we knew what was going on.

"But isn't that good?" asks Ian. "We set the zombies free. We saved them."

"Oh, and *what*?" snaps O'Dea. "They were gonna turn to dust or just crawl into their graves? Leave magic to the experts, buddy." O'Dea shakes her head and lets out a long, low-pitched growl; then her arms drop at her sides. "Number one priority of a Warden is containment," she says, her voice as quiet and hard as a rock. "Whatever the cursed place spits up, we keep it here. The land's already ruined and destroying the monsters is forbidden, so it only makes sense to just store them here. If they get free, though . . ." She points down to the valley below us, surrounded by the mountains. "The only reason that countryside isn't swarming with zombies is because of the totem she just threw in the fire. Now the spell's broken, and they're free to go anywhere."

"Oh no," I whisper, because I've seen the movies; I know what that means. "It'll spread, won't it? The people they get to first will come back, and the ones *they* get to, and . . ."

O'Dea nods and puts her hands on her hips. "Ah, geez. I'm in trouble."

The look on Kendra's face is breaking my heart—complete despair, and the knowledge that it's all her fault. "But . . . but we found the diary. It told us that by breaking the web—"

"Oh, I heard about your diary," snaps O'Dea, giving me a stink-eye. "Tell me something, that part about destroying the dream catcher, was it written backward?"

Kendra responds with a pained squeak.

"Yeah, figured that," says O'Dea. "You thought you were playing Nancy Drew, figurin' out a secret code that O'Dea can't understand, being some *mountain witch*. You know when people write backward? When they're *demonically possessed*. That wasn't a person telling you to destroy my seal; it was something else, something dark that you can't see but that lives in this woods, and it was communicating through a *dead girl*. And they left it in the cabin hoping someone would find it."

Kendra's head sinks slowly until she's looking at her feet. Tears stream down her cheeks.

"So okay, new plan!" shouts Ian, trying to salvage the day. "How do we stop them?"

"Stupid kids," laughs O'Dea. "You saw how hard they are to kill, boy. Hell, your buddy here had to drop a tree on one of them just to stop it."

Ian cocks an eyebrow at me. "Did he, now?"

"They don't die," says O'Dea. She lowers herself in front of the fire, face as gray and hopeless as the darkening sky. "Once they break free, it's over. The Crow Indians used to call them the *unstoppable demise*. Don't

240

believe the movies—hitting them in the head only makes 'em look nastier." O'Dea shakes her head again. "The Wardens' Council is gonna have my head for this. That isn't a colorful saying, either; they actually do that. Put it in a box, throw it in the river."

I'm speechless. Our all-wise mountain guide has backed out on us. Kendra Wright is a shattered mess, her arms wrapped around her chest. Ian is staring from one of us to the next expectantly, waiting for an answer that's not going to come. And here I am, wishing I was home.

And then I think of Kyra, my little sister. My little sister is somewhere beyond this mountain, and soon, the zombies will be, too. If the curse gets out into the world, it'll spread, and it won't be just our problem, it'll be *everyone's* problem, the whole country's, the world's. And suddenly, I imagine Kyra in her bedroom, hiding under the bed with tears in her eyes as the door swings open and rotting feet slowly move toward her, and she's wondering where I am to help her. That's all it takes to get my mind working.

"We've got to stop the zombies from reaching Home-room Earth," I tell O'Dea. "If we can't reconstruct the seal, then destroying them is the only option we have left. There's got to be something we haven't thought of. There won't just be dead trees for me to drop on zombies left and right."

"Really, dude?" asks Ian.

"What else has enough power to just completely destroy a zombie?"

Kendra mumbles something. When we ask her to speak up, she squeaks, "Moisture generally speeds up decomposition. We could attempt to . . . rot them to death, if you will."

"Gross, but okay. Are there any hot springs around here, O'Dea? Maybe a geyser we could lead them into one after another?"

O'Dea shakes her head. "It's a nice idea, kids, but it ain't gonna happen. It's dry up here, with the mountain air. That's why their bodies are so dusty and well preserved—not a lot of moisture at this altitude."

"We saw a couple of creeks—"

"You gonna hold their heads underwater?" She squawks a laugh. "You'd have to submerge 'em completely, and what if one of them got ahold of you?"

"Come on, O'Dea, give us a hand here!" I tell her. "There's no magic Warden protocol for this kind of thing?"

"Not since we got rid of the Gravediggers," she says.

"The what?" I ask.

"There used to be two classes—Wardens and Gravediggers," says O'Dea. "Gravediggers were the soldiers, the killers. The Wardens kept the evil contained, but if it got free, the Gravediggers were sent out to handle it. But the Wardens' Council got rid of them nearly sixty years ago. We haven't had a breach in ages, so we didn't need them. I even voted against them. I was so good at containment . . . never thought one of those stupid things was gonna *write a diary* that gave away all my secrets. Guess the dark forces always find a way to escape. We might as well just make some dinner and wait for the gunshots and the screams."

"Well, great," says Ian, flopping to the ground, "now what do we—"

A scream cuts through the air, and we all go scurrying around the clearing, trying to locate the source of the crackling wail, until O'Dea grabs hold of Ian's pocket. Ian digs around and pulls out, oh thank you God, my handheld camera, giving off a high-pitched scream in my voice.

"Sorry," says Ian, clicking it off and holding it out to me. "You dropped this in the woods. I must have sat on the button just now. Here."

"You should be careful with that," I tell him, taking my camera back. "If the zombies were still around . . . they . . ."

WAIT.

". . . they'd be drawn . . . to the sound . . ."

There's something about the feeling of the camera in my hand that focuses me, gets my brain lined up just right, and—

Wait a second, this . . . this could work. No. Wait. Yes. Yes, it's all coming together in my head, the zombies, the camera, my scream, the zombies, wait, I got it, yes yes YES!

"That's it!" I yell, shaking my camera at Ian. "Don't you see, *this* is how we're going to stop the zombies!" I crouch in front of O'Dea. "You said they're stupid? They have rotten eyesight? So they'll have a hard time distinguishing one person from another, right?" Slowly, the Warden nods. "And the only way to get rid of them is to completely tear them apart until there's nothing left. But we need something strong enough to do that, meaning we need something stupid enough to get near them."

She shrugs. "Yeah, so?"

"So let's fight fire with fire."

"We've set enough fires," mutters Kendra, still lost in her embarrassed head.

I explain my plan, and one by one my friends come in close and listen. Color comes back into Kendra's face, O'Dea begins nodding, and Ian cracks his neck and stretches his knees. My strategy is a long shot, but it's all we've got right now, and given the unspeakable horror that we've just unleashed, it will have to do.

CHAPTER NINETEEN

Ian

Who thought cowardly little PJ would come up with the idea that might save us all? One minute, he's trembling in front of this cave, like the big stone mouth is going to clamp down and chew him up, and the next he's huddling up with the old witch, or Warden, whatever that is, and he has the Plan, man, the sixty-million-dollar answer. It's really simple, and it sounds like it actually might work. When he finishes a basic outline, even Kendra signs off on it, though she still looks like someone let all of the air out of her.

What can I tell you? I figured burning the dream catcher was the right move too, but I guess we didn't know jack. So PJ's right, if we made this mess, we have to help clean it up.

He's also good with O'Dea, the magic zombie Warden, who I guess was the victim in the whole Pine City Dancers fiasco, which is hard to believe because man, she is one tough customer, quick and strong and more intimidating than Coach Leider on a bad day. While we prepare for PJ's plan, she rushes in and out of the woods carrying sticks, leaves, bones, berries, all the nonzombie ingredients to make a new dream catcher. She still keeps a mean eye on me and treats Kendra like dirt for releasing bloodthirsty zombies into the world, but she and PJ have a real vibe going on between the two of them. Again, how my little mousy friend was able to buddy up to the scary mountain witch is anybody's guess, but she won't listen to anyone else. She must be impressed by his tale of crushing the undead by pushing over trees.

For the record—I don't care how the rest of us remember it—I came up with the idea of dropping that tree on that zombie. I'm just letting him have it 'cause he almost died, okay? Least I can do.

The first job is to make a recording of our voices. We stand in a circle around PJ's little handheld camera, and when he presses the Record button, we get going.

"Hey! Hey, zombie!"

"Hey pal! Over here!"

"Over here, you ignorant savage!" ("Ignorant

savage? Come on, Kendra, tough it up!")

"Right here! Thaaat's it, see me? Huh?"

"Mm-*mmm*, tasty humans!"

"Come on, you . . . you smelly moron, eat me!" ("See, Kendra, you're getting it.")

"Eat me! Eat my face, ya jerk!"

"Choke on it!"

"Whatsamatter, you scared?"

"Right here, slowpoke!"

"We're serving human tonight, hot off the grill!"

When we play it back, it's a solid two minutes of cat-calling and attention getting, but Kendra says we need more. "Think about it timewise," she says. "You've got at least twenty, uh, dancers and hikers, and then at least six or seven of the rotten Indian skeletons, and let's say it takes each one thirty or forty seconds to be . . . dealt with. That's twenty-seven creatures, with thirty seconds apiece, which means we need at least ten minutes of sound."

This is why it's good to have a brainiac around. We do another round, this one for twelve minutes, which doesn't sound that long, but by the end we're hoarse and our insults sound bored.

Pretty soon, I'm getting antsy—this is all taking too much time. Those zombies were booking it pretty hard when they left, so they could be anywhere by now. O'Dea won't come with us—some Warden rules about not interfering with the natural order of blah blah blah, sounds like an excuse to me but whatever—though she describes the area the zombies should have reached about now ("If your calculations are correct," mumbles Kendra, which gets her a dirty look) and a nearby opening in the forest that will work for our plan.

"And if this all goes smoothly," says PJ, "you'll have enough material to make a new seal?"

"Oh yeah," chuckles the Warden darkly. "If this works, I'll have enough to make a new quilt."

"Gross," he says.

"You'll need a guide," O'Dea says. "Hold on."

She gives PJ a slap on the back, then puts her fingers in her mouth and whistles hard, and the bushes begin crunching and rustling, and out of nowhere comes the buck, *my* buck, standing huge and proud in the fading sunlight, chest thrown out, head reared back, just as gorgeous as when we first saw him.

"Whoa," says PJ.

O'Dea walks over to him like it was nothing, and the buck lowers its head down to hers. They talk (or whatever) for a moment, and then she pats his neck and turns back to us. "He says they're only about halfway down the mountain at this point," she says. "He's going to lead you to them while I take care of things here."

"Wait," I say, "halfway down's a pretty far hike—"

"You better keep up, then," she says. She slaps the

buck's spotted hindquarters, and he goes bounding into the woods, and we go barreling into the woods after him, and of course I'm in the lead, but I keep my eyes over my shoulder and wouldn't you know it, the other two are doing just fine, PJ especially, his eyes bright with action.

The buck is a flicker of white tail and brown hooves for a while, and somehow we manage to stay on its heels, dodging between trees and bounding over rocks and burrows, and even though their breathing gets heavy and their collars turn damp, PJ and Kendra keep pace perfectly. This is amazing, running after the buck, but with a purpose this time, a mission, not just some stupid what's-going-on-let's-see kind of plan like the one I had before.

Suddenly, we turn a corner of the path and a steadily marching group of bony dead backs appears in front of us. The buck skids to a halt, and we duck into the trees on the side of the path, doing our best to tread lightly and barely breathe. The zombies are power walking now, too stiff to really run but hobbling with a vengeance, probably desperate to get down to Homeroom Earth before we catch up with them.

I look at the buck again, his antlers lowered, his nostrils flared. He glares back at me with those black glassy eyes, then nods toward the zombies, like he's saying, *I did my job; time to do yours.*

"Thanks . . . ?" I whisper to him.

He snorts, then vanishes with a quick leap into the thick woods.

PJ waves us up ahead, and we stealth creep from behind one tree to the next until we're right alongside the horde, doing our best to keep pace with their new supercharged death march.

PJ hisses at us and holds up three fingers, and we count down: three, two, one. I go first: "HEY!"

Next is PJ. "HEY! OVER HERE!"

We glance out from behind our trees. Nothing. They don't even look up, just move forward like getting off the mountain is all they can think about.

This isn't part of the plan. We make noise, they come after us—that's how it's worked for the whole time. Without the magic barriers, they must know there's bigger game out there than three eleven-year-old kids.

"What do we do?" I ask, no longer bothering to whisper.

"I have an idea," says Kendra.

"Whenever you say that, everything goes wrong," I reply.

She shoots me a stink-eye and then digs Deborah's diary out of her pocket and flips through it for a second. "Let's try . . . BILL?"

The fat zombie from the basement stops in his tracks and slowly, reluctantly raises his milky gray eyes into the air.

"GRACE! LEONARD! CHELSEA! AARON!"
One by one, the zombies turn and look toward the woods, eyes frozen in recognition, faces slowly twisting into furious snarls. Hearing their names must remind them that they were people and now have to wander around as disgusting sacks of dead meat. Or maybe because they could use a snack. Doesn't matter; it works. The other zombies begin slowing down with them, bumping into their backs and following their stares to our section of woods.

Come on, zombies, don't just stand there. This needs to happen now. If you're as dumb as we think, the rest of you will follow. At least I hope you will.

Kendra leaps into view and goes nuts: "PINE CITY DANCERS! COME ON, YOU FAT HIPPOS, LET'S GET DANCING!"

Yikes, that does it. The Pine City Dancers turn their ugly gray faces away from hauling down the mountain and run snarling into the woods, and the rest of the horde follows, swept up by brain-dead mob mentality. At first, we're all smiling at one another, patting Kendra on the back for making the plan work, and then a zombie comes howling at us, eyes gone, mouth open, and we shut up and run like crazy.

My legs are killing me. My calves feel like they're about to split off my bones and stop for coffee. When we get home—and I never thought I'd say this, but—I'm going to take a week off from physical activity of any kind.

They're harder to outrun than they used to be. Even the ones limping on busted legs are keeping up. But this time around we don't have a wounded PJ, so the three of us manage to stay ahead of them.

"This spot O'Dea mentioned should be right up ahead," says PJ over the moaning and cracking underbrush. "Big oak with lots of sturdy branches there."

"Perfect," says Kendra. "You'll be all right climbing—" Then her voice turns into a shriek that punctures our eardrums. A zombie in a red flannel jacket hobbles out from behind a tree and grabs her wrists with his stiff gray hands. Kendra kicks at the ground and pulls herself as far back as she can from the dead man, who moans and slobbers as he drags her fingers toward his open mouth—

"Come on!" yells PJ, and whoa PJ, Mr. Scared of His Shadow, puts every underdeveloped muscle in his tiny body behind his right shoulder and slams into the zombie like a defensive lineman. The walking corpse releases Kendra and falls to the ground with a moan. I bolt over to PJ, help him to his feet, and then we're kicking the zombie over and over, shoving our feet into his gray, lifeless face. His nose breaks, his teeth fall out, but there's no blood, just little clouds of dust and bits of face.

"Guys!" shouts Kendra. "I appreciate the help, but

they're getting closer!"

PJ and I stop and stare at each other, wide-eyed. His face is redder than I've ever seen it, at least when he isn't crying, and there's a toughness in his eyes that's so not PJ. "The plan," I pant at him. "She's right. Quickly." He nods, and we're off.

We charge back into the forest, and soon the trees open up into a clearing, huge, sunny, floored with leaves and centered around a sturdy old oak tree with its first spring foliage popping out fresh and green between the beams of golden sunlight. It's the kind of place where you'd have a picnic—afternoon sunlight pours in gray and green between the branches, and the ground is soft and flat beneath our feet, nice for sitting and snacking.

But this is no picnic.

Kendra and I give PJ a hand up to one of the lower branches, and he starts scrambling up the oak. Once he's a good twenty feet off the ground, he gives us a thumbs-up, and Kendra and I hide behind a couple of trees at the edge of the clearing and wait for the horde.

There are no silhouettes in the distance or far-off footsteps this time—within seconds of us hiding, they come marching in, heads raised, mouths wide open like they're ready for a buffet. When PJ screams out their names, the forest of hands stretches up toward him like maybe, if they reach hard enough, they could extend their arms and drag him down. That hippo crack did a number on them, too—they're not just hungry, they're *ticked off*, screaming and scrambling against one another with genuine rage.

Maybe the sad, sorrowful moaning that drove me crazy on the path was bad, but this, the shrieking and gurgling, makes my blood run cold. Soon, the last of the skeletons stumbles into view, and the clearing's packed with the entire horde, moaning for a quick snack before they hit Homeroom Earth and start in on the main course.

"Come on, guys!" calls out PJ. "Come and get it! Grade-A man flesh!"

Just like PJ expected, they huddle around the tree, clawing at the bark with their rotten hands or snatching blindly at the air. Across the clearing from me, Kendra holds up her palm—*Wait for it*. Once the group is tight packed at the base of the tree, she gives me the thumbs-up, and I pull PJ's handheld camera out of my pocket and go tiptoeing up behind the nearest zombie, the big guy with the half face, his ham fists pounding angrily on the tree trunk.

My hand slowly drifts toward the zombie's back pocket and I ready my finger on the camera's red Play button.

"*Hurgh!*" Next to me, a skinny zombie with a bushy beard turns away from the tree long enough to spy me trying to slip the camera into Half-face's pocket. He claws a bony hand at my chest, and my heart skips three beats, and then I'm back behind my tree before I know it, only I don't have the camera, I dropped it in the clearing, I never pushed the button, I—

Oh no! I've ruined everything. The plan's gone out the window. Ian, you idiot, you can't even *run* right! You can't even put a piece of plastic and metal the size of a candy bar into someone's back pocket! Now PJ's up a tree with a crowd of hungry corpses underneath him, and you've let him down *again*, and you've probably alerted the entire zombie population of this mountain that this kid up a tree is part of an elaborate scam, and Coach Leider is gonna have to tell your dad that he found your half-eaten leg somewhere in the woods.

I expect to see Kendra either glaring at me with superintense *You let this happen* eyes or staring in horror at the fallen camera as one of the zombies learns how to climb, but instead, she's got her palm up again, telling me to wait. She's focused on the clearing, and when I follow her stare, I see why.

The bearded zombie isn't running at me and moaning *It's a trap!* in zombese or whatever. He stands there with PJ's camera in his hand, staring at it like it's a photo of someone he can't quite remember, running his big gray thumb over its face. I can almost see the rusted gears turning in what's left of this thing's brain.

And like he's reading my thoughts, the zombie

furrows his brow, puts his thumb on the big Play button in the middle of the camera, and presses it. There's a loud beep, and the recording starts blasting out of the tiny device.

The plan officially goes into action.

Easily the most disgusting thing I've ever seen.

CHAPTER TWENTY

Kendra

If this mountain is permeated with bad luck, as O'Dea the overly hostile Warden claims, then the confluence of events we're currently experiencing means that we have tapped into some sort of vein of good fortune running through the landscape. First, the creatures have enough of their brains left to remember their names, but not enough to expect the ambush we have planned for them, and now they've proven that they're semi-intelligent enough to operate simple technology, but not so much as to discern one humanoid from another.

If our lives weren't in peril, I'd consider someday writing a dissertation on the selective memory of the reanimated human body.

But I'm *ideating* (and that's five). Back to the plan:

The bearded creature presses the button on the handheld camera, and the speakers crackle to life with our voices—"Hey! Hey, zombie!" "Hey pal! Over here!" One by one, the other creatures turn away from PJ in the tree and slowly focus their eyes on their bearded cohort, who doesn't seem to notice, just stares at the camera in wonderment as the audio recording of our voices echoes through the woods. There's a pause, a moment when the other creatures silently consider their options, and then one of them lets out an angry snarl and the horde descends on him as one. The bearded creature looks around in blank astonishment as his reanimated brethren mistake him for a screaming human being and tear him to pieces.

It isn't pretty, but I make myself watch as they pull the creature to shreds. There's no blood, only dust and rot, but it is nonetheless unnerving, and the whole forest stinks of old books and bad meat. It isn't until the rib cage comes loose that I have to turn away, breathing through my shirt sleeve in the hopes that I don't lose my breakfast of peanuts and termites.

Finally, the tearing sounds cease, and when I turn back, the creatures stand around, hands caked with black filth.

Now to see if PJ's long-term plan is plausible.

One of the other creatures, the woman in the pink spandex, leans down and picks up the screaming camera, staring at it dumbly.

The heads turn, the creatures moan, they come at her all at once, and the carnage starts all over again.

I repeat: there's nothing pretty about what happens. The skeletons go rather quickly—they're basically bones held together by mummified dirt—but the Pine City Dancers still have a lot of dried meat on them, and it isn't until the other creatures tear them completely apart that the ones foolish enough to pick up the camera stop twitching and moving. After a while, it's just repetitive, and I sit with my back to the fighting, listening to excited snarling and moaning, ripping and crunching, and the tinny electronic voices of my friends and me loudly yelling things like "pus bag."

Soon, the outcries die down almost completely, and when I turn around, I see a wiry woman with no lips and one eye holding the head of one of her undead contemporaries. After a moment of staring into the empty sockets, she tosses the head aside and bends down, retrieving the screaming camera from a gnarled gray hand detached from its body. For some reason, I'm surprised to see that the one surviving creature is female. I'm not sure why that seems so strange to me, but staring at her now, eye white beneath clumped bangs, gore-covered hand sprouting from a tapered-waist flannel shirt, I'm stunned. In the many sequences of this plan I ran in my head, the last of them was always a male.

"That's it, come and get it . . . ," says prerecorded Ian, sounding tired.

"Is that enough?" asks PJ's voice. There's a crackle and a beep, and the noise dies out.

The creature shakes the camera, holds it up to her ear, and then drops it onto the ground.

"Uh, guys?" yells PJ. "What do we do about the last one?"

"You didn't think of that?" asks Ian from behind a tree.

"Guess not."

Ah.

This is, conceivably, a serious problem.

All our voices are, of course, not helping the peace of mind of the last remaining creature. Her head whips from one shout to another with a series of howls and grunts, snapping her rotten teeth under her cracked, desiccated lips. The more she realizes she's surrounded, the more agitated she gets, until finally she gives PJ one last stare and then turns away from the old oak and launches herself into the woods, heading back to the path.

"We've got to stop her!" yells PJ as he begins shimmying down the tree. "Do something!"

Ian and I are on our feet and after her in seconds, following the bony back in the skinny flannel as it moves swiftly through the forest (somehow, I wish we could have rigged PJ's plan to leave us with one of the creatures with a broken leg, but the time for wishing is long gone). Ian gets to her first, putting his shoulder down in the hopes of toppling her the way PJ knocked over my attacker earlier, but she seems to expect that, and Ian is swept off his feet by a rotten backhand. When I reach her, I grab one of her wrists, my fingers pressing sickeningly into the crusty dried skin, but the bone underneath it is powerful and yanks away from me.

"HEY!" A pair of skinny arms appears around the creature's neck as Ian jumps onto her back. She screams and spins, snarling at the top of her deflated lungs as she reaches her clawed hands over her shoulders. At first, it seems like she's going to capture him, but then she wises up, and her hands simply snatch one of the arms around her neck and pull it toward her mouth while Ian's eyes go wide and he yells, "No no no *no no*—"

In seconds, I've grabbed Ian by the waist, and I'm pulling him, playing a twisted game of tug-of-war with the furious corpse in front of me, her hand still drawing Ian's arm to her lipless maw, my arms yanking at Ian's feet, Ian himself screaming like his life depends on it as he goes horizontal between the two of us, probably feeling the beginnings of a dislocated shoulder.

"Let GO!" I hear myself scream. My eyes clench shut, my teeth grind to the point of pain, and I put every ounce of energy I can muster into my feet, digging them into the ground, leaning away from the creature—

—and then she listens to me and opens her hand. Ian and I go flying backward. The base of my skull hits something hard, and a pillow seems to cover my eyes, ears, face. Somewhere, I hear Ian yelling my name, and then the world swirls into night.

"*Wake up, girl.*"

The voice snaps on a light in my brain, beating away the shadows with a blinding flash. As I sit up, my head pounds, my stomach knots, and my hands fly to my hair, fingers digging into my curls.

Easy, Kendra, sort your thoughts. Take a deep breath, tear the cobwebs off of your brain, and assess the situation. "What happened?"

"You got knocked unconscious," says Ian, putting a hand on my shoulder. "Your head hit a rock and you were out cold."

The world comes into focus. The afternoon light is dim enough to keep the pain in my head from throbbing too hard. Ian and PJ crouch around me, O'Dea staring down contemptuously from a few feet away. The cold stone beneath me and the fiery warmth at my back tell me that we've returned to the Warden's cave, that I'm safe, that the abyss of snapping teeth and rotten hands and white mindless eyes that I just barely escaped existed only in my unconscious mind.

"Yeah, she's all right," says O'Dea. "Maybe a concussion, nothing serious."

"A concussion's *nothing serious*?" says PJ.

"Not in this business, it ain't," says O'Dea, throwing another handful of sticks on the fire. "Girl, you stay awake, got it? No napping. You gonna throw up?"

It's a distinct possibility, but it feels inappropriate to be coddled like this, so I say, "No, I'm all right," and then, *Come on, Kendra, drag yourself back into the now.* "Did we get her? The last . . . creature?"

"Gone before I got there," says O'Dea.

"I'm such an idiot," curses PJ. "Of course there'd be one left. You can't expect a zombie to destroy *itself.*"

"We got a couple of hours," says O'Dea. "This here's a big mountain, and as fast as she may be moving now, she won't be getting too far. First things first: we eat. Then we get cracking, make sure your buddies down there don't have a run-in with her."

"How can you eat at a time like this?" says Ian.

"Son, looking at you kids is painful," says the old woman, jabbing a twiggy finger into Ian's ribs. "You're the palest bunch of malnourished train wrecks I've seen in a while. Can't have you fainting. You eat, then you go. Settle down."

O'Dea ambles into the cave, mumbling about supper. PJ and Ian help me to my feet, brush bits of dirt and leaves out of my hair and off my back, and give me a nice fraternal pat on the shoulder.

"Are you out of your mind?" PJ laughs. "No one just attacks a zombie, not even in the movies, not unless they're totally insane—"

"—yanking me like that," babbles Ian. "Like, seriously, if I had any idea you could get that kind of heel traction, I would've told Coach to get you on the girls' JV team ASAP—"

It's hard to concentrate on the exact words, what with the buzzing of a recent concussion still in my head, but somehow I recognize what's happening, and it causes a feeling in me that I'm not accustomed to, a warming sense of courage and strength that I have not felt in . . . maybe in my entire life. Through all this hardship and terror of the past two days, my plan to make friends has come to fruition. A smile crosses my face, and a similar look of amusement and glee crosses the faces of my co-adventurers.

"Thanks, guys," I manage.

"Thank *you*," says Ian Buckley.

"Seriously," says PJ. "Careful, don't trip over that."

I nearly walk into a canvas sack made huge and bulky with content, the bottom stained blackish green. A sweet, nauseating smell rises from it.

"What's that?" I ask.

PJ grimaces. "That's the . . . makings of O'Dea's new

seal. She gathered it up before we brought you here."

"Makings?"

Ian hisses through his teeth, "Mixed zombie debris."

"Ah."

"Yeah, at least you were unconscious when she was picking it up," says Ian. He nudges the bulging sack with his foot, and then shudders when it responds with a soft squish. "I don't think she needed to take all this much. Went a little overboard, if you ask me."

It's only grilled cheese and chicken soup, but it's easily going to be the best meal I've ever eaten after the mix of little to eat and high-energy activity that's marked the past thirty hours. Berries and nuts are good for you, but nothing compares to warm protein and carbohydrates!

While O'Dea makes the food, the three of us watch like hungry dogs, licking our lips and pacing, and when she hands us our lunches, they're gone almost instantly.

As we suck soup from our spoons, O'Dea gives me a light slap on the shoulder and beckons me toward the cave. Ian and PJ share a glance but remain silent.

Deep in its depths, the cave's stone ceiling flickers orange from a torch the Warden has fixed to the wall, and on the floor in front of a three-legged stool sits a ring of wood and reeds—the beginnings of a new dream catcher. O'Dea plops down onto the stool, picks up the ring, and begins weaving more leaves into it from a pile by her feet. It's bigger than the last one, at least three feet in diameter, probably to accommodate all the pieces in the grisly canvas bag outside. My backpack sits at her feet, the remaining contents strewn about carelessly.

After a few moments of her weaving silently and me standing there, she holds out a hand, callused and bony. "Let me have that diary you kids have been talking about," she says.

My hand immediately goes to the lump in my pocket. "Why?"

"I'd like it very much."

"Maybe I should hold on to it. It might come in use—"

Her eyes rise up from her weaving, and there's a hard white light in them that causes my breath to catch up in my throat, sends cold through my veins and heat through my face, blurs everything around us except those beads glittering in the darkness. It's something familiar, like when I first took the dream catcher in my hands, electricity that reaches all the way down into me, into my soul.

"Give it here."

The words are oppressive—I have to obey. Without even meaning to, I pull the diary from my pocket and lay it in her hand. Then she sets it on her knee and takes her eyes off me, and the humming power is gone, leaving me breathless, unsure if I can stay on my feet.

"Much obliged."

"What . . . what was that?" My head swims, and I lower myself to the ground slowly and carefully. "Was that . . . *magic* you just used on me?"

She nods. "Evil Eye. Oldest gag in the book. Doesn't take much, just the right stare, the right genes."

"How did you do that?"

"Wish I could tell you," she says, putting down the new seal and looking at me with nonelectric eyes. "Been able to weaken knees with a look since I was your age, and it's not just my beautiful face." She grins and motions to her cheek, a road map of wrinkles. "It's in my blood, just like whatever made those poor dead folks walk around is in the earth. Some things just have a power about them."

My face feels hot. Being overpowered by a stare is embarrassing. "Well, there's your diary. Can I go?"

"Not quite yet." She cracks her knuckles and sighs. "It occurs to me that . . . I was a bit hard on you when you burned up my old seal. Laid into you real good. And looking back, I'm not all that sure I needed to do that."

"But . . . I ruined everything. Thanks to me, there's a horrible creature making her way toward my classmates right now."

She nods. "That may be. But look, girl—"

Enough. "My name is Kendra."

"*Kendra?* That's no name for a girl."

"You are easily the first O'Dea I've ever met."

"Fair enough," she says. "Look, *Kendra*, you did something stupid, and you got us in a real pickle here. But at least you made a move. You stood your ground, you went through on your threats, and you did your best to help your pals. If you're going to screw up, then screw up trying, and you tried as hard as you could. No fault in that. Those two out there"—she hikes a thumb toward the mouth of the cave—"those *boys*, they'll always listen to what you have to say, what you're *thinking*, but they'll always want the action for themselves, got me? Especially the blond one. I can see it in his eyes. You better make sure you stand your ground, no matter who says they can take care of the problem or what terrible beast comes stumbling out of the woods to eat you. Being smart is great and all, but the real sweet stuff is in the *action*, you know, the, eh . . ."

My heart swells, and my eyes sting. "Adventure."

"Right. Boys think they should have it all. Prove 'em wrong."

Her knees pop as she stands, and her neck cracks as she twists her head, and suddenly, as she's looming over me with her wild hair and bright eyes, I feel a kinship with this woman. She knows about adventure not because she has gotten tattooed or gone bungee jumping once, but because she lives every day fighting against evil. She holds out a hand, and I take it, envying its strength and hardness.

"Here," she says, handing me the torch. "Getting dark. You'll need it."

Outside, the sun is almost down behind its cloudy curtain, and Ian and PJ are champing at the bit, wringing their hands and tapping their toes in anticipation. When Ian sees me, he smiles goofily. "You sure you want to be waving that torch around?" he says. "Only you can prevent forest fires."

"I'm fine," I say, and then, "but if you want it, you can have it."

He shakes his head. "Nah, it's probably best that you have it. You're pretty official when it comes to things like this, and I'm kind of a klutz."

"How do we beat that zombie to Homeroom Earth?" asks PJ, raring to go. "If she's taking the main path, how do we get there before her to stop her? Is there a car?"

"No car," says O'Dea, "but there're shortcuts in the woods, if you know how to navigate 'em."

"Navigating the woods is not our specialty," says Ian. "Can you come along and show us the way?"

The Warden shakes her head. "No can do. I've got work to do cleaning up this mess you've made for me. But I can help. Remember when I brought PJ up here?" She crouches, digs her fingers into the ground, and twists something circular and heavy. With a grunt, she pulls a huge disklike rock out of the clearing floor to reveal a black hole in the ground. "I got tunnels carved all through this mountain. One of them will lead you back to your school trip."

"Are you kidding me?" asks Ian. "We can't navigate the woods, much less get around in a bunch of underground tunnels—"

O'Dea dips her hand into the ashes of the fire, then takes PJ by the shoulder and draws a symbol—a circle with a cross coming from its top—on his forehead. She mumbles something low and guttural, and PJ's eyes go wide.

"Whoa," he says, "that feels . . . funny."

"Follow that symbol," she tells him. "If you see it in the dark, it means you're going the right way."

"Now wait," says PJ, "will it glow, or will there be some kind of—"

"Enough talking!" she yells, and shoves PJ into the hole, where he collapses with a grunt. She nods to Ian and me, and before I can allow myself to think twice, I'm leaping in after him, going after that last zombie and, hopefully, our destiny.

CHAPTER
TWENTY-ONE

PJ

For a second, the tunnel is just a dark, root-ceilinged cavern flickering orange from Kendra's torch. Then the ashes on my forehead fill with a cold, vibrating light that extends down into the backs of my eyes, and suddenly a symbol—a ball with a cross on top of it—glows a faint blue along the wall down one shadowy tunnel.

"There," I say, pointing toward it. "Where that glowing sigil is painted."

"I don't see anything glowing," Ian replies.

"Lead us," says Kendra, handing me the torch, and I walk toward the twinkling blue sigil, then jog, then run after it.

If only I could film this. Words like *awesome* and *epic* don't do it justice.

Scraggly thick roots and pointed stalactites go rushing overhead, small rodents and insects scurry underfoot, but I keep running, following the shimmering magic symbols etched into the walls, my friends running behind me to stay within the orb of light the torch provides. Every time we reach an intersection of tunnels, the sigil appears against one wall, pulling me farther down at greater speeds, my sneakers pounding hard against the soft underground earth. Yesterday, I would've been content to film this, edging warily through these tunnels inch by inch, but I'm in love with this feeling—my calves taut, my arms pumping, my eyes pulling me deeper and deeper into the tunnels in the direction I know is right.

Then, just like that, flecks of yellow light dance in my vision, and Ian, Kendra, and I burst through a wall of sticker bushes and into the cool fresh air. A few yards away sits the Homeroom Earth parking lot, glowing obnoxious yellow beneath halogen streetlights. Just beyond it, the mess hall shines warmly. I wipe at the electric sigil on my forehead until the ashes have smeared away and my second sight fizzles out of my eyes in a little burst of pins and needles.

"Do you think we made it before she did?" whispers Ian.

"Hard to tell," says Kendra. "She could be anywhere on the premises. We could have passed her using the underground shortcut. They're slow moving, after all."

"They *were*," says Ian, "before you torched the dream catcher and they got loco."

"This conversation gets us nowhere," says Kendra.

Something colorful catches my eye on top of one of the cars in the lot, and a distinct sense of *uh-oh* rushes through me.

"Let's split up," I say.

"It's my belief that splitting up is a bad idea," says Kendra. "With our concerted efforts—"

"Look," I say, and point to the red-and-blue plastic lights on top of two of the cars in the parking lot. Two police cruisers sit on one side of our bus. "We've been lost overnight, remember? They've got the cops here looking for us, and if we get caught running around trying to find this runaway zombie, we aren't going to get far."

"We could tell them the truth," suggests Kendra.

"Grown-ups never believe the truth," Ian counters. "Especially teachers. PJ's right; we need to split up. If they catch one of us, the other two can keep looking around and trying to find the zombie."

"And when we find her," asks Kendra, "what then?"

"*Then* we get an adult," I say, "and tell them to bring the cops. We trap her someplace, lock the doors, and go looking for help." I reach out and touch Ian's shoulder. "*Don't* try to fight her, okay? I know that seems like a good idea, but it's not worth the risk of getting bit."

Ian nods calmly. There's hope for him yet. "Good call, man. Meet back here in twenty minutes if you haven't found anything."

We stay low, tiptoeing past the parked cars and into the courtyard of Homeroom Earth. A uniformed police officer stands in front of the bonfire pit with his back to us, surveying the area. The only lights that are on are in the windows of the mess hall, from which I can hear the rumbling of voices.

"Perfect," I whisper. "Everyone's at dinner. If we stay out of sight, no one will know we're here."

"All right," says Kendra. "Ian, you take the boys' bunks. I'll take the girls' bunks. PJ, you take the arts and crafts building. Keep your eyes peeled, and if you see anything, call for help. Let's go."

Ian and Kendra dart off toward their assigned bunks, leaving me to sneak around the policeman by the fire pit and walk as slowly as possible up the porch steps of the arts and crafts building. At one point, my foot lands on a weak step and a long, high-pitched creak breaks through the silent air. I duck down low, but the cop only looks around a little, makes a face, and checks his watch. The door to the building opens slowly and silently, and it isn't until I'm in the darkened hallway that I dare to stand straight up and walk around like a human being.

The arts and crafts cabin is quiet and still, draped in concentrated darkness. Moonlight pours in through big front windows, but it's barely enough to see by. Half of the room is broken up by long tables with benches around them, while the other has a wraparound counter with sinks and art supplies lining it. The whole thing is bathed in oblong shadows that merge with my horror movie knowledge to drive my imagination wild—the paint-flecked tables look like giant coffins, and every brush-filled cup seems like a shrunken head on the counter, spiky hair standing up in fright.

Every bone in my body begs me to go find Kendra and Ian, to turn on a light so the place won't look so creepy and twisted, but I take a deep breath and swallow as much of the fear as I can. That's the old PJ, the PJ who didn't run with twelve-point bucks and body-check the living dead. This new PJ is hard, brave, ready to fight anything in his path—

Something scratches around in a supply closet and I nearly pee my pants.

All right, I need to step back, be careful. If the zombie's in there, she's going to come lurching out with her arms up, ready to grab me by the neck and take a big old bite out of my face. I'm going to yank the door open really quick and step back, and if I see a rotten claw come out of it, I'll run like my life depends on it, which makes sense, seeing as it does.

Three, two, one—

"Now," I whisper. I grab the knob and yank the closet open, ready for anything.

There's another scratch, and a mouse comes scurrying out onto the linoleum floor.

Classic. My heart feels like it's punching me in the ribs over a stupid mouse. It's never felt so good to exhale. "Shoo," I say, kicking my foot out at the mouse.

The rodent squeaks at me and patters across the floor of the art room.

Watching it, I finally notice the footprints.

And the smell.

Out of the shadows, a tattered foot, caked with filth, stomps down on the mouse with a squishy thud, and she steps into view, ragged lips quivering in hunger, remaining eye shining cold lunar white out of the dark pit of its socket, body a heavy swaying mass of dead skin and slack tendon. My breath leaps into my throat and grows three times too big. She bends over with a sickening pop and closes her hand around the mouse under her foot. The poor thing squeaks the entire time she takes it in her cold dead grip, stands back up, and shoves it into her mouth. The yellow teeth hang open for a moment, and then the jaw moves, there's a crunch, and the squeaking stops. O'Dea's lunch tickles the back of my throat.

The zombie chews the mouse for what seems like

forever, and then she's silent, and my body is all ice-cold and every one of my joints starts quivering at once, and we just stare at each other, there, in the cabin, me shaking like a leaf, her still and quiet as the dead.

And I think, *Maybe she's full.*

The mouth opens and lets out a blood-curdling scream. The hands rise, and she comes at me. I duck out from under her grasp and switch places with her, backing up toward the long art tables.

"*HELP!*" I scream over and over, but if anyone hears me, they don't come.

The zombie turns back around and lunges in my direction. The benches hit the backs of my legs, and then I'm climbing backward over the table and falling off the other side, putting as much stuff between myself and the zombie as humanly possible, but then she's climbing over the table, snatching out at me with her rotten hands, and I scramble down to the end of one long table and run back across the room.

This arts and crafts room is probably big enough to fit a whole class of kids, but when it's you and a blood-thirsty zombie playing a game of tag in it, it shrinks, and it's impossible to get away from the cannibalistic psychopath in the middle of the room. The zombie and I circle each other for what seems like ages. I scream for help until my throat is sore. Every time I get to the door to try and run away, her dry, bony fingers brush my hair and I dart away from the doorknob just in time to not get bitten. Soon, I'm exhausted, but there's no time to catch my breath before she comes at me.

Finally, I duck beneath one of the long tables and scurry down its length until I'm huddled in the corner of the room. The zombie gets down on her hands and knees and comes crawling at me, and the dead tree we used to kill Deborah comes to mind. I put my hands up under the table and push as hard as I can, push with my whole body, and slowly it lifts, then goes tumbling over, landing on its side and slamming down onto the zombie's waist like a heavy, blunt guillotine.

But now I'm trapped.

The zombie is pinned beneath the table—but she's still coming, her outstretched claws and snapping teeth only inches away from me, horrible noises of popping bone and tearing flesh coming from where the table has split her in half. And now I'm backed into a corner, legs against my chest, with nowhere to go.

"PJ?" The door swings open and Kendra pokes her head in, glances at me, then stops dead, her eyes turning huge. "Oh my God."

"Get help!" I scream. There's a snap, and the zombie stretches a full inch closer to me. Her guttural snarls become rhythmic like panting breaths—*NYARGH, NYARGH, NYARGH.*

Kendra begins breathing hard, looking around the

room, then back out the door, and then looks at me with a glint of hope in her eyes. "I have an idea," she shouts.

"No more ideas!" I scream. "Get help!"

I hear the sink running and water splashing, and Kendra reappears over the overturned table with a paint-smeared art bucket of steaming water, and I remember what she and O'Dea said about speeding up decay.

There's a horrible ripping sound, and the zombie's torso comes free of her lower half. She crawls forward on her elbows dragging a tail of sinew behind her, the yellow teeth slowly open wide, and a blast of cold rotten air bursts out at me in the form of a bone-chilling moan. Kendra leaps on top of the table and pours the hot water over the zombie just as her talons close around my throat.

Sure enough, the dry mummified flesh bloats white and begins dripping off her zombie bones like gobs of frosting, but all through Kendra's pouring, those teeth stay unchanged as they gape wider and wider in their descent toward my face.

CHAPTER

Ian

All of twelve seconds after I've secured the boys' bunks and the surrounding area, I hear PJ screaming bloody murder in the arts and crafts cabin, and I go bolting down toward the main courtyard of the Homeroom Earth campsite. At first, I'm thinking that if *I* can hear him way over by the cabins, then the police officer by the bonfire pit should be on the job, but when I get there, there's no sign of him, and PJ's still shrieking *"HELP!"* between these crashing sounds and angry moans.

My feet are screaming, *LET'S GO—HE NEEDS YOU*, but out of nowhere, my brain comes in and skids me to a halt, and I think about the past couple of days, how when I ran after the buck or went down into the basement or picked up the dream catcher, it just made things a lot worse, and this is weird, because it actually works. My brain grabs my feet, and I decide that I'm going to get the teachers and bring them to PJ, because that's what he told me to do, because maybe I need to change it up sometimes and not run right into things.

I know, what's wrong with me?

The mess hall doors fly open with a bang when I hit them, and the cop from outside is standing there with a slice of pie looking totally blankly at me, and then windows and hallways rush past me and I'm in the mess hall, brightly lit and filled with the entire fifth and sixth grades who're sitting around eating dessert, and suddenly I've jumped up on a sixth-grade table and all the clinking and talking in the room goes silent with a gasp, and Coach Leider and Professor Randy are on their feet and looking relieved that I'm not dead, and Sean and Mitch and the rest of the kids in my grade are staring at me like I've just descended from heaven in a chicken suit, and for a moment I think about how filthy and ragged I must look, and then I remember PJ and say the first thing that comes to my head.

"YOU HAVE TO HELP US!" I scream at the top of my lungs. "SHE'S KILLING HIM!"

Guess that might have been a little much, because every girl in both years and at least two of the teachers,

Ms. Dean and Señora Alanzo, scream like crazy people. Everyone in an obnoxious yellow Homeroom Earth shirt comes rushing for me, almost as scary as the zombies with their angry looks and crackling walkie-talkies. The cop from outside is joined by a second person in uniform, and they both put hands to the guns at their sides. A big arm wraps around my legs, and Coach Leider drags me off the table.

"Buckley! Where have you been?" he yells.

"Arts and crafts building, now!" I yell back at him.

"What's he talking about?" asks Professor Randy,

"PJ's in danger!" I shout, moving toward the door and praying that my best friend has somehow managed to hold his own. "We need to help him! Please, Coach!"

Coach stares at me dumbfounded, and then he springs into action, running alongside me with his shoulders down. "Take me to him," he booms, and over his shoulder calls, "Randy, bring the cops!"

The screams have stopped as we scale the porch stairs and burst into the arts and crafts cabin, Coach next to me, the rest of Homeroom Earth hot on our heels. An ugly smell comes from down one hallway, and I sprint toward it. Sticky black skeleton footprints on the floor lead down a hallway to the door labeled DAYROOM. From under the door comes a steady stream of smelly water. Is it blood? Am I too late?

When I yank open the door, a wall of steam and

moldy stench hits me in the face, and I throw my arm across my mouth to keep from losing my lunch. PJ sits huddled in one corner of the room, trembling and panting, while Kendra is draped over the edge of an overturned art table, a bucket clutched in her shaking hands. On the floor in front of them is a chunky pile of horrible black stuff and human bones, slowly spreading out into the pool of water that sits on the floor. The skull among the gooey blackness lies at PJ's feet, mouth opening further and further until everything holding it together is breaking up into the puddle, melting like the Wicked freakin' Witch. PJ's watching the whole dissolving process with an intense grimace, like he's afraid it's going to suck back up into a body again and leap toward him.

From over my shoulder, I hear the Homeroom Earth staff reach us and gasp aloud.

"What the hell is going on here?" shouts Professor Randy in a voice that sounds nothing like the supernice guy who introduced himself to us a couple days ago.

"Wilson, Wright," says Coach. "Status report. How you doing?"

Kendra and PJ finally look up at us, their eyes wide with panic.

"I, uh," says Kendra, "was attempting to . . . give PJ a bath." She nods at the bucket in her hands, the muck on the floor.

"Yeah," says PJ. He nudges the skull on the floor with his sneaker. "I was . . . dirtier than I thought."

I try not to laugh, but I'm riding on this wave of excitement that they're still alive and this storm of embarrassment that's coming off Coach, so I start cracking up right there, my hands on my knees, my eyes tearing up, just laughing and laughing. And then Kendra and PJ start laughing, too, clutching their stomachs and whooping to the sky. Kendra laughs so hard, she nearly slips in the goo at her feet, and that only gets PJ and me laughing harder.

No one else finds any of this funny.

Of course, we get in trouble. Big trouble, the kind of trouble a sixth grader hears about but thinks will never happen to him.

Ten minutes later, we're sitting in the office, which doesn't have a single cute student-made piece of art in it, just a desk, a bulletin board, a couple of phones, and a gigantic coffee maker.

For a moment, the grumpy horde of counselors and teachers turn their backs to us, and I look over at my friends.

"How'd it go?" I ask.

"We got her," breathes Kendra. "Hot water. Melted her dried-up flesh."

"PJ, you okay?" I don't ask if he got bit, but—

"No bites, no scratches," he says with a relieved shudder. "Though I did watch her eat a mouse whole."

"Sick."

Then it's chew-out time. First up, Ms. Brandt does the talking while Mr. Harder stands behind her, arms crossed.

"You didn't once think," she squeaks, "of how I'd feel when I found three of you gone, did you? You assumed I'd be enraged, which I *was*, but you never thought about how worried I'd be, knowing you three could be out there alone in the forest with no one to—" Her voice cracks, and she covers her eyes with her hand, her face curling up like she's about to cry.

"We . . . didn't mean anything by it" is all I can say. Never thought I'd feel like such a goon for making a teacher cry.

Then we get Professor Randy, flanked by Homeroom Earth counselors.

"I gotta say, I have dealt with some bad apples in my day," he says, pacing, "but what you did was the most *dis*respectful *fool*hardy shenaniganery I have ever *seen*. I gave you a measly *four rules,* and you couldn't obey *one* of them."

"What'd I tell you?" whispers Kendra, staring at her feet.

Coach Leider brings up the end, and he's actually pretty cool about it.

"You three are back at base, safe and sound," he says, waving a huge hand in front of us like he's wiping our records clean. "That's all that matters. I'm officially pleased. But we've got an art room full of liquefied human remains over there, troops. So forget whose fault this is. I could care less. No one's in trouble yet. But I need to know *what happened* back there."

And we don't say squat. I sit there and feel like a huge idiot, and the look on Kendra's face tells me she's doing the same—being in trouble feels like a weight pressing down on you, especially for kids like us, who don't see the inside of the principal's office much—but we never say word one of the truth. We know better. Coach is right; we're lucky to be alive. It would only ruin the moment to start saying the dead walk and end the day in straitjackets.

Finally, Coach Leider and Professor Randy step aside, and two cops, all blue and silver, hands on their belts, step in. They smile at us with chubby faces, and their voices make it sound like we're six years old.

"Well, guys," says Cop One, "we've got a bit of a situation on our hands here. First of all, which one of you is Ian Buckley?"

Uh-oh. "Me," I say, or croak, more like it.

Cop Two gives me a *Sorry, kid* smile and says, "Your father's on his way. Should be here any minute."

This is the worst news I've gotten all trip, easily

worse than finding out zombies are real. Next to me, PJ clucks and scratches his head. He knows about my dad—the dude is unmovable, impossible to argue with, totally hard-core. I'm in trouble.

"Second," says Cop One, getting out a pen and a small pad of paper, "we need to hear about what happened on that mountain—specifically, what happened to result in a puddle of human bones on the floor of the arts and crafts building."

We glance at one another but stay silent. What do we do from here?

"The . . . Pine City Dancers," says PJ softly. Professor Randy goes a shade paler and the cops are all ears.

"That can't be," says one cop, taking his hat off. "We scoured the countryside, kid. They're not up there."

"Who are the Pine City Dancers?" asks Coach Leider.

"Well, we, uh, lost a few hikers around here last year," mumbles Professor Randy, glancing at the floor.

"You *what*?" bellows Coach. "Were you going to tell us about that at any point?"

Professor Randy mumbles something like "Bad for business."

"We found them," says PJ. "Up on the mountain. But they weren't dead. They . . ." He freezes, his mouth open, knowing what will happen if he says—

"Zombies," says Kendra.

The back of my neck prickles. PJ hisses through his teeth. The adults in the room share a glance, then look back at Kendra. "Excuse me, Wright?" asks Coach.

"You couldn't find the Pine City Dancers because they became zombies. Ambulatory corpses. The living dead."

Another silence falls over the room, this one loaded with a little more weird disbelief, and the truth about what happened feels more and more like a bad joke with every second that the punch line is out there.

But then my dad bursts through the door, so I have a whole new set of things to feel gut-wrenchingly embarrassed about.

My dad isn't a big listener. He doesn't ignore me or tell me to shut up or whatever— he's a cool dad and all— he just has this big tough front to him, like a wall you can't break through, and it's impervious to any excuse or alibi. When my dad has an idea about something, no one's changing his mind, even if he's wrong. When he thinks something needs to be taken care of, he takes care of it. And if he's angry, wow, forget about it.

And here he is, charging through the door, and he is *way* angry.

"Ian, my God," he booms, and throws his arms around me, yanks me to his chest. Then he pulls me out at arm's length and gives me a once-over. "You okay? You hurt? Did you get bitten by an animal or anything?"

Or anything. "I'm fine, Dad," I say.

"Excuse me, Mr. Buckley," says Professor Randy, "but your son's friend just told us something of importance—"

"No more questions!" shouts Dad, jabbing a finger into Randy's face. "Not without my lawyer present! How dare you interrogate my son after what he's been through? You better hope I don't sue you for utter incompetence, letting him run off like that! You, too, Larry!" He points at Coach Leider. "My son's on your JV team, for Pete's sake, and you let him get stranded in the woods? Ridiculous."

Everyone falls quiet, shoulders raised, mouths clamped shut. No one can talk back to him.

"Ian, get your things. We're leaving." Suddenly, I'm standing up, even though I don't want to. He points to the door and I walk toward it. Who's the zombie now? "You better thank your lucky stars that Coach Leider called me when you went missing. Without me here, the police would've—"

"My parents aren't here, are they?" whispers PJ.

"Not another word out of you!" snaps Dad. "Not another *word*, Wilson! You stay away from Ian from now on, got it? My boy doesn't need people like you getting him lost in the woods for days! And *you*!" he says to Kendra. "You're the girl who hit Ian with a book, aren't you? Oh, I remember *you*, missy. I remember that *hair*."

"Dad," I say.

"You two better tell your fathers that if I see them anytime in the near future, I'll let them know what I th—"

"Dad, it was my fault."

"Ian, I'm talking."

"No, *I'm* talking!" I yell, my voice going all high and whiny. It gets Dad's attention, though, and he looks at me like *What's wrong with you*, so I keep at it. "It was my fault, okay? I saw this deer in the woods, and I wanted to see it up close, so I ran into the woods and made PJ and Kendra follow me. They tried to hold me back, but I went anyway." Kendra and PJ both beam at me, although PJ looks a little amused that I'm putting myself this much on the line. I nod to them, and Kendra salutes back.

"Ian, you don't have to do that," says Coach Leider.

"*Did* you call their folks?" I yell at Coach. "Huh? Or just mine? Just the kid on your team?" Coach opens and closes his mouth a couple of times. Dad looks ready to explode. "This is all my fault, so if anyone should be getting yelled at or punished, it's me!" I yank my shoulder out from under Dad's hand and walk back to my folding chair next to PJ and Kendra, my friends, and I sit back down, staring at my dad and Coach, and for the first time in forever I feel like I'm doing the right thing.

"Well, now that we've settled that," mumbles one of the cops, "would you mind telling us about these . . . *zombies*, young lady?"

Dad's eyebrows go up, but he says nothing.

TWENTY-THREE

Kendra

Ian's heroics are heartwarming, especially given how petrifying his father is, but it's all a bit futile. We're in trouble, and the truth is proving ineffective.

I explain the past two days of our journey to the adults present. Their disbelief is staggering. Sure, even I'm feeling foolish finally using this awful, sophomoric, obnoxious word, but it's the only one that will best describe what we encountered up there: there were *zombies* on the mountain. Dead bodies reanimated, instilled with a hunger for human flesh. At first, Ian and PJ blush as I admit to our encounters with the supernatural, but a hardness develops in their eyes after a bit, an understanding that as long as the truth is being put out there in some form, it might as well be the whole truth, no matter how implausible it might sound.

The more we explain the zombies and O'Dea the Warden, the further the faces of the adults sink. After a few minutes, Professor Randy says, "Excuse me," and motions for the cops to leave the room. Coach Leider watches them go, then turns back to us, his face full of worry but hardened into resolve.

"At the end of the day, it doesn't matter what happened up there," says Coach. "You broke explicit orders from a superior, and that calls for punishment." He sighs and shakes his head. "Can't believe I'm doing this—Ian, since you were the ringleader here, you've got three months' detention and . . . no more recreational sports for the rest of the year."

Oh no. My heart aches as I watch Ian deflate with a breathy sigh. It's a death sentence for a middle school athlete.

"Larry, let's not go overboard here," says Mr. Buckley.

"Sorry, Vince," says Coach, "but it's the only way he'll learn." He turns to PJ and me. "For you two, two months' detention. Wright, your library internet privileges are revoked."

"That's hardly fair!" I sputter. "I—what about school research—you can't—"

"Should've thought of that before you ran off," he

says. "Stick to books. Wilson, I'll be talking to your teachers, and if they see anything even resembling a camera on your person, they're taking it. We clear?"

"Crystal," grumbles PJ.

"Good," says Coach with a nod. "Sorry, guys. We're really happy you're all okay, but rules are in place for a reason." He observes us for a minute longer, then says, "All right, let's get you kids back to the bunks and into bed. It's been a long day."

As we trundle out of the office, we pass Professor Randy, Ms. Brandt, and the police a ways down a linoleum hallway. Professor Randy is explaining something in whispers and big hand motions. I'm almost ready to ignore him in favor of sleep, until I catch two words:

". . . shared hallucination . . ."

"Excuse me!" I say, marching toward them. Professor Randy turns around and holds up his palms in front of his goatlike face.

"Easy now, little camper," he says. "What's the problem?"

"Are you telling these people that we *hallucinated* my story? Is that it?"

His mouth goes tight—caught red-handed. Slowly, he lowers to his knees to give me a patronizing smile. "You see, sweetheart," he says, "I've got a degree in child psychology, and under stressful situations, young people have been known to come up with a false idea in their heads—"

"I *know* what a shared hallucination is," I say. "I've read about post-traumatic stress disorder and schizophrenia. We didn't imagine anything. There were zombies up there."

"Young lady," says one of the cops, "zombies aren't real."

"You think I don't know what?" I snap. "Of course they're not real. I've been saying that for the past two days. But they were up there nonetheless. How do you explain the human remains in the arts and crafts cabin?"

Professor Randy opens his mouth, but nothing comes out—he *has* no explanation. Finally, one of the police officers saves him: "Little girl, do you have any other proof?"

Against all my better judgment, I know what has to be done. "Tomorrow morning, we go up on the mountain. There's a diary written by one of the missing dancers that proves everything I'm saying."

"Whoa, hold on!" PJ comes running up behind me. "Kendra, we just got *off* that rock. Do we really want to go back, just to prove a point?"

"PJ, they think we're crazy!" I tell him. "If we go up there, we can show them otherwise! O'Dea can explain the truth to them!" PJ stares off into space but finally nods along. When he looks back at Ian, Ian gives him a weary nod and a thumbs-up.

"Tomorrow morning," I say to the cops, "we'll go up. Be ready." Then Ms. Brandt puts a hand on my shoulder and leads me to the bunk, my face hot with rage and determination. I won't let anyone say I'm some stress-crazed hallucinating crackpot. They'll see.

The bunk is dark, though one or two girls are illuminated in their beds with flashlights and books, and a few of them go so far as to give me a half-whispered "Hey" when I come trudging in. I nod back to them, but my eyes are focused on something else, something off in the next room that I've been dreaming of since our compass first failed us.

The shower water is scalding hot, almost to the point of discomfort, but it's beautiful. As it washes the soap off me, I think of every filthy patch of mud I've fallen into or slept in these past two days. I think of every long-dead hand that's wrapped itself around my arms and legs, of the cloud of awful bacteria that must have been released when, not ten yards in front of me, a zombie was torn to shreds by other zombies. These mental images keep me under the stream of hot water as long as possible, until the heat begins to subside and I hear Ms. Brandt stage-whisper, "Kendra, it's time for bed."

My sleeping bag might as well be made of imported

silk, and the thin waterproof mattress I'm lying on could easily be filled with swan feathers. Compared to what I've just been through, this bed is heaven.

As the bunk turns to pitch-black, it dawns on me that somehow, through this horrifying experience, I actually fulfilled my main objective on this trip. I made friends—two of them, even—and had an adventure. A smile creeps across my face at the idea, and then sleep waves its hand over my eyes, and I'm gone.

Its hand closes around my wrist. It is stronger than any grip I've ever felt. When I follow the unmovable arm to its body, I see Ian Buckley, face gray, eyes missing, mouth wide—

My body rockets into action. My limbs flail. My fist beats at the grip. A painful feeling comes out of my mouth as I scream.

"Kendra!"

The voice is familiar, and human, not far off, close, hanging over me.

Easy now, Kendra. You're going to hurt somebody.

Ms. Brandt holds me by the shoulders and steadies me. "Okay, honey, okay. Just a nightmare. Take a deep breath." I do as she tells me, and the room evens out. The bunk is empty, save our troubled English teacher and a single goofy-looking police officer who looks terrified of me.

"Where is everyone?" is what comes first. The beds are all empty—no sleeping bags, no luggage.

"They're at breakfast," she says. "Everyone packed their things earlier. We figured you might want to sleep in a little. But the sheriff says if you kids still want to go up on the mountain . . ."

Outside, the sun is blinding, and my body feels slow and *lethargic* (that's going on the list), glutted on the most sleep I've had in the past three days. Professor Randy is standing with a tall, broad-shouldered man whose star-shaped brooch and mirrored shades label him the sheriff. Immediately, I'm anxious—maybe I shouldn't have said anything.

What can you do, Kendra? These people were worried sick about you, and you said it was because of zombies.

PJ and Ian wait next to them and wave to me as I approach. It's pleasant to see them again, though I can sense they share my mix of embarrassment and worry. Both appear to have had as poor a night's sleep as I did, but poor Ian looks especially miserable. The reality of his situation must have dawned on him today. Even though Mr. Buckley is nowhere to be found, his invisible hand seems to weigh down on Ian's shoulder.

The sheriff sees me and grins. "Morning, little lady," he says. "Man, look at that hair. I had a girlfriend in college with hair like that."

"Good morning," I reply in my iciest tone.

"Professor Randy and I have talked to the policemen who interviewed you," he says, "and he says you were pretty adamant—sorry, you were *very sure*—"

"I know what *adamant* means."

The sheriff's grin disappears. "They said you said *zombies*," he says coolly. "Your boyfriends over here"— a cheap shot—"are saying the same thing. Professor Randy thinks you made it all up, but you seem pretty *adamant* that I come all the way out here and hike up that mountain. Now, I don't care if the Tooth Fairy is making moonshine up there. But my boys also mentioned that your buddy here knew about a gang of lost dancers from Pine City, and Randy said you mentioned a diary. So I'm here. I'm interested. What's the story?"

Ian glances at me, and through his fatigue he looks stalwart. PJ smiles and cocks an exhausted eyebrow; I think he finds this funny.

"Let's go up the mountain and find out," I finally answer.

"Young lady," says the sheriff, "I am serious."

"There's a wall," I tell them. "An old Indian stone wall, about a mile up. Covered in old symbols and vines. Do you know it?"

The sheriff frowns, but Professor Randy nods coolly. "Yeah, I've heard of it. The locals don't like it. They say it's cursed."

"Then that's where we'll start," I tell him.

Everyone turns toward the parking lot. I say hi to Ian and PJ. Ian marches rigidly, head down, so PJ and I fall as far back as we can and whisper.

"He got it bad last night," says PJ. "His pops yelled at him for two hours after we went to bed. We could all hear it from inside the cabin."

"That's terrible."

"Yeah, well . . . look, what do we tell O'Dea?" he murmurs. "When we show up with the cops? I doubt she wants us blowing up her spot like this."

"She'll understand," I tell him. "Maybe if we show them the truth, they can do something about it. Set up some fences to keep people from wandering up there and turning into monsters."

We pile into a state police SUV—Ian, PJ, Professor Randy, the sheriff and I. We roll out of the parking lot and onto the mountain road leading to Homeroom Earth, and a few yards in, Randy says, "Stop right here." He gets out and unfastens a chain across a dirt hiking path winding off into the woods, a path I never would have seen if not for Randy undoing the chain. He gets back into the car, and the sheriff turns us into the woods.

We drive for a while, taking tight curves through the impervious line of trees on either side of us. At first, I'm almost bouncing with excitement at the prospect of being the first human being to provide proof of the living dead. Soon, though, watching the heavy trees pass us brings back nauseous memories of our trip, and my stomach turns sour. Finally, the road ends in a small cul-de-sac, and Professor Randy urges us out. The soft earth underfoot and the smell of pine needles and decay are sickeningly familiar.

"It's right up here, if I remember correctly," he says, motioning to us.

The walk we take can barely be called a hike, but the movement of treading my way up the mountain brings back even more vivid recollections. All three of us feel it and are doing everything not to turn and run. Ian kneads his hands. PJ wraps his arms around himself and glances at every tree.

At first, I wonder if it's a lost cause, but then I see the wall in the distance, its gray flatness bisecting the brown-and-green forest floor. "There," I say, pointing, and suddenly Ian and PJ and I are jogging toward it, drawn to its reality after doubting our own for so long.

When we reach it, it's the same wall, choked with plant life, glistening with rum. This time, however, there are orange signs on posts in front of it reading PRIVATE PROPERTY—KEEP OUT—TRESPASSERS WILL BE SHOT—O'DEA FOREE, OWNER.

"That's one way to go about it," says Ian.

I drink in the forest on the other side of the wall. It looks no different from the woods we're standing in, but there's a cold, looming quality to it, as though the curse itself stands at the wall staring down at us, inviting us in. Slowly, my foot goes to the top of the wall, ready to launch me over it and into the insanity of the mountain.

We could be lost for days. But then again, it would mean so much—

"Wait," says PJ. "Look."

He kneels down at the base of one of the signs and rises with his handheld camera in his grip. Ian and I huddle around him as he presses the Play button.

The video is shaky, made by an amateur. We see trees, sky, hard rock floor, and then a gnarled hand rises into view holding something—a dream catcher, huge, the size of a truck wheel, strung with finger bones and teeth and a million and one other pieces of zombie detritus. The camera pans over to a bonfire, roaring with twigs and leaves, and then it lifts something else into view—Deborah Palmer's diary. A hard, gravelly voice mumbles, "Sorry," and then the hand tosses the book into the flames.

"*NO!*" I scream as the pages blacken and curl. Professor Randy and the sheriff come trundling up behind us. The breath feels yanked out of my chest. PJ lowers the camera to his side, shaking his head and sighing.

"No," I moan, "no, no, no, *no!*"

"She all right?" asks the sheriff.

"She's fine," says Ian. Then: "I . . . don't think we

need to go any farther than this, guys."

Ian's words sting me. All we need right now are facts, and yes, O'Dea burned the diary full of all the facts we had, but there has to be proof somewhere on the mountain. Doesn't there? "What? No, wait," I say. "We can still go up there!"

Ian looks back at the sheriff. "Can we talk alone for a second? Just the three of us. You two head back to the car."

"Don't try to pull a fast one on me here, son," says the sheriff.

"I promise we just want to talk to her." Reluctantly, the sheriff and Professor Randy shrug at each other and head back to the SUV.

"We were here," I say. "She was here. They attacked us." I hold out my hands to PJ, who just stares at his camera. "*Zombies!* See, I said it! Zombies! They're real! If we go up there and introduce them to O'Dea, she can—"

"Kendra, what'll happen if we go up there?" says Ian, pointing over the wall. "We'll get lost again. O'Dea will have to save us from dying out there, and this time we'll be bringing attention down on her, too. We can't do it."

"But we didn't make this up! Walking dead people, magic, curses! PJ, this is your chance to—"

But PJ is staring at his camera with a defeated look on his face, and I can already see that he agrees with Ian.

"We can't risk going back up there," he mumbles. "We're okay. Compared to never seeing our families again, this just . . . doesn't matter."

"It *does* matter! It matters to *me*!" *Try not to break down, Kendra. You've been so good about it so far.*

"Maybe things weren't what we thought they were," says PJ. "Maybe O'Dea wasn't as good a witch as she said she was. I mean, burning that diary, our only proof of what happened . . . it doesn't look good. And Ian's right, we don't want to get *more* people lost up on this mountain."

"Let's just go home," says Ian. "All that matters is that we're safe. Right?"

"But I—" Then I lose my composure and begin crying, like a baby. It's involuntary. I wanted to show the world that horrible, impossible things *were* out there, and instead I have nothing except three missing kids talking about movie monsters. It's too much, and I am overwhelmed by tears.

And out of nowhere, Ian Buckley, the biggest jerk in my school, whose face I once bashed with a textbook for being a sexist, comes over and gives me a bear hug while I cry, and that only makes me cry harder.

"It's not fair," I sob repeatedly into his shoulder.

"Oh, it's totally lame, no question," he says. Once I stop shaking, he holds me out at arm's length. "But you know what these woods are capable of." He smiles.

"You've got to swallow that pride. There are more important things."

His words warm my heart enough to overcome the tears. Once I've sniffled a bit and wiped at my eyes with the sleeve of my sweatshirt, I say, "What do we tell them? We knew about the Pine City Dancers, and the stone wall . . . how do we explain that?"

Ian looks to PJ. "Any ideas?"

PJ thinks for a moment, his mind mapping out the plot of our next act. "We tell them that Jeremy Morris told us about the Pine City Dancers," he says. "Then we say that we accidentally ate some wild berries. They were poisonous and caused a hallucination."

"You can probably do better than that," I say. "If a movie ended like that, you'd be angry about it."

PJ laughs but then shakes his head. "Maybe. But right now, I just want to get out of here. These woods still give me the creeps."

"Okay," says Ian. "Let's head back and make ourselves look dumb."

"Not yet," says PJ. He gives me his handheld camera. "I want to do something before we go."

CHAPTER
TWENTY-FOUR

PJ

"To whom this may concern," I say into the glowing red light and the shiny round iris. "My name is Peter Jacob Wilson." Nothing sounds worse than my full name. "I'm eleven years old. Me and my two friends broke off from a class trip and got lost in these woods, and we were attacked and hunted down by . . . something. Something evil, and unnatural. So if you've found this, take it as a warning. Turn back." Our whole journey flashes before my eyes, and a chill shudders through me.

"You're not okay, are you? Everything feels wrong, doesn't it? That's not you; it's this place. These woods want to hurt you." Ian wraps his arms around himself. Kendra nods, never taking her eye from the camera screen. "I know how you feel. Something about whatever's on the other side of this wall seems cool, even if it feels strange and scary. Trust me when I say this: there are better adventures, and there are worse things out here than you can imagine. Turn around, and head downhill, and you should reach camp. It might take a while, but you should be okay. Do it for your family and your friends." I'm out of stuff to say, but I feel like I need to send them off. "I'm not afraid of this place anymore, but you should be. This isn't a movie; it's real. Get out now."

There's a pause, and then a beep as Kendra presses the button. "Got it," she says. "Now what?"

This is the part that kills me. "Leave it here."

Kendra blinks. "Just . . . leave it here?"

"For whoever finds it." *God*, this *sucks*. It's taking everything in my power not to snatch my device from Kendra's hands, pocket it, say forget the whole thing. But this needs doing. If we aren't going to blow this thing wide open—and we can't now, not with the diary gone and O'Dea who knows where—then we at least need to try and help people. "Let's just . . . leave it and go, okay?"

"Really?" says Ian. "Dude, that's your camera."

"Well, yeah," I say, "but . . . I think I'll be okay

307

without it." No, I don't think; I know. It's just a thing, a gadget. I'm safe. We're safe. "But wait. Does one of you have a pen?"

"Actually . . . ," says Kendra, and hands me a felt-tip pen. On the side of my handheld device, I scribble WATCH ME TO LIVE in big letters, then place it gently at the base of the wall.

Over by the car, the sheriff and Professor Randy are admiring the view of the mountain from up here.

"You guys have a little talk?" asks Sheriff Mc-Mustache.

"Yeah," I tell him. I look at the other two, and they both nod. "I guess it's time we went home."

We have to pack up quickly, as everyone else has already gotten ready to get on the bus and get out of there (from what little I've heard, Homeroom Earth was pretty lame, seeing as most of the outdoor activities were canceled once we disappeared; apparently, there was a lot of movie watching in the mess hall).

As Ian and I stuff our clothes and stuff into our backpacks, Coach Leider comes to the cabin door. "Wilson, Buckley, front and center." When we approach him, he hands me my camcorder, and though I've learned that life can't be lived behind a camera, its weight and buttons feel delicious in my hands.

"Wilson, we should talk at some point," he booms.

"Bet the JV basketball team could use a good videographer, get some practice footage for us to study."

"Sure thing," I tell him, surprised but kind of excited. Is this how male bonding feels? I'm unsure.

"Got to say, I'm not psyched about your disappearing act," he says. "That said, I just wanted you to know that I'm impressed you made it off that mountain unharmed. Really shows what a wolf pack you two are."

"We three," says Ian. "Kendra Wright really saved our butts out there, Coach."

"I'll talk to Coach Arnholdt about recruiting her for a team," says Coach. "Maybe rugby. We'll see. Just . . . do me a favor, guys, maybe keep the zombie talk down. Makes you guys look a little soft in the head."

"Gotcha," I say.

"Good," he says, motioning us out the door. "Come on, they're waiting."

The buses rattle and rumble in the parking lot. In front of the sixth-grade bus, the sheriff hands me my backpack. I'd almost forgotten about it.

"We found a book, too—a picture book, for little kids—but it had all that muck on it," he says. "We had to throw it away."

Ugh. It's like a punch in the heart, but I can't freak out about it too much. These things happen in zombie warfare. "Has anyone looked into those human remains?"

The sheriff kicks a rock. "We gotta send the teeth in

to be studied. Gonna be a while, but they say it might be one of those poor dancers who got lost up there last year. They've never seen anything decay this fast, is all." He stares hard at me, almost smiling. "Wish I knew what you three kids're hiding."

"Just don't let anyone hike on that hill," I tell him. "Make it illegal. Put up a fence. I don't care."

"Wilson!" yells Coach Leider from the bus. "Let's get going."

"Gotta run," I tell him. "It's been real."

"Watch it, kid," he says.

Once we're on the bus and the teachers are safely twenty-eight rows away from us, half of our class huddles around Ian and me and starts firing off questions—what actually happened, did we really tell the cops we saw zombies, was there actually a body in the art room, what's the deal with that Kendra girl. Before I can say anything, Ian goes off, spinning this weird half-true tale of what we just went through. Note to self: consider Ian as a screenwriter.

"This big cat comes around a tree in front of us, right?" he's saying. "It's a . . . Kendra?"

"A Canada lynx," says Kendra from a few seats away. She rests her head on the seat back, letting herself enjoy Ian's story even as she taps a zillion text messages into her smartphone. "They're native to these parts. Usually harmless."

"Right, so this Canada lynx, he's got his teeth bared, his fur up. Kendra and I have already scared one of them off, but this one's looking hungrier than the rest, a little skinnier, a little meaner, like he's, uh, uuuh—"

"Malnourished," says Kendra.

"What do lynxes eat, Kendra?" asks Jenny Dylan.

"What website are you on?" says Barbara, peering at Kendra's phone. "You should sit with us at lunch tomorrow."

"Sure, whatever," says Kendra, waving them aside. "Let Ian finish."

"Thanks. Anyway," says Ian, "he's growling, just *snarling* at us, and I'm thinking that this is it, this is a big mean-looking animal here, and he's going to gnaw my face off. Time to accept fate, right? And then there's this creaking noise, and this *crack*, and I look over"—he hikes a thumb at me—"and PJ is just putting his back into a dead tree. The tree falls over and *crushes* this lynx to death."

"No way," says Mitchell.

"I call shenanigans on that," says Katey Price.

"Scout's honor, guys," says Ian. "When all the dust clears away, there's just this huge termite-eaten tree on the ground with a big nasty-looking claw coming out from under it."

"Was this before or after the rattlesnakes?" asks Tom Richter.

"Way before," says Ian. "The rattlesnakes weren't until the next day, when PJ got lost way up on the mountain and Kendra and I had to find him."

"That poor lynx," coos one of the girls.

"Poor nothing. You should've seen these things. They were—" Ian pauses for a moment, mouth hanging open, and it's like someone just replayed him a video of the past two days, like he sees the army of reaching hands and moaning dead mouths all over again. His face goes a little white. "They were horrible," he says, a lot quieter. "Really horrible."

"That's a load of bull," says Sean Cunningham. "Never happened."

"Whatever, dude, you weren't there," says Ian.

"Doesn't matter. Didn't happen. You didn't fight any lynxes and that kid didn't knock over any tree." Sean folds his arms and sneers at me. "I mean, look at him."

Ian gets that look in his eyes, sort of like he did with the buck, like he's going to go rushing headfirst into a fight, and I figure he's in enough trouble already. "Shut up, Cunningham," I say. "Nobody asked you."

"Watch your mouth, Wilson."

"Or what?" I yell at him. "You're gonna beat me up? I just spent two days fighting off wild animals in the woods, you idiot. Just *try* making my life any worse than it's been for the last forty-eight hours."

Everyone laughs, and I feel like I've won. Sean gives

me this evil stare but goes quiet. Ian gets back to his story, moving on to the part where he and Kendra accidentally fell down a gorge and got separated from me. Kendra fills in the blanks, and sometimes corrects his grammar.

Back at school, Ian's dad is waiting outside the bus. Before we can even say good-bye to him, Ian is whisked into the family car and driven away. Ms. Brandt finds Kendra and me and leads us to our homeroom, where our parents are waiting.

Our folks look a little funny, sitting at our desks and drumming their fingers. When Kendra and I enter, my mom bursts into tears and rushes over to me, throwing her arms around me, then touching every part of my face and shoulders like she's checking to make sure nothing's broken.

"You had us pretty scared for a little bit there," says my dad. He's trying to sound at least a little angry, but mostly he just looks grateful.

Glancing across the room, I see the Wrights talking to Kendra. They both wear angular business clothes and worried but stern expressions. Her mother stands behind her, one hand on her shoulder, while her dad crouches in front of her, engaging her in soft, intense conversation. When she sees me glancing her way, I get a thumbs-up, leading her parents to shoot me a sidelong stare and a faint smile.

"I'll contact you tonight," says Kendra as my folks usher me out.

"Who's that?" asks my mom as we head down the hallway.

"My friend Kendra," I tell her.

I expect the car ride home to be a lot of chewing out, but it's quite the opposite—my parents mostly ask if I'm okay, if there's anything I need. They ask a few questions, but I do my best to avoid details. When I talk about chasing the buck, my dad gets all indignant.

"I'm going to call Vince Buckley when we get home," he says softly. "Give him a piece of my mind."

When we pull into the driveway, my mom smiles back at me and says, "There's someone here who's going to be very happy to see you."

I'm barely in the door before Kyra rushes down the stairs to greet me, all chubby face and mussed brown hair. When I hug her, I almost cry my eyes out and squeeze the life out of her.

"You said you were gonna call home and read me my story," she says. "You didn't. Mom says you got in trouble."

"I know," I say. "I'm sorry. I got lost in the woods instead." And even though she's way too young to understand it, I tell her anyway: "I missed you a lot, and it helped me get through it. You kept me going for a while."

"I missed you, too," she says.

Over dinner, Mom and Dad grill me about how I made it through the night. Mom tears up three different times, at the lynx, my twisted ankle, and us having to take shelter from the rain (obviously I keep my mouth shut about O'Dea, evil curses, and the living dead). More than anything, they're interested in Kendra Wright. When I first mention her, they look at each other with this stupid *Our son hanging out with a girl?* expression, like they're already planning on sending out wedding invitations. They ask about her parents, her friends, how she is at school. When I explain that we call her Queen Brain and that she once cracked Ian in the face with a textbook, Mom says, "I like her already."

After dinner, Dad tells me to go to my room and stay there until it's time to read Kyra her story. I head upstairs and begin fiddling around with my camcorder, sturdy, heavy. If only I'd had this on the mountain, I could've been the biggest viral video sensation on earth. Maybe it's better this way, though. I can't explain why, but maybe this is my story, Ian and Kendra's, too, but no one else's.

A few minutes later, Mom pokes her head in and says I have a phone call.

"How you doing, man?" asks Ian. He sounds beat.

"All right. I'm getting interrogated pretty hard."

"You have no idea, man. My dad's on the warpath.

Apparently, your dad just called him and gave him the third degree, and Kendra's mom called him earlier and explained to him the exact steps she could take tonight toward suing him. Guess I've never been in trouble like this before. Anyway, I'm not allowed to hang out with you anymore or whatever."

"Like that'll happen."

"Right? Listen, I decided not to tell them anything about what really went on. Figured the less they know, the better. Plus, if I tell them the truth, I'll probably have to go see the school counselor."

"That sounds good. Let's stick with *We made it all up* if the z-word comes up again."

"Right on." There's shouting in the background on the other end. "I gotta go. See you at school."

We hang up, but before I can get to my room, my mom comes out of her office and taps me on the shoulder. "You have someone who wants to talk to you."

"At the door?"

"On the family computer," she says. "In the future, if you could ask your friends not to hack into our home PC, that'd be great."

When I sit down at the computer, it's blank except for a green line. "Hello?"

"Is Peter Jacob there?" says the line, vibrating with each word.

"This is he."

Click—the line disappears, and Kendra's face pops up. She pulls something up on her phone and looks at me through the screen. *"Revenant."*

"Sorry?"

"My friend Mia from Atlanta just emailed it to me. A *revenant* is a person or creature that has returned, *supposedly*, from the dead. The root is the French word *revenir*, meaning 'to come back,' or 'to return.' It is usually presented as a reanimated corpse that terrorizes the living, and can mean anything from a vampire, Frankenstein's monster, or even the legendary Haitian *zombi*, which is actually a hoax caused by people under the influence of mind-altering drugs." She says it like a textbook word, *zum-BEH*. "Your *zombie* is a creation of modern-day cinema, a faceless stalker born primarily out of the rampant atomic fear of the 1950s—"

"I got it. Congratulations on finding the right word. I know that means a lot to you."

"Thank you." There's a pause, and then, "What have you told your parents?"

"Nothing. I just got off the phone with Ian, and we both think we ought to keep the truth to ourselves."

"I concur."

"Good. How are your folks treating you?"

"They're . . . confused. I haven't been punished since I assaulted Ian last year. They're unaccustomed to dealing with bad behavior on my part."

"There's a first time for everything, I guess."

"Yes." Another pause. "Perhaps tomorrow, if it wouldn't bother you, I could show you some of the zombie research I've done since getting back home. Ian as well, if you think he wouldn't mind."

Kendra Wright, reaching out to us? Hey, the dead walk, so who's to say what's what in this bonkers world? "Sure. Come find us at lunch."

"That sounds nice," she says. "Till then." She clicks her mouse, and the screen returns to its normal wallpaper of a dog popping out of a Christmas present. Kendra Wright, Queen Brain. What a freak. I love it.

After another half hour in my room, someone knocks at my door. Kyra peeks around the corner, her face blank and pleading.

"Are you going to read me my story?" she whispers.

Ugh. It's time for me to ruin my sister's childhood, and I can't even tell her the truth, that her favorite bedtime story dissolved in a pool of corpse goo. "Kyra, your book . . . I lost it while I was in the woods."

"Oh," she says, then stares blankly at the floor and nods to herself. "That's okay. Burly Bunny is for babies, anyway. Are you in a lot of trouble?"

"Oh yeah," I say. "Mom and Dad were really scared about me being lost in the woods. No one knew where I was for a couple of days."

She runs into my room and hops up on my bed,

sitting cross-legged in her feety pajamas. "Did you see any animals?"

"Yeah, actually," I tell her. "We saw a lynx, which is a big cat, and we saw a big buck. A deer."

"Tell me," she says.

Now, *that's* an idea.

So I came away from hell without any footage to show for myself—but my memory of what happened is terrifyingly clear. And okay, my parents, my teachers, none of them believe me, but my little sister, that's another thing.

"Listen," I tell her, "I'll tell you about me and my friends getting lost in the woods. But this is our secret, okay? No telling Mom and Dad, no telling anyone. Promise?" She nods. "Okay. So, Ian, me, and this girl Kendra are picking flowers together out in the woods."

She gives me a six-year-old's half-toothed grin. "You were picking flowers?"

"The teachers made us. It felt pretty dumb then, too. Anyway, Ian, you know Ian, well, he sees this deer, a big twelve-point buck, standing between the trees. And for some reason, he decides that we have to follow it. . . ."

It's after midnight when the noise shakes me awake. It takes a moment for me to rub the sleep out of my eyes; a whole day of getting yelled at by every adult you know can wear you out. At first, I figure I'm having another nightmare that somehow crept into my waking mind, but after I sit up in bed and sip some water, and listen, I can still hear it.

Somewhere downstairs, there's a click, and then creaking, ever so light, but getting closer, moving through the house, coming up the stairs, coming right to my room. In the crack under the door, I see a light, yellow and flickering, and suddenly it's streaming in through the cracks all around my door, illuminating four perfect lines. The thing in my throat is either my heart or my stomach, I'm not sure, but it's keeping me from screaming.

The door to my bedroom clicks, and then swings wide, revealing a figure holding something, some kind of torch, with a light so bright and yellow that it's both blinding and impossible to look away from, like a miniature sun. The muscles and tendons in my face stop working, the fear dies down in my throat. A warm feeling spreads through my whole body, like when I was in the tunnels and could see that glowing sigil. Even though my mind is telling me to run and scream and fight, all I can do is stare at the burning light in front of me.

There's a sharp breath, and the light goes out, and I'm back in control of myself. Before I can scream, the skinny figure pulls back its hood and gives me a kindhearted smile.

"Geez, O'Dea," I exhale, "you scared me half to death."

"Sorry, PJ," says O'Dea. She closes the door behind her, then pulls my desk chair out and sits. "I had to get in here somehow. Figured it was this or break a window."

A million questions race through my mind, but the first one out of my mouth is "How *did* you get in?"

She tosses me her torch. It's waxy and hard to the touch, and more a candelabra of sorts, with five small candles coming out of some kind of larger—

"Oh, *gross*," I say, tossing the gray wax-coated thing to the floor with a thud. "That's a hand!"

"Hand of Glory," she says. "A candle made of a condemned man's hand. The light opens any door in a house and paralyzes anyone who looks on it. Usually you need the hand of someone hanged at the crossroads, but looks like it works with zombies, too." She jabs her chin out at the appendage on my floor. "That's from the girl you dropped that tree on. Found her last night. You can keep it."

"Thanks . . . " Note to self: find a really good hiding place. If Mom finds this, she'll have a heart attack. "What are you doing here? We saw your signs, and the video of you burning the diary."

The Warden nods. "I had to do it, PJ. That thing was trouble."

"But now no one knows about the zombies. They think we made it all up."

"Perfect. This way, no one's sticking their nose where it doesn't belong." She shoots me a stink-eye. "Last three kids who did that caused me a hell of a lot of trouble."

"Sorry."

She nods. "Point is, everything's taken care of on the mountain," she says. "Put new bones in my cabin, put a new seal over the graveyard—a big seal, mind you, dream catcher the size of you. The bad juju up on that mountain's on serious lockdown now."

"So we've got nothing to worry about."

She hisses between her teeth. "Not exactly," she says. "See, karma's a balance. You gotta have the bad with the good. Well, you kids tipped the balance by killing those zombies, not to mention burning my seal. You played a hand in this game, and karma ain't the kind of game you can just up and quit. The forces of darkness remember people."

"What does that mean?"

"Means you and your friends're marked," she says in a voice that feels like a concrete slab. "You're Gravediggers now—zombie slayers."

"What? No!" I say. "We never decided on that!"

"Doesn't matter," she says. "You tipped the balance in your favor, and you've been chosen. You should be honored—we haven't had Gravediggers for a long time now. Word'll probably get out fast about you three." She smiles and shakes her head. "Look at that. They always come in threes, to this day."

"But . . . but . . . what do we *do*?" I ask her. "We don't know the first thing about killing zombies! I just made up a plan with the tools at hand!"

"Exactly," she says, smiling. "A good Gravedigger shows initiative."

"We're *not* Gravediggers!" I say, mostly trying to convince myself.

She ignores me. "Don't you worry about what to do from here on out. If trouble comes your way—and I'll be honest, PJ, it's *gonna*—I'll be around to help you out."

"Where will you be?" I ask.

"Around." She pulls her hood back over her wild hair, and her face disappears into shadow. A flick of her hand, and my window pops open on its own. "Be careful, PJ. You three are good kids. Sorry you have to be a part of this, but there's no going back now."

"That's all right," I say. "I guess this isn't the end of the world."

"Not yet," she mumbles, and then she leaps out of my window and the black mouth of the night devours her whole.

Christopher Krovatin was raised in Hoboken, New Jersey, birthplace of Frank Sinatra and the Oreo cookie. At thirteen, he moved with his family to New York City, where he sought out trouble and adventure in its many forms. At this age, he also discovered the music of Rob Zombie, which would color his interactions with society at large from then on. He has a BA in theater from Wesleyan University, which he finds indispensable in the outside world, and is the author of two YA novels, *Heavy Metal and You* and *Venomous*, as well as countless articles about horror culture and heavy metal music. He lives in Brooklyn, New York, where he enjoys lángos, long walks in the cemetery, and blaring death metal. Follow him on Twitter at @chriskrovatin. He's kind of a weird dude, so he might not respond to you, but if you want to talk about Slayer or Bela Lugosi, he's usually down.